A CERTAIN SMILE

A CERTAIN SMILE

THE DONNELLY CABIN INN BOOK 4

JOANNE PENCE

QUAIL HILL PUBLISHING

Quail Hill Publishing

Eagle, ID 83616

Visit our website at www.quailhillpublishing.net

First Quail Hill Publishing E-book: June 2023

First Quail Hill Print Book: June 2023

CHAPTER 1

S ophie Evans drove her car, a fifteen-year-old red Volkswagen Beetle, to the garages of the Donnelly Cabin Inn. With a quick push of the remote, a garage door lifted, and she parked the car inside.

For the past month, Sophie had enjoyed the cozy comfort of the inn. She needed the serene surroundings and peaceful seclusion it offered, and as days went by, the cabin had become more than a bed-and-breakfast to her. It was the only home she had at the moment.

She had learned about it by chance at a party she'd attended in Milan, Italy, some months before her life as one of the top fashion photographers in Italy fell completely apart.

At the party, she had met a thriller author on a European tour, Alex Townson, and his wife, Carly. The couple had regaled her with tales of how they had met at a quaint cabin which had recently been turned into a bed-and-breakfast in the mountains of Idaho. In that far corner of the world, the inn was shrouded with rumors of hauntings and ghostly mischief.

Sophie had found the story of the inn charming, but had

put it out of her mind until after leaving Italy and returning to the US. She had gone first to her parents' house in Chicago, but that had been a mistake. Her mother had bombarded her with questions about life in Italy, why she no longer had a job, and why she'd never married her rich, handsome boyfriend of many years—-the man she'd been living with for over six years.

Finally, Sophie decided she needed to get as far away from everyone, family as well as co-workers, and thoughts of the small bed-and-breakfast in Idaho came to mind. She wasn't sure she could even find Idaho on a map. To hide away at a cabin like that seemed ideal.

She contacted the Townson's, and learned the inn was undergoing an expansion, but if she didn't mind occasional noise, she could stay in one of the already finished rooms. The new manager of the inn, Carly Townson's Aunt Maggie, was already living there and would appreciate some company since the place was a bit remote. And since Sophie would be there under less than ideal conditions, she would get a reduced rate.

She took it.

She bought a used VW Beetle the owner was practically giving away, loaded it with as much of her photography and computer equipment, clothes, and books as could fit in the tiny vehicle, and drove westward to Idaho.

The cabin provided exactly what she needed, a secret oasis where Sophie could escape the pressures and disappointments of her former high-profile career and concentrate on a new beginning. There, she spent four weeks of quiet, filled only by reading, taking nature walks, and shedding buckets of tears over a broken heart and shattered dreams.

But all the solitude she'd enjoyed would end the very next day. Then, the inn would re-open and take in additional guests.

Sophie picked up the three bags of last-minute groceries and supplies she had gotten for Maggie, who was in a dither about receiving her first "real" guests at the inn. "Maggie, I'm back," she called as she entered the foyer.

"Thank goodness!" Maggie hurried to her from the kitchen area and took one bag to carry. "I shouldn't be so nervous, but what if the guests hate the place? Or hate me? What if nobody comes? What if all this was just a colossal waste of time and money? What if the sisters decide to close the inn?"

By "the sisters," Maggie meant her three nieces who had inherited the inn from their mother, Roxanne Donnelly. They decided to make it a bed-and-breakfast, and Maggie, a widow, was thrilled to manage it for them.

"Calm down," Sophie said as they placed the groceries on the large kitchen island. "First, anyone who doesn't like you doesn't deserve to stay here. And I'm sure people will love it. I do, and I've stayed in some of the fanciest hotels and resorts on four continents."

"Yes, but yours was a special case, due to your, uh, situation."

Sophie began putting things away. She hated it when Maggie referred to her situation since she was doing all she could to forget about it. And mostly, over time, she was succeeding.

Other than that, the older woman was a decent companion. She had filled Sophie in on the history of the cabin, built in the 1890s by Elijah Donnelly, and handed down through the Donnelly family to the present day.

"Tell me about the ghosts," Sophie had asked as Maggie, whose full name was Margaret Donnelly Banks, gave her the cabin's history.

"There's nothing to tell, since it's not true," Maggie said.

"Who's supposed to be haunting the place?"

"They say it's Elijah, his wife, Hannah, and their son, Lucas. But as I said, none of it is true."

"Well, of course it isn't, but it's still a fun story," Sophie said. "Why did people think the cabin was haunted?"

"As best I can tell," Maggie said, "one of the current owners, Mallory, was trying to drum up business and wrote something about the ghosts being match-makers because many Donnellys over the years have found love at the cabin. Her story went viral, and lots of people came to the inn hoping for help from the ghosts."

"Did they get it?"

"Not as far as I know. So, in time, the story faded. It's my hope, when new people come here, it'll be for a comfortable bed and a hearty breakfast. Nothing more. If they come, that is."

"If? Of course they'll come!" Sophie insisted.

But Maggie's nervousness about her new position increased. One guest was scheduled to arrive the very next day, another the day after, and a young couple about a week later. The inn only had four guest rooms, so with Sophie staying, soon all rooms would be booked. And Sophie's peaceful existence there was about to end.

At times, Sophie had to chuckle at how she, Sophie Evans, once an internationally acclaimed, award-winning fashion photographer, was content living such a simple life.

But for now, at least, she was.

That night, Sophie went into the great room to listen to the silence one last time.

A long couch faced the fireplace. Sophie lit a fire, then sank down into the plush cushions. Her gaze wandered up to the mantle that displayed some American pewter pieces from the late 1800s, and over it, the oil painting of the man who built the original cabin.

Elijah Donnelly peered down at her, his expression stern. He was only twenty-eight when he lost his wife during the birth of their son, and apparently had spiraled into a deep depression until his death a year later. The son had been raised by relatives, but died after contracting tuberculosis while serving in the Army during World War I.

Sophie felt nothing but sorrow that Elijah Donnelly's family had faced such suffering. She wished his story had had a happier ending, and that he could have somehow garnered the comfort and peace that his cabin—for some reason she always thought of this as Elijah's cabin—had helped her feel with each passing day.

"Do you really want all these strangers invading your space, Elijah?" She whispered, half jokingly. She knew it was silly, but as the fire crackled and the shadows danced on the walls, something about the way his eyes had been painted made them seemed to stare at her, almost as if he was with her, listening, and silently watching her every move.

But the strangest thing, instead of finding it creepy, she found it comforting and, strange as it was, she enjoyed talking to him. It was almost as if she sensed in him another lonely but understanding soul.

Truly, she thought as she shut the lights and made sure the cabin was locked down for the night, she had been spending far too much time alone.

———

The next afternoon, Tray Bowman drove his Ford F-150 onto the Donnelly Cabin Inn's driveway and pulled up next to a red VW Beetle with an Illinois license plate.

If that don't beat all, he thought. He guessed the tourists had already found their way to the Idaho mountains. It was a cute little car, but he couldn't imagine many men would rent or buy it. He probably couldn't even fit in it, being about 6'4" tall, not counting his rolled brim cowboy hat.

He got out of his truck and pulled his two duffel bags from the back seat. The VW told him that everything he'd heard about this bed-and-breakfast was true. It was comfortable, inexpensive, and usually fairly empty except for an occasional female and sometimes male, who sincerely believed some ghosts inhabited the place who might help them find true love. What malarkey.

He was there because of the location and the price. Fairly inexpensive with a substantial free breakfast, and located in Garden Valley: check and double check.

So here he was, and unless he found something annoying about the place, here he'd stay until he finished his task.

He marched into the foyer, dropped his duffel bags onto the floor, removed his hat, and boomed out a quick, "Hello?" In a matter of seconds he heard footsteps on the stairs and saw an older woman hurrying down them.

"Good evening," she called. "You must be Mr. Bowman. I'm Margaret Donnelly Banks—and you can call me Maggie. I'm so glad you made it today. Everything is ready for you to settle in and relax, which is what the Donnelly cabin is known for."

Tray heard "Donnelly" in her name and guessed she must be a relative of the pioneers who built the cabin. "Thank you. I suppose I should sign this register?"

"That's right." She handed him a pen. "Are you here on vacation?"

"I've heard the cabin's reputation about its ghosts," he said, giving her a slight grin, "but believe me, I'm here on business."

She smiled back. "Not a problem. That's the way it is for most folks who come here. Hopefully, your trip will be successful."

"Thank you, ma'am." He put down the pen.

She led him up the stairs to what she called the Mountain View room. It appeared cozy and comfortable. When she explained that he had the run of the downstairs, including whatever was stocked in the refrigerator and in the pantry, with all it offered, he felt he'd made a good choice coming here.

He hoped it also offered some luck, which he sorely needed. He went to the window and looked out at the tall Idaho mountains that edged this valley. As his gaze drifted over their familiar contour, he realized how much he'd missed them.

CHAPTER 2

Sophie steeled herself before heading downstairs for breakfast. She'd heard that the cabin's first new guest had arrived the day before, but she hadn't met him yet. She wasn't one for talking to strangers first thing in the morning and hoped the new visitor wasn't chatty.

Now, she brushed her long, curly brown hair, then pulled it back with a rubber band and headed downstairs. The new guest sat at the dining table, his back to her.

And so it begins, she thought.

Maggie stood like a maestro behind the kitchen island, overseeing the variety of breakfast foods she had put out for her guests, all two of them—yogurt, granola cereal, fresh fruit and pastries, plus she was ready to cook up eggs, bacon, sausage, pancakes, or waffles, whatever the guest desired. "Good morning, Sophie! Coffee is in the carafe, but I can get you hot water if you prefer tea or hot chocolate. Would you like some bacon and eggs? And I've got a hot-off-the-griddle pancake for you." Maggie all but sang out the words, causing Sophie to cringe at so much cheerfulness so early in the day.

When it was just Maggie and Sophie, they had a much simpler breakfast, usually fruit, yogurt, and cereal or eggs, plus, on occasion, a few items for "taste-test" purposes from the newly opened Pastry Corral bakery.

"Morning," Sophie said as she helped herself to some blueberry yogurt and then looked over the pastries. "I'll just have this and maybe a scone."

"I've got something even better," Maggie said. "One of my huckleberry pancakes. I already cooked up this one, in fact. If you don't want it, just leave it." She then put a humongous pancake on a plate. "Huckleberries, you probably don't know, are best if grown wild, not cultivated. Since they don't do well on farms, they're fairly special."

"I had no idea," Sophie said. Maggie had been a school librarian until she retired, so she often sounded as if she was trying to stuff reams of information into a child's skull. "Of course I'll try it."

Taking the pancake and her yogurt, she turned toward the dining table, then paused. The man who sat there hadn't turned to greet her or even face her yet.

Her gaze skimmed over the way he was dressed, from the light blue checkered shirt to jeans to cowboy boots. And she couldn't help but notice his broad shoulders, tapered waist, and long legs. His hair was dark brown and wavy.

She stood, plate in hand, and hesitated. His breakfast plate was high with pancakes, scrambled eggs, bacon, and a buttered biscuit. He couldn't possibly eat all that, she thought.

As she marched forward and put her plate on the table, facing him, he looked up at her. His eyes were a startling light green color in a burnished face, as if he spent a lot of time outdoors. Between those amazing eyes, high cheekbones and straight nose, he might have been attractive except that the rest of his expression formed a frown.

"Good morning," she said. She placed her camera beside her plate—she'd flung its long strap over her shoulder that morning as she came downstairs, planning to take some outdoor shots after breakfast.

Sophie might no longer be working as a fashion photographer, but she still enjoyed taking photos. And this area offered completely different views from the high-fashion, big city world she was used to working in. In fact, she was developing a plan for a travel article on the Donnelly Cabin and similar "haunted houses" and ghost towns in the American West.

The stranger gave her a quick nod and then dropped his gaze back to his plate, where he shoveled in food as if he hadn't eaten for a week.

Maggie walked over to them, gave Sophie a glass of orange juice and gave the man a fresh glass, taking away the one he'd already emptied. "I saw how much you enjoyed it," she said with a pleasant smile, as if she liked the guy. "Fresh squeezed. Did it myself."

"Thank you, much appreciated," he said. "And your breakfast is quite fine." His voice was surprisingly deep.

"You're most welcome," Maggie said, then stared at Sophie and cocked her head in the stranger's direction. Sophie shook hers, which caused Maggie to purse her lips.

Finally, Maggie said, "I should introduce you two." Both looked up at her. She gestured first at one, then the other as she said, "This is Sophie, who's here from Italy, and this is Tray, from Montana. You'll both be staying awhile, so you may as well say hello."

She then returned to her spot behind the island.

"Good morning," Sophie said with a slight smile. Her photographer's eye couldn't help but notice everything about him cried cowboy even without the hat or spurs. Her fingers itched to grab her camera and snap away, although she realized that these days, he was more likely to be a used car salesman than a genuine cowboy.

His expression was unreadable. "Morning," he said, then went back to eating.

He might be even more quiet than she was. Good. She didn't want to talk, anyway.

She had eaten pancakes in the past and never saw the appeal of them. The syrup was always too sweet and the pancake itself seem to either stick to the roof of her mouth or it was so dry she could barely swallow it.

When she was a kid, the closest her mom ever came to pancakes was to stick Egg-O Waffles in a toaster.

But Tray had put a lot of butter on his as well as syrup, and often mixed some egg or bacon with a bit of pancake on his fork. The way he was relishing his breakfast made it look delicious until, to her horror, he added some hot sauce to his eggs. What manner of Western US perversion was that? She didn't think she'd seen any Tabasco sauce the whole time she was in Italy, and definitely not anywhere near eggs.

Just thinking about the combination made her shudder, but he now acted as if his eggs tasted even better.

Nonetheless, out of curiosity, she slathered butter and syrup over her pancake and cut a piece with her fork. At least it didn't feel hard. She found the huckleberries had a slight tartness to them that lessened the sweetness of the syrup. Also, Maggie used real maple syrup, which had a deeper, more interesting flavor than the imitation brands Sophie had tried in the past.

Before she knew it, the pancake had vanished from her plate. She put the fork down. Despite telling herself she didn't want to talk, she was curious about her fellow lodger. "So, what brings you here, Tray?" she asked.

He looked up, surprised at her words. "Not much. Just

looking around." His gaze went to her Nikon. "That's quite a camera."

"I'm a photographer. A travel photographer." She was trying to get used to saying "travel" rather than "fashion," testing the word, and found that she liked the way it sounded. "I go to different places, take lots of photographs, and if any are good enough, I'll sell them to a magazine."

He nodded and went back to his breakfast.

Not only was he less talkative than she was, he also wasn't in the least bit interested in what she had to say. Although maybe, this being the West, he didn't want to be intrusive. She'd heard a lot of cowboy types liked to keep to themselves.

"So," she said, causing Tray to look up once again from his nearly finished meal, "I'm trying to find places that might be interesting to photograph around here. Have you been here before? Do you know the area?"

He swallowed the last bite of food, then wiped his lips. "Long ago. But it's all changed."

"I'm interested in natural scenery, far from people, which I'm pretty sure won't have changed. But I don't know this area at all. And Maggie's also quite new here. Maybe sometime you can point out some interesting areas for me to photograph."

"I don't know that I'll have time." He drained his coffee cup and stood. "Good luck to you."

Then, without another word, he walked away.

Well, she had hoped she wouldn't end up with a chatty person at breakfast, and she certainly got her wish.

As soon as Sophie finished her coffee, she went out to take some photos in the morning light, and headed for a footpath that ran near the river, the Middle Fork of the Payette.

A neighbor named Anna often used the path for a morning walk. After noticing each other on the path a couple of times, they began to talk, and found they enjoyed each other's company.

Anna, who once told Sophie she was twenty-three years old, had a delicate build and fair skin. Her eyes were brown, and she wore no makeup. Her light brown hair was parted in the middle and twisted into a low bun or worn as a single, very long braid down her back. Anna lived with her husband and son, and seemed to know little about the world beyond Garden Valley.

Yet, to Sophie's complete astonishment, after walking together a few times, she had practically spilled her soul to Anna, as she explained what had brought her to the cabin.

Seven years ago, she'd had a job as a photographer on the staff of a New York City based travel magazine. Someday, she had hoped, she would rise to the ranks of a full travel photographer, doing photoshoots about exotic and interesting places all over the world. But she had to pay her dues first, and work her way up to that level of trust.

One such dues-paying job was to stand on a sidewalk and take photos of the fashion designers, the models, and others going into and out of the hotel where a huge, international fashion week event was being held. She was dutifully snapping away, moving this way and that, all the while peering into her camera, when a man heading her way and also not looking where he was going, walked into her. Or she backed into him—she was never sure which. Anyway, the lid to his coffee cup flew off, and his coffee spilled all over her expensive camera.

She was upset since the camera belonged to her boss; he felt bad and tried to help her dry it and make sure it still worked. His name was Sergio Genovese, and as the new owner of an Italian fashion magazine, he was in the city to attend the event.

One thing led to another, and before Sophie knew it, she had fallen head over heels in love with the dashing, sophisticated Sergio. After a year of long-distance dating, where just about every penny she earned went towards flights between Milan, Italy and New York, she agreed to move in with him and to take a job with his magazine as a fashion photographer.

He'd been her Prince Charming. But for her, being Cinderella wasn't in the cards. For the past couple of years, she could feel Sergio pulling away from her. More and more reasons came up for him to spend time in Rome, where he eventually opened an office and took an apartment.

When Sophie heard he wasn't always alone in that apartment, she confronted him. She wanted to know where they stood. By then, she had reached the "old" age of 32, not an age that was old in the "real" world, but few fashion models still worked at that age. Sergio was already 40. She'd assumed he was ready to settle down.

Instead, he said the way they were living was fine. He saw no reason to change anything. She wanted a marriage and children. He didn't.

She stayed with him for another six months, hoping they would grow closer, but instead they grew farther apart. Finally, when she told him she was leaving, he said he thought that was for the best.

His coldness broke her heart.

And now, here she was. No job. Nothing. She was starting over and trying to work out what she wanted to do with the rest of her life.

Sophie found Anna to be remarkably understanding of her sadness over the end of a seven-year relationship and the destruction of all she had once thought her life would be. She was especially grateful for Anna's empathy because Sophie had attempted to hold some "life and love" type conversations with Maggie, only to find Maggie was fairly clueless about such things. She'd married her high school sweetheart, raised a son who was single and now living in Seattle, worked in a school library, and then retired.

What Maggie had offered Sophie as help or advice was so Pollyanna-ish and unrealistic, Sophie may as well have been talking to one of the cabin's ghosts.

To Sophie's surprise, Anna seemed to understand her, despite their many differences. Sophie guessed Anna possessed what she'd heard called "an old soul."

Sophie had once asked Maggie if she knew Anna. Maggie said she didn't know anyone by that name, but had looked troubled by the question for no reason Sophie could discern.

Now, as so often happened, when Sophie was on the footpath, she saw Anna headed her way. "I'm so glad you're here!"

"I was glad to get away—home has been quite busy," Anna said as she approached. She smiled, but as usual, her smile never quite reached her eyes, as if she had a deep sadness. Sophie had asked her more than once if there was anything wrong, or if she'd like to talk, but Anna always responded that all was well.

"What's kept you so busy?" Sophie said.

"We have visitors," Anna said. "It'll be fine, I'm sure. But how are you doing?"

"My life here is changing," Sophie said as they slowly strolled.

"In what way?"

"The cabin, too, has visitors. One new guest has arrived, and I heard another is showing up today."

"Isn't that a good thing?" Anna asked. "It must have been lonely in the cabin. Maggie sounds nice, but quiet."

"I know you find it hard to believe, given the supposedly exciting and hectic life I used to lead, but I've enjoyed being here this past month. Maggie has been an excellent housemate for me, since she keeps to herself, and that's exactly what I'd hoped for."

Anna chuckled. "I'm glad you've decided it's okay to talk to me, at least."

Sophie's eyebrows rose at the Anna's words. "I guess consistency isn't my strong suit."

"Or you're still trying to figure out what it is you really want."

"True," Sophie murmured. Again, Anna seemed to hit the nail on the head. She couldn't help but go back to the morning's breakfast, when she found herself wanting to talk to the stranger at the breakfast table.

"I'm sure you'll get used to the newcomers," Anna said. "And maybe there's someone you'll like among them. I'm surprised you don't already have a dozen single men lined up at the cabin to meet you. I've asked my husband to be on the lookout for a good man for you. He's an excellent judge of character."

"Please, no thank you! I've already told you, I suspect it'll take me years, if ever, to get over Sergio, the slime!"

Anna shook her head. "You say that, but when the right guy comes along, you'll feel differently."

They reached the spot along the path where Anna always left her. There, they both stopped, and Anna faced her. "You said nothing about the cabin's first guest. Is he or she interesting?"

"I'm not sure yet. The guest is male, from Montana. But so far, he's very guarded. Maggie said he'll be with us awhile. Maybe I'll find out more about him, or he'll remain as quiet as he was this morning. Time will tell."

"Single? Young, old? Good-looking?" Anna asked with a grin.

Sophie chucked. "You're an incorrigible romantic. He looks around my age, maybe older. Definitely good-looking if you like the rugged, outdoors type. No ring, so maybe single, or allergic to wedding band material. I have no idea."

Still smiling, Anna added. "Well, I'll look forward to your next installment. I'd better get back. See you soon."

"Bye now," Sophie murmured and watched a moment as Anna continued to the spot where the path curved and she was then lost from view.

A while back, Sophie had concluded Anna must be a part of one of those distinctly rural American religious or spiritualist sects that keep to themselves and lead modest lives having as little as possible to do with technology. Not that Anna wore long dresses or rode a horse and buggy. Baggy slacks and a loose shirt were her favorite clothes. But she had made it clear that she didn't want Sophie to walk with her to her house, and she didn't want any photos at all taken of her, ever. Her only explanation was that she "didn't like them."

Although Sophie couldn't imagine living that way, Anna seemed quite unbothered, so Sophie kept her opinions to herself.

Alone now, Sophie walked back to the cabin.

CHAPTER 3

T ray Bowman didn't know what had possessed him that morning to tell that photographer that he had ever been in Garden Valley before. It wasn't her business or anyone else's.

He wondered if she had been drawn to the cabin because of the story of love and ghosts. At the same time, with her looks, he didn't think she would need much help to find a partner. The woman was pretty.

Pretty, and pushy, most likely. He'd heard stories from buddies "in the dating game" that women were getting stranger by the day. He hadn't thought it was true, that the fault was more the guys, but their words had encouraged him to continue in his solitary ways. Not that it was difficult because, since his wife Charlene passed away four years earlier, he hadn't met anyone who interested him in the slightest. He guessed that meant Charlene was the only woman for him, ever.

Life was lonely—he'd admit that—but nothing had happened to cause him to change.

He thanked God every day for their boy, Brody.

His son, back in Montana and living with his uncle's family, was the reason he was here. The boy was also the reason he didn't want some photographer tagging along with him to look at "natural scenery"—as if there were any other kind— while he searched the area for the right piece of property. She hadn't asked to go with him, but he knew no way to describe how to reach some of the photo-worthy spots in this area, and even if he did, there was no way she could find them.

But he had to admit he'd been drawn to Sophie. He suspected it might have been because of the way she'd looked at him with her big brown eyes.

His wife also had beautiful, soul-searching brown eyes. He'd never really thought about it before, but he guessed he was partial to them. Of course, he'd also loved Charlene's jet-black hair, thick and straight as a line drawn with a ruler. She'd usually worn it plaited in one or sometimes two braids, espe-cially when they would visit her mom and other friends and family on the Crow Reservation near Billings. But when they were home alone, she'd often unbraid it, and he loved the way it felt. Sometimes he'd brush it for her, especially when she grew too sick and too weak to brush it herself.

Fortunately, as the years had passed, remembering that time didn't hurt the way it once had. But he still hated to think back on how it had felt to watch his wife slowly leave this life and to be unable to help her live, which she had so desperately wanted to do.

Tray shook his head, needing to stop thinking about times long past as he reached the center of town and crossed a bridge over the river. As he was driving along flat land used for pasture and crops, he kept an eye out for street signs.

Finally, Tray saw the street he'd been looking for and turned onto it.

Raising a teenager was difficult, which was why he was

here. His son was a good boy, with his mother's black hair and his green eyes. Charlene always loved that their son had gotten his father's green eyes. She said they were going to have to keep a close eye on the boy as he grew older because the girls were going to find Brody very attractive. Tray noticed that even though Brody was only fourteen, the girls were already taking notice. Brody, mercifully, was a lot more interested in sports. So far.

Tray headed toward the home of the only remaining relative that he knew, his sister, Maeve. Many years ago, they'd had a terrible falling out.

He was here to make amends, but exactly what he'd say to her, he still hadn't settled on.

He slowed as he reached the address he'd been looking for. A split-rail fence marked a property line. He saw a truck parked in front of a one-story ranch house that looked to be some forty or fifty years old, in need of paint and, likely, a new roof. Toward the back he saw outbuildings and maybe a couple of acres of land. There were no crops, of course, this time of the year. They were high enough in the mountains that the snow had only recently melted off, and a late storm could blow in at any time. As a boy, he had seen a few snow storms as late as May. And it was now only April.

He slowed, trying to get up the nerve to pull into the driveway and knock on the door, when he saw a man and a couple of boys come out of the house. The boys ran to the truck and got in, and the man followed.

Since he'd heard that Maeve had married and had four sons, he guessed they were her husband and two of her boys.

He stepped on the gas and kept going down the road. In case that was Maeve's husband, he didn't want the fellow to think his family was being spied on. Slowing down, from his rear-view mirror he watched the truck head toward the town.

He made a U-turn back toward Maeve's property, telling himself it would be good to see her with few others watching their interaction.

Before he changed his mind, he forced himself to turn onto the driveway, stop the truck, hurry to the door, and knock. He heard the barking of a couple of dogs, but nothing more.

After a while, he knocked again, and then tried a third time.

Finally, he went back to his truck, feeling relieved. She wasn't there, and any ugly confrontation he might have had to deal with was put off for another time.

He decided to stop for a cup of coffee in town before he drove around to look at a few more parcels of land for sale. Time wasn't his friend.

———

As Sophie drove through the town of Crouch on the way back to the Donnelly Inn, she noticed "The Pastry Corral" bakery had the lights on and the door was open. She was just returning from Boise where she had met with an advisor in a local bank to help her move her money from Italy to the US, and not pay a fortune in euro-to-dollar conversion fees.

The day was bright, but chilly, the VW's heater was weak, and a nice warm caffe latte with a pastry on the side sounded inviting. Besides, since the bakery had just opened, she suspected visitors would be most welcome.

She parked and hurried into the shop. The first thing that struck her was that it was pleasantly warm. The second was that it was empty except for a young man standing behind the counter and looking anxious. He was about six feet tall, slim, with a muscular build. His blond hair was stylish—fairly short on the sides, but the top was longer and fell in attractive waves —and he seemed too young to be the owner of the place. "Hello," she said as she wandered over to the glass counter displaying the pastries.

As she checked them over, she grew warm and took off her furry hat and stuffed it in her Gucci tote, and even unbuttoned her coat. She had dressed stylishly for her Boise visit, wearing a cream colored midi-length coat over a white turtleneck, short black skirt, and over the knee black boots with high heels. She couldn't help but notice the young man gawking at her. Most people in town wore—as she usually did—jeans, walking shoes or boots, and a heavy pullover or puffy jacket.

"Anything I can help you with?" he asked.

"I think I'll have an almond croissant and a latte."

"To go?"

"No, for here. I believe I've had these pastries at the Donnelly Cabin Inn. I'm staying there, and your owner would bring us pastries now and then to try out before opening this shop. Everything was delicious."

A friendly grin lit his face. "That was me. I'm the owner, Josh Zalaski. So, you must be Maggie's guest. Nice to meet you. You two were a great help. Maggie mentioned that the woman staying with her had lived in Europe and knew good pastries. I took a few pastry classes there, whenever I could afford to go."

"Really? That explains a lot," Sophie said with a smile. "My name is Sophie Evans. It's nice to meet you, finally. I hope you weren't offended when I'd suggest a little more of a flavoring, like apricot or raspberry, and sometimes a little less sugar."

"Not at all. It was what I needed to hear. It's the balance that's important, not to have one overwhelm the other. I appreciated it."

"I'm glad. And your almond croissants needed no improvement. They're among the best I've ever had."

His smile grew even wider. "I really appreciate hearing that. Baking can be a lonely business. Say, if you're not too busy, I'd love to take you to dinner sometime. Mama's Folly, just down the street, is great. It'd be my way of thanking you for trying out all those pastries and giving good advice."

She laughed. Much as it was nice to be invited out, dating was not on her agenda. Besides, he was far too young, and not at all her type—whatever that might be now that Sergio was no longer in her life. "Believe me, the pastries were thanks enough."

"In that case, how about just as a way for me to talk to someone who's probably been to places in Europe where I went to study how to make a perfect puff pastry?" he asked with a wide-eyed look she found charming.

She couldn't help but find his suggestion tempting. "Okay. That sounds like fun. I'll join you, but to be clear, this isn't a date and I'll pay for my own dinner. Let me know when."

"Are you busy tonight?"

"Not at all."

"What if I pick you up at seven-thirty?"

She heard a slight cough behind her. "That works."

Josh looked past her—apparently for the first time since they'd begun talking—because he seemed as startled as she had been that a second customer was now in the shop. He put the croissant on the plate for her. "I'll bring the coffee to you as soon as it's ready. You can sit anywhere. Obviously." His tone cast a sad note about his empty shop.

"Don't worry. As soon as word gets out how delicious everything here is, you'll have people lined up out the door."

He looked relieved. "I sure hope so!"

Another "ahem" sounded behind her. She picked up the plate and as she headed for a table, turned to see who was being so impatient. Behind her stood her fellow lodger, Tray Bowman.

"Oh, hello," she murmured.

"Ma'am," he said brusquely, then stepped up to take her place at the counter. "Coffee. Black. To go."

CHAPTER 4

Sophie sat in the great room by seven twenty that evening, her hands clutched together so tightly, her knuckles were white. A wood fire—a real one, not a gas insert—burned in the fireplace, and soft classical piano music came from compact discs played on the stereo system. The internet connection was so unreliable at the cabin that music streaming services simply didn't work well so the older method was used.

Sophie could have kicked herself for having accepting the baker's dinner invitation. She didn't want to leave the cabin. Why, she asked herself, had she agreed to go anywhere with a total stranger? What had gotten into her?

She guessed her bruised and battered heart appreciated attention from the opposite sex, no matter what the reason, and that was why her mouth had opened and a "Yes" came gushing out. Plus, she recognized it really wasn't healthy to stay hidden away like she had done this past month, enjoyable though it had been. Still, she really didn't care about going out with the guy.

Thankfully, before she had a complete meltdown, she heard a knock on the front door.

She stood and smoothed her dress. Since Maggie was nowhere to be seen, Sophie went to the door and opened it. Sure enough, it was Josh, looked quite handsome in a brown leather jacket, jeans, and blue pullover. On his feet were white running shoes. Yes, she thought, he definitely was young.

"Right on time," she said, trying to sound cheerful.

"Of course. I've been looking forward to this all day." He gave her a smile that made her realize why she'd accepted his invitation. His light blue eyes all but sparkled in a tanned face that, at the moment, was eying the foyer. "Say, I've never seen the inside of this place. Mind if I take a quick look?"

"Come on in."

He slowly wandered into the great room.

The seating area and stone fireplace were closest to the entrance, followed by a dining table and beyond that, a large kitchen island with tall chairs for seating, and a modern stainless-steel kitchen. Double French doors between the living and dining areas led to a back porch.

His head constantly moved side to side and up and down. She wondered if he thought he might spot a ghost flying around on the ceiling or something.

"It's a whole lot prettier and up to date than what I'd imagined," Josh said. He turned to the fireplace and moved closer, staring at the oil painting over the mantle. "That must be Elijah Donnelly, the one who built the cabin, right?"

Sophie had heard that the whole town knew the story of the cabin, so Josh's words didn't surprise her. "That's him."

"People say he haunts the place to this day," Josh announced. "Elijah looks like he's scowling at the world in that portrait. What an odd way to paint him."

To her, Elijah didn't seem to scowl at all. "Perhaps," she murmured.

"Well, if he's the matchmaker they say he is, he could be scowling at me because I'm standing here talking about him instead of taking you out to dinner like I promised." He finally cast an appreciative gaze at her slinky black dress and high heels. "You look beautiful, by the way. A little classy, maybe, for where we're going. But that's okay."

"Thank you, I guess," she said. She'd never been out of the cabin at night except a couple of times to run down to the grocery store, and she hadn't given much thought about how to dress for dinner here. A simple black dress was common, not especially classy, in her world.

They left the cabin for the short ride to Mama's Folly. She had only seen it in daytime when it looked empty and verging on shutting down. But as they walked in, the place was hopping. To one side was a bar area with what appeared to be mostly a singles' crowd. In the opposite direction was the dining area, and between them was a dance floor with a country-western band playing. Several couples were dancing.

She'd had no idea Mama's Folly could be so lively.

A young, pretty waitress walked up to them, her focus on Josh. "Hey, handsome. Can't stay away from me, can you?"

"You know I can't. Especially when chicken-fried steak is on special," he said.

"Like that isn't every night!" A dimple appeared in one cheek when her smile broadened, and the more attention Josh paid to her, the happier she became. "All right, you two, follow me."

She then led them to the only empty table in the place. Josh ordered a beer, Sophie a whiskey sour, and they both opted for the chicken-fried steak dinner, something Sophie hadn't eaten the whole time in Italy.

She found Josh to be pleasant company. As promised, they talked about Florence, Vienna, and Paris, where he'd taken courses over the years on creating great pastries. Sophie had spent time in each city.

He talked about his love of baking and his excitement at starting his own business, while Sophie told him a little about her prior work as a fashion photographer. Neither talked about anything more personal, which was fine with Sophie.

Still, she couldn't help but notice the once-overs she was getting from several of the younger women there. Some gave her a look filled with daggers, as if they wished they were the ones sitting with Josh, while others looked at her with pity, as if they might have dated him in the past and it hadn't ended well.

They had both finished their main course when the band began to play the slow, romantic country song, "Amazed."

"I'm not ready for dessert yet," Josh said, and held out his hand. "How about it?"

Sophie always enjoyed dancing in the past, and Sergio was a great dancer. She didn't exactly feel like dancing, but she was pushing herself to "get out there," and after some hesitation, placed her hand in his.

They began the dance some distance apart, but as the song continued, he drew her closer. She had to admit it felt good to dance, and the scent of his aftershave was pleasant. For the first time she wondered if, someday, she might possibly meet someone who could cause her to forget Sergio.

Just as she was relaxing in the dance, a young woman came up to Josh and tapped his shoulder. He stopped dancing and faced her. "What are you doing here?"

"I need to talk to you!" she cried, as tears filled her eyes.

Sophie watched, curious, her gaze jumping from one to the other.

"I'll be right back," he said as he took hold of the woman's arm and hurried her from the restaurant.

Nothing like being abandoned in the middle of the dance floor, Sophie thought as she headed back to their dinner table. It crossed her mind that the woman seemed awfully young, even young for Josh, who she guessed was in his late twenties. But these days many people looked increasingly young to her.

Back at the dinner table, Sophie sat to wait for him to come back. As the minutes ticked by, she wondered what she should do if he didn't. She also hated sitting there, the center of attention from the cadre of women who'd been eying Josh so intently. As she sat, waiting, she had a feeling that the looks of pity she'd previously noticed had now changed to smirks.

When fifteen minutes had gone by, she decided to simply pay the bill and leave. Since there were no Ubers in town, she hoped Maggie wasn't already in bed.

The waitress came over to their table, her blue eyes swiveling from Sophie to Josh's empty chair to the exit door Josh had gone out of. Clearly, she'd watched the entire embarrassing show. "Can I get you anything?" she asked.

"Just the check, please," Sophie murmured.

Her lips pursed, she looked ready to say something, but after a soft "Okay," she walked away in silence.

Sophie used her credit card to pay the bill and had just finished adding the tip and totaling the bill when Josh returned and sat in his chair again. "Sorry about that. You didn't pay for the dinner, did you?"

"I did." She wasn't angry or even upset, just annoyed that what had been a nice evening had ended on a sour note. "I didn't know if you'd be back. It appeared things might have gotten rather involved."

"I'm sorry," he said. His face was slightly flushed, and he

looked and sounded uncomfortable. "Although I am going to have to cut our date short. It's just that—"

"It's okay." Sophie stood. To be honest, she was just as glad the evening ended. In retrospect, the way he'd begun to hold her closer as they'd danced—nice as it had seemed at the time—wasn't a good idea at all. "You don't need to explain. But I would appreciate a lift back to the cabin."

"Of course," he said as they left the restaurant. He looked and sounded like a kid who'd been sent to the principal's office. "I feel bad about the dinner check. I'll take care of it next time."

Next time? Fat chance of that, Sophie thought. "It's no problem."

He opened the door for her to get into his truck. He then jumped in the driver's seat and turned on the engine, putting the heat on high. Finally, he looked at her, his expression quizzical. "I should have introduced you, except Piper was so upset."

"It's fine. Is she your girlfriend? Did she get the wrong idea, seeing you with me?" Sophie couldn't help but ask. Okay, maybe it wasn't her business. But she had always been too curious by half.

"Girl—? No. Piper's my sister."

Sophie did a double take. "She is?"

"Shoot! I should have realized you wouldn't know that," he said. "Plus, I still think of her as a little kid. I mean, she's nineteen, but she's still a kid to me." He started the drive back to the cabin as he explained. "Piper had a nasty breakup with her boyfriend, and our parents aren't exactly the best people to go to when you need to talk or need comforting. She lives with them in Boise, but every chance she gets, she hangs out at my place. She's there now, crying her eyes out over some jerk. That's why I've got to get back to her."

Sophie studied his expression, a mixture of embarrassment

over his predicament, love for his kid sister, and the trial of being the big brother who needed to comfort her. She liked that about him more than anything else she'd learned about him that evening. "I'm sorry. I really had no clue what was going on."

He glanced at her, a look akin to hero worship on his face. "Of course you didn't. Let me get you home, take care of Piper, and then I can think about making this date up to you."

They were back at the cabin in a matter of minutes. He walked her to the door and then reached for her. She was astonished that he'd think that, after their evening, she would want to kiss him. She turned her head and his kiss landed squarely on her cheek.

"Good night," she said, and reached for the doorknob.

He stepped back, clearly disappointed. "Good night." He then headed down the walkway to his truck.

She was about the shut the door when she saw Tray Bowman on the walkway step aside to let Josh go by.

She held the door open for him and wondered if he'd seen the awkward goodnight display between them.

After he walked past her, muttering a quick "thanks" that she'd held the door for him, she shut the door and then turned to face him. But he was already halfway up the stairs to his room, much to her relief.

CHAPTER 5

W hen Sophie went down to breakfast the next morning, she had to face two people at the dining table instead of just one.

Across the table from Tray Bowman sat a sleepy looking young woman with red hair pulled back in a ponytail, bangs that reached past her eyebrows, wearing violet-framed glasses, and eating a chocolate croissant.

"Good morning, Sophie!" Maggie called out with way too much cheer. The only times Sophie had ever heard Maggie use that particular tone of voice was when she was forcing herself to act cheerful instead of complaining. Sophie couldn't help but wonder if the latest lodger was a bit of a challenge.

"Morning," Sophie said as she helped herself to some scrambled eggs, crispy bacon, and an English muffin, then walked to the table.

Maggie followed her and said, "Sophie, meet our newest lodger, Bree. And Bree, this is Sophie."

Bree looked up at the sound of her name, and the two women greeted each other.

Sophie and Tray also mumbled greetings to each other, and then he went back to concentrating on his belly-busting breakfast.

"What brings you to the cabin?" Sophie asked Bree.

"Nothing much," Bree said with a one shoulder shrug. "You?"

"It's quiet and relaxing."

"That's what I hoped," Bree finished her croissant, then went to the Island, picked up a chocolate chip muffin, and again sat across from Sophie. "Croissants have a lot of air, which makes me question why businesses charge so much for them."

Sophie was tempted to point out the difficulty in making them light and flaky, but instead decided to eat. She also noticed Bree wore a green and purple dress that barely reached her thighs, well-stretched green leggings, and low-heeled black pumps. Not the best choice for this area, she thought, but again, she kept her opinion to herself. A month of living at the cabin had taught her that heavy jeans and boots were the best way to protect herself from being stabbed, scratched, or otherwise bloodied by the thorny, thistle-like and otherwise prickly plants that covered the area. Most of them appeared to be dead but were apparently waiting for springtime to turn green and to soften, at least a little.

"The pastries are from a new bakery in town," Maggie said to Bree. "The owner tested his pastries by bringing a few here for the cabin's breakfasts. I think I gained five pounds trying to be helpful. And now, we're official customers each day."

"They aren't too bad," Bree mumbled, wiping muffin crumbs from her lips.

"And speaking of pastries," Maggie said to Sophie with a twinkle in her blue eyes, "how was your date with the handsomest baker in all of Idaho last night?"

"Well, it wasn't really a date, and he was quite nice. Mama's Folly is certainly lively."

"Yes, it is." Maggie said.

"So does you having a date with a local guy mean that a there's truth to the story about the ghosts and this inn?" Bree asked. "And they're already trying to find a match for you?"

Sophie all but choked on her eggs, and she was quite sure she heard Tray give a mild snort at Bree's question. "That's all nonsense," Sophie said.

"Are you saying you've never seen anything odd?"

"Not a thing."

Bree looked disappointed and then stood. Without a word, she left the table. But apparently to drown her sorrow, to go from the table to her room, she backtracked to the island for a cheese Danish.

Sophie shook her head at the woman and went back to eating. She noticed Tray scarcely looked her way and for some reason she didn't understand, that bothered her. She poured herself some coffee, then spoke up.

"How was your trip yesterday? Did you find what you're looking for?"

"Nope."

When he didn't elaborate, she took a swallow of coffee. "Does that, by chance, mean you're going to be traveling around again soon to look over the area?"

"You could say that." He took a moment from eating to refill his coffee cup.

Sophie took a few more bites of breakfast as she summoned the courage to continue to question this strangely recalcitrant man. "Are you doing that driving and looking all by yourself?"

He took a moment to answer. "Since I don't know where I'm going or how long I'll be there, I can't see anyone wanting to tag along." He didn't bother to look her way as he spoke, and then he cut more pancake, stabbed it with his fork, and dipped it in his sunny-side up egg yolk before eating it. Something about the way he was cutting and dipping and eating, at times adding a little bacon to his fork, made it look surprisingly tasty.

He had almost cleaned his place when she decided she needed to speak up if she hoped to take advantage of this opportunity. If she was going to produce a proper travel article about the Donnelly Inn and the area around it, she needed pictures taken off the beaten path that showed interesting and beautiful nature shots of the area. "All I was planning to do today was to drive around to places I don't know and take pictures," she said. "But I really, really don't know anything about this area, and frankly, I know even less about driving on mountainous roads. From what I've seen, my choice of a car, a VW Beetle, might not have been the brightest for an area like this. I actually thought I'd be mostly in cities when I bought it, not that it matters, or that you'd have any reason to care, of course. Anyway," not sure where all those nervous sounding words had come from, she sucked in her breath and added, "if you wouldn't mind, could I possibly ride along with you?"

He immediately looked up at her with a frown, causing her to quickly add to her argument. "I promise to keep my mouth shut and not bother you in any way. I mean, other than once in a while to roll down the window and take a picture. And, whenever or wherever you stop, I'll quietly get out of your car, truck, or whatever you drive, and take a few pictures. You won't even know I'm there. I promise."

Tray continued to glare at her as if she were crazy.

"I wouldn't even talk if you don't want me to. In fact, I'd ride in the bed of the truck if that's what I need to do. Well, maybe I wouldn't go quite that far. But... please?"

Tray shook his head at the torrent of words and then finished the last few bites of his breakfast. He pushed the plate off to the side, and drained his coffee cup. Finally, he cast those unnerving green eyes in her direction. "Actually, that's not a half-bad idea."

She was speechless and wondered if she'd heard him right.

"If you don't mind taking a few photos for me of places we see," he added, "it'd help me remember what I saw and where. Sometimes, when looking at land, after a while, it all kind of merges together."

"That's no problem at all." Her voice was bursting with enthusiasm. "I can easily do that. I'd like to, in fact. I already do something very similar for myself, so I know where I was when taking my photos for documentation or if I'd ever want to go back."

"Good." He stood up from the table.

She did as well. "Can I ask you what is it that you're looking for? That would help me to take the right kind of pictures when you say we're somewhere you want documented."

He thought a moment before answering. "I'm looking for a piece of land to purchase, with or without a house."

"What kind of land?" she asked. "For what purpose?"

"I'm not sure yet. Got to see what's available. But maybe for a ranch."

"A ranch? You really are a cowboy then!"

He gawked at her comment a long moment then slowly, his lips curved into a half smile, the kind that spread over only one side of his face, and caused laugh lines to form along the edge of only one side of his mouth, but it was more of a smile than she had seen from him during that morning's breakfast or yesterday's. It softened his features nicely.

Since he made no response, she changed the subject. "I can be ready to go whenever you are. What time do we head out, pardner?"

His lips scrunched, and he shook his head at her awful

attempt at a cowboy accent, but his words were teasing, "No time like the present, li'l lady."

When Sophie came out of the cabin with her Nikon, camera bag, and wearing a down jacket, she saw Tray waiting beside his truck. She hurried to the passenger side. "Sorry to have kept you waiting."

"Wasn't bad at all. Gave me time to come up with a route that'll let us see a fair number of properties."

For Sophie's photographs to be published in a travel magazine, they needed to be exceptional, above the standard fare any amateur could take. Seeing the growth of population in this area, she had already decided that her article and the photos that accompanied it would capture the beauty of this rugged land before progress turned it into shopping malls and parking lots—along with the hook of ghosts and ghost towns. The hauntings would give the public a reason to want to read the story, but preserving the beautiful land should be the take-away. Sophie had already contacted an editor about the article and received a positive response to the idea.

As they rode along, Sophie was sorry that she had promised Tray she would remain quiet. It was difficult. Even more than questions about where they were going or why, she was curious about the man, such as how long ago was he last here? Did he live here or just visit? And if he had lived here, why did he leave?

She hoped he'd relax so she could start up a conversation, but the way he kept staring forcefully at the road with his mouth a grim line, made her decide if she didn't want to end up abandoned on the side of that road, she'd better stick to their agreement for silence.

As they left the highway and traveled over narrow, rut-filled dirt roads, she realized she could never have made it in her VW. All in all, keeping quiet and taking much wanted photos was probably the best plan for her.

The first place he stopped was on the south side of the river. Some acreage was ringed by a barbed-wire fence with a big "For Sale" sign attached.

Tray walked along the fence, staring hard at the land beyond it. "Take a photo or two, would you?" he said.

"Absolutely!" She started with the "For Sale" sign, which would give her as good a marker as anything else she could think of. She also noted the photo number that began the sequence of shots. Clearly, Tray had never worked with a real photographer. She found it all but physically impossible to take "a photo or two" of a subject. Instead, as he looked over the land, she followed him around using different lenses and different magnifications, but she also took many simple shots, ending up with somewhere around forty. Maybe she had over-done it, she realized, as she stopped taking photos and saw that it was actually a rather dull, flat piece of land.

"So," she said, "is this the kind of land you want to buy?"

"Yup."

"You don't want a house on the land?"

"Could always build one." He headed back to his truck.

"Right." She hurried after him.

He got in the driver's side, and she quickly jumped into the passenger seat. She knew when someone didn't want to talk to her, frustrating though it was.

They made two additional stops to look at land without houses. Tray was growing increasingly unhappy, grumbling that the land parcels were way too small and too expensive for anyone but a pinheaded big-city type who wouldn't know arable farm land from a patch that's so depleted it couldn't grow healthy weeds.

They were deep into a back road, traveling along the creek off the Payette River when Sophie couldn't hold back. "Could you stop a moment? I'd like to take a photo of the creek."

"A creek? You're joking, right?"

"I took a bunch of photos for you," she said. "All I'm asking is two minutes to take some for myself. Two brief minutes. Consider it a bathroom break."

"It's time, something I don't have a lot of!"

"Fine! Forget it!" He was definitely the most sour-tempered man she'd been around since... since Italy. She folded her arms and stared straight ahead, not saying a word.

He continued, but she noticed that the truck slowed and he glanced her way more than once.

"All right." He pulled onto the shoulder. "Go take your photos."

He surprised her by this change. She was about to get out of the truck when she looked back at him. "You aren't going to ditch me here, are you?"

"Don't tempt me," he muttered.

Her eyebrows rose. She hoped he was joking, although he never had before.

"Thank you!" she cried as she sprang from the car and ran down to the creek.

These would be some of her best photos that day.

When she got back into the truck, Tray announced it was time for lunch. The closest restaurants were in a town called Horseshoe Bend. As they drove by a Mexican restaurant, they saw enough cars parked in front to be a good sign. They stopped and went in.

As they ate burritos, Sophie asked, "Are you finding anything that looks hopeful?"

The look Tray gave her said everything before he finally answered with a curt, "Nope."

"Do you have more places to look at?"

"Yup."

He finished his burrito. She was only half done with hers, so she bolted a few more bites. "Okay, I'm done," she said.

"I warned you it wouldn't be interesting." He sounded glum as he pulled out money to pay the bill. She scrounged through her handbag. "Put your money away. I've got this," he added.

"No, not at all." She pulled out her wallet. "I asked to come along. You don't need to feed me as well."

"It's the gentlemanly thing to do." His tone was both firm and final.

"Thank you, then," she said. "And I'm actually finding this quite interesting. I'm getting exactly the photos I'd hoped I would. I never would have ventured off onto all those narrow dirt roads, and besides that, you actually seem to have some sense of which way you're going. I'm afraid I might have become completely lost on those fire trails."

He actually looked pleased when she told him she was enjoying their day, then walked up to the cashier, paid for their meals, and headed out the door. Once back in the truck, he drove westward along an arm of the Payette River.

They were now fairly well south of Garden Valley. New housing developments were being built along the Payette, so she guessed they were getting close to the suburbs that were forever expanding around the city of Boise. But once Tray turned off the highway, they were again back in much emptier territory.

Without a word of explanation, Tray pulled over to the side as much as possible on a narrow road and stopped the truck. Sophie didn't see any For Sale sign and wondered what was going on. He met her gaze with a smile and then pointed out the windshield. "Antelope. Do you want photos of them?"

She looked where he directed, and her breath caught. "Oh, my God! They're beautiful." She quietly opened the car door and slid out, doing her best not to attract any attention to herself as she changed the camera's lens and took some twenty or more shots of the three antelope eating and cavorting in the distance. Finally, she got back into the truck and shut the door. She couldn't help but look at Tray with wonder that he had been paying enough attention to realize that such a sight was exactly what she wanted.

"Thank you," she said. "That was truly special, and it was thoughtful of you to stop. It's odd that after a childhood of singing about a place where the deer and the antelope play, I'd never seen one except in photos."

He nodded, then started up the truck again. "All I can say is, I'm glad nobody's decided antelope make good eating, so we can still enjoy them."

She grinned. "So true." Had he actually made another lightly humorous comment? Two in one afternoon? Had she been mistaken about his character, his sense of humor? Maybe he wasn't quite as dour and moody as she'd thought. No, scratch that—he was definitely moody.

They looked at one more parcel of land for sale and then returned to the cabin. Tray wasn't happy, but would only say that the land he'd seen so far was unacceptable to him.

CHAPTER 6

T ray was in the great room, trying hard to concentrate on a book about alpaca farming. He'd heard raising the beasts was often profitable, so it was one of the many options he was considering. But then Sophie entered the room and, to his dismay, his heartbeat went into overdrive. He shouldn't be feeling that way about a woman who wasn't his wife... should he? He'd adored Charlene. She'd been gone for four years now; four years in which he hadn't looked twice at another woman.

He couldn't imagine that changing, although his buddies back in Montana had told him it was time to move on. They knew he would never forget Charlene, but they said he was still a fairly young man and that he needed to live again. The problem was, without Charlene, he didn't know how to do that.

Still, even he had to acknowledge that Sophie Evans was smart and attractive. Not with the exotic and delicate beauty Charlene once had. No, Sophie's looks were more earthy and strong, even raw in their pure sensuality. He should be able to appreciate that about her without infringing on his feelings for Charlene.

That meant it was fine for him to notice but how Sophie's dark, curly hair cascaded past her shoulders in a wild and enchanting mass, and how it swung from side to side as she glided with long-legged strides into the great room. It was equally acceptable for him to notice that her breasts were full and her hips wide, while her waist was small. Involuntarily, he sucked in his breath before turning back to his book. But the letters seemed to have become scrambled, making no sense. He lifted his gaze to her again.

She faced him with a smile, and his pulse quickened. Despite himself, he'd enjoyed having her with him that day, enjoyed her discovery of the area he'd once called home, and found it fascinating to view it through her eyes as she selected scenes to photograph.

Now, with her in the great room, the book about alpacas didn't stand a chance.

He took a deep breath. "What's up?"

"I'm heading to the store to pick up something for dinner," she said. "Can I get anything for you? Or would you like to come along?"

Would he ever! But he heard himself reply, "No thanks, I'm fine."

"Are you eating here?" As she turned those big brown eyes on him, capturing his gaze, food was the last thing on his mind. Stop this right now, he told himself. He forced a scowl as he said, "I've got some cold cuts for a sandwich. I need to do some reading tonight."

To his surprise, a hint of disappointment touched her expression. He had to be mistaken. Weren't she and the pretty boy baker an item? What was it Maggie had called the guy? The handsomest baker in the state?

Sophie gave Tray a quick goodbye and left.

He let out a sigh, but if it was one of relief or disgust at his behavior, he didn't know.

He tried to go back to his book about raising alpacas, but the words swam before his eyes as his mind reran their day together. As the day continued and he came to know her better, he couldn't deny the pure sensuality that seemed to radiate from her in the close confines of his truck's cabin. Maybe because he hadn't had such a day in so many years, it meant far more to him than, in reality, it was. But throughout, he was keenly aware of her energy simmering just beneath the surface. He'd found himself intrigued by her every movement, by her every expression. At times, the way she looked at him sent shivers down his spine. Ironically, the more she strove to remain quiet as she had promised him, the more drawn to her he'd felt.

More than once when he'd be out walking on flat land to check it out, he'd turned around and discovered she was halfway or more up a mountainside taking pictures. It was as if the gal had a streak of mountain goat. A couple of the places she went even made him gasp as he wondered where the nearest hospital might be if she took a tumble. But somehow between her boots and, he had to suppose, her experience at hiking around to take photographs, she stayed pretty well glued to the mountainside. For that, he was grateful.

Much as he didn't want to admit it, her nearness had caused him to use all his powers of concentration not to run them off the road.

He was going to look at property again the next day, and he guessed he really ought to do it on his own. After all, he wasn't here for companionship. He was here for business. And the worst thing one could ever do with business was to mix it with pleasure.

In fact, he couldn't help but wonder if that was why he had

found nothing that day. Maybe he'd been overly concerned about her wellbeing as she took photos. What if it was her fault that nothing looked good enough for him to consider buying? Could it have been that if she hadn't tagged along, he might have found a piece of property that he liked?

It's not that she had distracted him. No, obviously, it was that he had found it difficult to look at land and, at the same time, to worry about some fool woman running all over the place and most likely paying more attention to views through her camera lens than to look at where she was stepping.

How many times had he heard of some idiot tourist trying to take a selfie and backing off the edge of a cliff? Or walking into a herd of buffalo to get a closer photo and not knowing that male bison were every bit as dangerous as bulls?

That did it. He wasn't taking her anywhere with him again, no matter how sweetly she asked.

He shut that door. And good riddance.

As Sophie drove to town, she decided to have a nice meal rather than to simply buy something from the grocery store and bring it back to eat at the cabin. She headed for The Rusty Nail, a brewpub that she heard served an excellent meal without the price, music, or people that filled Mama's Folly each evening.

A large Western style bar ran along an entire wall. Men, either wearing cowboy hats or having one nearby, stood talking to each other in small groups. A few women were also in the place, and most sat at tables. She looked around, not sure if she should wait to be seated or what.

The bartender, an older man with white hair and a big grin almost hidden by his wide, thick mustache, noticed her predicament. "Take a seat at the bar or an open table. Your choice," he called out. "And welcome."

"Thank you." She noticed several of the customers turn her way to see who the newcomer was who didn't even know she could sit anywhere she pleased. She chose a small table. Before long, a server, an older woman wearing a dour expression, came over. She was the like the yin to the yang of the cheerful bartender.

"Hey," she said. "I've got a menu if you're interested in something to eat or maybe you'd just like a drink."

"I'll take a look at the menu," Sophie replied. "And I'd have a cosmopolitan."

"We don't serve those. Bartender don't make 'em."

"Oh?"

"We serve mostly beer. Or whiskey, straight up. Pendleton's real popular. But we can make you a margarita, or if you like such things, a martini. Tastes like gasoline, if you ask me, but enough people order 'em."

Sophie found the attitude perplexing for a cocktail waitress, but said simply, "I'll have a vodka martini."

"Got it." She then pulled a menu from one enormous pocket in her apron and utensils wrapped around a paper napkin from the other, put both on the table and walked off.

Everything on the menu was a variety of hamburger or breaded chicken. Sophie placed her order as soon as the martini showed up.

At the moment, a relaxing drink seemed to be what the doctor ordered, if the town even had a doctor. She took a sip and then gave a heavy sigh, wondering exactly what she was doing in a town where the drinks depended on the bartender's taste? She could imagine Sergio's reaction if the waitress had given him that answer.

Looking around, she felt completely out of place here.

Fortunately, a short while after she finished the martini, the grim-faced waitress brought out a thick hamburger with Swiss cheese, bacon, and mushrooms, some sweet-potato waffle fries on the side, and an iced tea to help wash it all down. One bite, and she was in heaven.

As she ate, a fellow sitting at the bar kept looking her way and smiling. She tried to ignore him, but couldn't help but notice that he was good looking, probably around her age or a little older, with straight ash blond hair and blue eyes. In other words, he was the opposite from the dark-eyed fellow with wavy black hair she had left behind in Italy.

Or, more accurately, the guy who had destroyed her hopes and dreams about their future after she had lived with him for over six years.

Just thinking about Sergio made her want to do almost anything to put aside memories of him. She watched as her admirer chatted amiably with a number of acquaintances as they entered or left the bar, but eventually, he would go back to sitting alone. Still, they seemed to like him, so she guessed he wasn't some crazed pervert or anything like that.

Finally, unable to stop herself from glancing at the man, when she finished her burger and was enjoying the waffle fries, she gave him a smile. He took it as an invitation, which it was, if she were being honest. He picked up his drink and strolled over to her.

Suddenly, she wasn't sure she was ready for this encounter, and gave serious thought to leaving.

"Hello," he said. "The name is Carter Waterton. Doctor Carter Waterton. I couldn't help but notice you sitting here eating alone, and I was sitting over there drinking alone, and I thought it might be nice to join you, if you don't mind, that is."

A doctor? No wonder so many people in the pub seemed to know him. She relaxed, a little. "No, not at all. I'm Sophie."

He took a seat. "Can I order you something from the bar? That iced tea looks a bit watered down."

Tempting as it was to leave, she knew she had to get used to talking to people—to men—again, even to get back into the whole dating scene. One drink would be all right, and then she'd leave. "Well, they make a good martini. I guess I have time for another."

Carter waved over the server and placed the order, then turned back to Sophie. "Are you new in town?" he asked.

"Just here for a vacation."

"At least you found the best burger place in the area," he said pleasantly. He seemed nice enough, she decided.

"I'll admit, my dinner was delicious."

The server brought over Sophie's martini and another scotch and water for the doctor.

"It's a little early in the season for many tourists to our little town, as I guess you've noticed," Waterton said. "It gets a lot livelier around here when the weather warms up."

"So I've heard."

"I take it you aren't from this area."

"Not at all."

"Your accent... it's not quite Western."

She smiled. "No. I'm originally from Chicago. I spent a little time in New York, and the last six years in Italy."

"How cool. Was it for work?"

"In a sense. I'm a... a travel photographer, so I'm always looking for places off-the-beaten path, so to speak."

He cocked his head slightly. "That's interesting. It sounds enjoyable, too. Although, if you've come to Garden Valley for captivating photographs, I hope you aren't too disappointed."

He gave her such a crest-fallen expression, she had to laugh, which then caused him to smile. She would have been lying if she didn't say, "It's getting more interesting by the moment."

"That's what I like to hear!" he said.

"But tell me," she asked, "Have I met the town doctor or the town veterinarian? Or maybe the town dentist?"

She threw in that last because he had the straightest, whitest teeth she'd ever seen, and considering who she'd been photographing the last several years, that was saying a lot.

"I work with humans, not animals or teeth," he said. "I'm the town's GP. My primary field of study was in internal medicine."

"I imagine the people here are glad to have you. I've heard from doctor friends that the lure of big city hospitals and being able to specialize are difficult to refuse."

"Maybe, but nothing compares to getting to know and care about one's patients. And there are always interesting cases in an area like this."

"Really?" That was news.

"Right. Sniffles, slivers that become infected, twisted ankles. Even a person getting stepped on by a horse or butted by a goat. Actually, those last two can be serious, although rarely. Anyway, you name it, and a country doctor has probably seen it as long as it's fairly common."

She was finding him fun to talk to. "It sounds like a profession that gets you a lot of thank you's, which I imagine gives you a good feeling."

His gaze grew more intent, as if he liked what he was hearing from her. "That's a really nice way of putting it."

A sudden discomfort struck her at the way he was staring into her eyes. She looked away and sipped her martini before asking, "Have you always lived in Garden Valley? Is that why you're here now?"

"Actually, I did my internship in Seattle, and then worked

for a while in Portland. A short stint in Missoula, and then moved here when I learned the former doctor was retiring."

She nodded. "How do you like it?"

"I love it," he admitted. "It's now home."

His words touched her. Home had a nice ring to it.

When she didn't respond, he asked, "Have you seen much of our town?"

"Not yet. But I hope to soon."

"Are you staying in town or renting a cabin?"

"I found an interesting bed-and-breakfast just down the Middlefork Road."

His eyebrows lifted, and then he grinned. "You aren't staying at the old Donnelly cabin, are you?"

She had a good idea why he reacted that way. "I am. Does your smile mean you've heard stories about it being haunted?"

"Believe me, everyone in town has heard stories about their matchmaking ghosts, so, if there's any truth to it, someone as lovely as you are—if you're single, or otherwise unattached, that is—should have an interesting stay."

"Well, I am single, and I am unattached, but right now all I'm doing is taking photos of this area and hoping a travel magazine will want to buy them from me."

"Hmm," he murmured, then added, "Actually, if you decide to stay in town awhile, and are interesting in taking photos of people, I know a place that could use a photographer."

That surprised her. "Oh? I definitely can take photographs of people. What are you suggesting?"

"We have a great weekend market that features our local artisans, plus local crops once they're ready. I've seen such markets with photo booths where people can dress up in Western costumes and have their pictures taken, and I've even heard tourists ask if there isn't a photographer in town who does that kind of thing. But there isn't. I think it'd be something the locals would also find fun. To go to a photography studio is expensive and a hassle, but to have someone at the market taking pictures when everyone is in a good mood sounds like a dream job to me."

She had to agree, and it would be child's play compared to the fashion photographs she normally took. "That's interesting. Thank you for the tip. If I stay here awhile, that actually could be fun."

"The market's slow now, but it'll grow as we get closer to summer. How about another drink?"

His suggesting another drink was her cue to leave. She decided this conversation had been pleasant, but wanted to end it before things turned in anyway complicated. "I think it's time for me to get back to the cabin. It's been nice talking to you. And thank you for the drink."

He stood. "It was nice to meet you, too. If you decide to stay in town awhile, feel free to drop into my office. I'd be happy to take you to dinner—and maybe we can find a place that's even better than this."

She placed money on the table to cover her dinner bill and he walked with her to her car. "If I stay, I'll keep that in mind," she said as she got into the car. "Goodbye now."

She drove off, pleased. Who would have expected a handsome baker and a handsome doctor in one little town like this? Maybe there was something to this ghost story, after all. *Take that, Sergio!*

CHAPTER 7

T ray stumbled downstairs for coffee and a big breakfast, ready to face another day. He'd been getting disturbing text messages from Brody's grandmother, Charlene's mom, that the boy had been acting up in school and with family. Brody was upset that he would have to leave his family and friends on the reservation if Tray found a home for them in Idaho. Tray knew it would be difficult to move a fourteen-year-old away from his friends, but he and Charlene had wanted to raise their son in both his world as well as hers, and right now, he was failing in his promise to do that. He realized too late that he'd been so upset and lost after Charlene's death that he'd pretty much turned his son over to his grandmother to raise.

Now Brody was in the ninth grade and attending high school, so he had moved from his grandmother's house to stay with his uncle, Charlene's brother, and his cousins. He would go home to Tray on weekends, but Tray realized he was becoming less and less important in his son's life, and knew their relationship would grow increasingly weak if he didn't do something about it. His fear was that he'd already waited too long.

"Good morning, Tray," Maggie called out as he entered the great room.

He went over to the kitchen island and made small talk as he asked for eggs over easy, sausage and pancakes. Then he took a seat at the table and got himself some orange juice and coffee.

Bree entered the great room right behind him. She was still in her pajamas. As she walked toward the kitchen island where the breakfast foods were placed, she kept peering over her shoulder at the portrait of Elijah Donnelly. Tray found that strange, especially since it caused her to walk into one of the barstools at the island.

The stool began to tip over. Tray stood to help, but fortunately, Bree caught the chair and herself before they both hit the floor.

"Are you okay, Bree?" Maggie asked as Tray sat back down.

Bree picked up a plate. "I'm fine," she muttered.

"Can I cook anything for you? Eggs? Sausage?" Maggie offered.

"No thanks," Bree said as she looked over the breakfast choices. "Hmm, are those raisins or chocolate chips in the muffins? They look like chocolate."

"They are. I can ask Josh to send some raisin muffins tomorrow, if you prefer."

"No, not at all." She took a muffin. "But I passed by his bakery and saw some éclairs in the window. That would make a great addition to breakfast."

"Éclairs?" Maggie repeated.

"My stomach's felt a bit delicate. All that nice cream inside would probably help settle it." Bree added an apple fritter to her plate and then sat at the dining table where she poured herself a cup of coffee, then added half-and-half and sugar.

"Morning, Bree," Tray said.

"Good morning," she mumbled. "I'm not feeling well. Too much fried food around here."

"Right," he muttered. He hadn't seen Bree eating anything but sweet pastries since she'd been there, but he told her he hoped she'd feel better soon.

She nodded and took a bite of the apple fritter.

Maggie put an overflowing plate of food in front of him just as Sophie entered the room.

"Good morning, Sophie," Maggie said. "Can I cook up something for you?"

"I think I'll just have a scone," she murmured as she took the pastry over to the dining table and the place setting across from Tray. She couldn't stop a groan as she sat and reached for the coffee.

"Big night, huh?" Tray said, using his fork to cut into a short stack of buttered pancakes dripping with maple syrup.

"Not really," she murmured as she poured herself a cup. "I think I'm just out of practice, although the Rusty Nail serves the largest martini I've ever had. How was your trip yesterday? Did you find what you're looking for?"

"Not really," he said, parroting her reply.

When he didn't elaborate, she took another a few swallows of coffee. Before long, her head cleared. "Does that, by chance, mean you're going to be traveling around again soon to look over the area?" she asked.

"So it seems," Tray said, as he looked at her breakfast. "Still eating as if you were in Italy, I see."

Sophie smiled at him. "It must make me the perfect B&B guest. They hardly have to do any work at all." She then turned large brown eyes on Bree. "So, Bree, how are you finding Garden Valley?"

"I haven't seen much yet. The weather's not very warm and I'm afraid to drive on the backroads. But the cabin is fine."

"Are you here on vacation?" Tray asked.

"Sort of."

"Sort of?"

"I mean, yes. I'm doing research."

"Oh? On what?" Sophie asked.

"Elk migration."

At that, Sophie simply nodded.

But Tray knew something about elks in this area. "What's to research? They follow their food—going higher up the mountains in summer and coming to lower ground in winter where the snow isn't so heavy and thick. Sometimes, they're practically in Boise."

Bree looked uneasy at his obvious question. "It's *where* they go that I'm watching."

He could tell she was lying. He had no idea why, and he frankly didn't care. He frowned and finished the last few bites of his breakfast.

"I've got work to do," Tray said as he moved his dishes to the island near the sink. "Have a good day, ladies."

Sophie also stood. "Could you use help today?"

"Thanks, but I don't think I'll be out long. See you later."

She nodded, then sat back down.

Tray noticed Bree's questioning gaze as her eyes jumped from him to Sophie and back again. He had no idea what that was about. He thanked Maggie for a delicious breakfast, as always, and quickly left the room.

After breakfast, and after being rebuffed by Tray, Sophie decided to go off and see the sights on her own.

In her room, she grabbed her camera bag, purse, and phone, but stopped when at the sight of a new email message on the phone. She guessed it must have downloaded during one of those rare times the cabin actually had cell service. It came and went. But mostly went.

She opened up her email and, to her surprise, the message was from Pasquale Valenti, an acquaintance as well as the editor at *Il Viaggiatore Felice*, or *The Happy Traveler*, magazine. He was the person she'd contacted to ask if he had any interest in a travel article with never-before-seen photos about ghosts and ghost towns in remote areas of the American West. He'd replied that he was definitely interested, quite interested, in fact. Of course, such an article would have featured the Donnelly cabin.

Why, she wondered, would he be writing to her now? She immediately opened the email.

The first surprise was that he wrote it in English. Nevertheless, she had to read the email three times before she decided it really said what it seemed to. She kept hoping Pasquale had muffed his translation. But she had to conclude he hadn't.

He had just been informed that the magazine was folding, going out of business, effective immediately. No savior had swooped in and bought it to keep the doors open and the staff employed. And all contracts for future articles had been severed.

Sophie didn't even have a contract to sever, just the promise of a good and careful read when she submitted the article. Since Pasquale knew and liked her work, she'd been fairly certain he would buy her submission. Plus, the magazine paid well.

She sat on the bed, wondering what she should do now.

Perhaps the best thing to do would be to jump on the next plane back to Rome to look for work with other magazines. After all, she had an excellent reputation in Italy. But then she thought of the other travel photographers—Italian photographers—who would now be looking for work because of the magazine's closure. And since her reputation in Italy was based mostly on her work for fashion magazines, she saw little reason the few remaining travel magazines would hire her.

Besides, Sergio was there, and the thought of seeing his smirk as she ran back begging someone to hire her made that option a non-starter.

This cabin was as good a place as any to stay to figure out what to do with her life. And on the bright side, to write the ghost towns article she would have had to leave the cabin and travel to other towns. Now she could remain here.

So far, she felt content being here. Or, as content as a person could be whose exciting life in Italy and whose great romance with the dashing Sergio Genovese had ended.

Looking back, she could see that over the years, their relationship had gone stale. She had tried to deny it and to overlook the obvious until it became clear that a lot of his late-night shoots had nothing to do with cameras. Apparently, he found her comfortable to go home to after the excitement of the newest, most exciting young model had worn off.

Yet, he swore he loved her. At the same time, he couldn't promise her that anything about their relationship would change. He was forty years old, and still not ready to settle down.

She was thirty-two and wanted, and needed, more than he offered. Of course she wasn't in the least bit "old," but she worked in an industry where youth reigned. Most models were washed up by age thirty, and being around that mindset weighed on her. As much as she wanted a commitment from him, Sergio wanted his freedom. He wasn't about to change, or if he ever did, her gut instinct warned her it wouldn't be with her.

Listen to your gut, she'd always said. It won't lead you wrong. And her gut was sending her all kinds of warnings about Sergio.

Finally, knowing their relationship wasn't going to improve, she did the only thing that made sense for her life and her self-respect. As much as it hurt, she left him, and Italy.

Now, her future career seemed even more uncertain. The best idea she could come up with at the moment was to continue on with what she'd planned. It could be a great travel magazine article. But for which magazine? Not for any American one. The story had been overdone in this country. Maybe a lot of Norwegians were thinking about visiting the American West and some magazine in Oslo would be ecstatic to get her proposal for a story. Or not.

She'd ponder it.

Fortunately, she'd managed to save and invest some money while living with Sergio. The easiest thing to do at the moment was to submit freelance articles and send out feelers that she was available for hire. All the while, she should live somewhere cheap. Somewhere like the cabin.

It wasn't Rome, but it was clean, inexpensive, and safe. She could remain there for a few more weeks as she perused opportunities for her future. She had experience and a name. It was time to use them.

Also, she hadn't forgotten the idea Dr. Carter Waterton had mentioned—that the weekend outdoor market could use a photographer. At the time he'd said it, the idea of setting up a simple photo booth had sounded like fun. Of course, she'd had two martinis.

But what if it really was a good idea? All she would need

were chemicals and photography paper to develop the photos, something she'd learned how to do while taking pictures of the best of the best. She would need a darkroom—and the laundry room in the cabin had no windows. Surely, Maggie would let her use it for a few hours from time to time.

Second-hand stores probably sold cowboy hats, necker-chiefs, and other Old West memorabilia to decorate her photo booth. And maybe some customers would want to put on hats or bonnets and such for their photos. Who knew how far she could take this idea?

It just might work.

And if it didn't and her money ran out, the Rusty Nail could certainly use a waitress with people skills.

She had to find out the town's rules about setting up a photo booth. She was going to phone the town's offices to ask if there were some forms she need to fill out, but by the time she reached a spot with a strong enough cell service to make the call, she was nearly at the offices.

There, she was more than pleasantly surprised that every-thing could happen for a fee of twenty-five dollars, plus instruc-tions about collecting sales taxes.

Once all the legal mumbo-jumbo was taken care of, she hoped to find local stores that could sell her photographer's chemicals plus materials to create an interesting backdrop for her booth, only to learn she needed to drive to Boise. She went, and found everything she wanted, including a bail of hay as a prop, except that it wouldn't fit in her VW.

Finally, as she headed back to the cabin, a riff on a quote from *The Wizard of Oz* came to mind, "Sophie, you aren't in Milan anymore."

CHAPTER 8

Tray was up so early the next morning, he'd even beaten Maggie, but he had too much on his mind to sleep. Since the inn was so quiet, he decided to leave it and walk down the river to clear his head. All of his "house hunting" had gotten him nowhere. This wasn't what he'd expected when he came to Garden Valley.

As he reached a little beach area, he saw a man fishing. He meant to walk by and not disturb him, but the fellow noticed him and waved. "Good morning!"

"Having any luck?" Tray asked.

"No." The man reeled in his line. He was tall and quite thin, probably just a bit younger than Tray, with brown hair and eyes, and oddly old-fashioned clothes—baggy brown slacks and an off-white loose-fitting shirt. His face was so pale, Tray wondered if he might be ill. "I don't much care for trout, anyway, so I throw back any I catch. Fishing mostly gives me a pleasant way to spend the morning." He then turned his eyes on Tray, eyes that had a strangely sad cast to them, as if the fellow had the weight of the world on his shoulders. "Do you fish?"

"Not often. Not anymore," Tray admitted.

The stranger gave a slow nod, as if understanding not only the words Tray had spoken, but the sorrow and worry that lay beneath them. "My name is Luke, by the way. I live down the road a bit. Are you staying at the Donnelly place?"

"I am. The name's Tray."

"Tray? Like the Stephen Foster song, 'Old Dog Tray'? It's one of my favorites." He softly sang,

"When thoughts recall the past
His eyes are on me cast
I know that he feels what my breaking heart would say
Although he cannot speak
I'll vainly, vainly seek
A better friend than old dog Tray.
It still brings a tear to my eye."

Tray was surprised to find anyone his age knew the song. His father liked the name because his own grandmother, Tray's great-grandmother, often sang it. "Luckily," Tray said, "when I was growing up, not one of my classmates knew I was named after a dog."

Luke chuckled. "Well, I'd say it's an honorable name. And it's good to meet you, Tray. Here vacationing with your family, are you?"

"No, afraid not," Tray replied. But, then for no reason he could discern, he found himself saying, "My son's in Montana and my wife passed away a few years back."

"I'm so sorry." Luke all but whispered the words.

Tray was irritated at himself. He'd never said anything so personal to a complete stranger, and had no idea why he would have said it now.

Luke coughed, a raspy, deep in the chest sound.

"Should you be out here in the cold with that cough?" Tray asked.

"It doesn't matter. I feel better in the fresh air than in a stuffy old house, anyway. What about you? This is an odd area for a fellow to travel to, isn't it? I mean, there's not much out here."

"I'm actually looking for some property to buy," Tray said. "I used to live out this way, and hope to come back." Again, he clamped his mouth shut. What was wrong with him spilling his guts this way? He was acting like he was being interviewed by Dr. Phil.

But he saw a pleasant smile touch Luke's features, although it still didn't quite reach his eyes. "Good luck to you," Luke said. And then, almost as an afterthought, added, "Just a suggestion. Try to find someone to go with you. Looking to buy a house and land can be such a trial with much to think about. It's often best to have a friend join you to help notice things you might have overlooked."

Getting such advice from the fisherman rocked Tray a bit because he'd been thinking about Sophie and how she seemed to want to ride with him. Now, hearing Luke's words, he had even more reason to let her come along. "Good thought," he murmured, then louder added, "Well, I'd better get back. Breakfast is probably on the table now."

"Good luck with everything you're searching for," Luke said, then turned back to his fishing and cast the line once more.

When Tray reached the inn, Maggie had breakfast set out. The other lodgers weren't there yet.

"Say, Maggie," he said as he piled hot-off-the-griddle pancakes onto his plate. "I met a guy down at the river this morning. He said his name is Luke, and he lives around here. Do you know him?"

Maggie looked momentarily stricken, her eyes wide, then she began to forcefully stir the pancake batter for her next batch. "Can't think of anybody by that name," she mumbled. "Maybe he has a house and only comes here a couple times a month or something."

"Maybe," Tray said.

Maggie put down the wooden spoon. "Why? Did he say something that troubled you?"

"No, not at all. Something about him just seemed a little... I'm not even sure what. Different? No, that's not it; I can't put my finger on it. Anyway, it's nothing, I'm sure."

They dropped the subject. Tray finished his breakfast and was about to leave to look at more property when he saw Sophie coming down the stairs. "Good morning," he said.

"I thought you must be already out looking at land for sale," she said, but gave no smile and had no cheerful "good morning," which was her normal greeting.

"I'm going now," he explained. She nodded and still said nothing more, which simply wasn't like her. She then took a step toward the great room

"What about you?" he asked quickly. "You going somewhere special?"

She stopped and glanced up at him. Now, he was certain she was unhappy. "No. No where."

"Is something wrong?"

She shook her head, but instead of denying there was a problem, she lifted troubled eyes to his. "I guess you could say that."

"I'm sorry."

"No need." She clasped her hands. "It's not really that big a deal. Not like life or death, or anything. A disappointment, that's all." When he said nothing, she added, "I shouldn't let it get me down."

As much as he wasn't sure what to say, at the same time, he couldn't ignore her and go on his way. The fisherman's advice came back to him. "If you're not doing anything special," he began, "and if you'd like to ride along with me, that would be fine. It might let you could concentrate on taking photos and not whatever this not-life-and-death bad news was."

She looked genuinely taken aback by his invitation. Did she see him as that much of an ogre? "Really?"

He shrugged. "As company goes, you aren't that bad."

She still didn't smile, but studied his eyes, and then asked, "Would you give me time to change my shoes?"

He looked at her soft leather pumps. "I'd hope so. I'll even give you time to eat your breakfast. How about we meet in a half-hour by my truck. Grab a warm jacket. We'll be heading north, up into the mountains, so it'll be a might colder up there."

"Thanks," she said, and this time she did smile.

As they left Garden Valley for the highway, Tray kept giving Sophie worried glances. "Want to talk about it?"

She lifted her chin. "It's nothing. Kind of silly, actually."

The further he drove, the less he was enjoying the quiet. The last time she rode with him she'd been aching to talk, and now, when he asked her to, she stayed mum. He wasn't sure what to do, but he remembered that one way to get people to talk was to tell them something about yourself first. "To open up," he thought it was called.

He wasn't one to do that. Usually, he was so far beyond "reserved" he was at times accused of being secretive. Not that he had any secrets to keep; he simply kept himself to himself. Especially after losing Charlene.

But that morning he'd told a complete stranger things about himself he normally would never had said, and it hadn't killed him. In fact, he felt better for it. This woman, who had never been anything but nice to him, was clearly hurting. The least he could do was try to help.

After another glance at her tight lips, he found himself talking. "Last evening, I got a call from my son's grandmother. That's never a good thing. I had to walk about a half mile down the road before I had good enough reception to hear everything she was complaining about."

Sophie glanced at him eyebrows raised. He wasn't sure if it was because he was talking or because he might not have told her had a son. "That doesn't sound good," she murmured.

"It wasn't."

"How old is your son?"

"Fourteen."

She nodded. "No wonder his grandmother is complaining. That's a difficult age. Any other children?"

"No. My wife and I were blessed with only the one, and he's handful enough for me." He saw her nod but then continue to glumly stare out the window. *Open up*, he told himself. It was harder than he thought, but he forced himself to add, "If you're wondering why the boy's with his grandma, it's because my wife passed some four years ago."

He said it bluntly, factually, and yet the words seemed to reverberate in the quiet of the truck. She glanced his way a moment, then murmured, "I'm so sorry."

"Thanks."

They rode in silence. So much for opening up, he thought. He couldn't bring himself to say anything more.

But then, after awhile, she asked, "Does all that, your son and your wife's passing, have something to do with you being here looking for property?"

"It does. And I suspect it's why he's acting up."

Her voice was soft. "It's not easy for a teenager to leave all their friends behind."

He grimaced. "So I'm discovering!" His words and exaggerated tone were wry.

She glanced up at him and he gave her a small smile. When she returned it, he actually felt good to have caused a little crack in the woeful armor she'd surrounded herself with that morning.

The road was a series of switchbacks up into the mountains, the Payette River on one side, cliffs that had been bulldozed to form the road on the other—and a lot of signs that said to watch out for falling rocks. Yeah, no kidding.

Just past one of those cliffs, the land flattened and a "For Sale" sign marked the entrance to a rocky, uneven dirt road. He pulled into it and stopped.

"Is this the land you were looking for?" she asked, clutching the dashboard.

"I'm sorry to say, yes. This was a wasted trip. Sorry about that. I doubt even bighorn sheep want to go up that hill just to get to the property. And I can see being stuck up there all winter."

"You're right," she said. "But since we're here, why not go see what it looks like? I suspect the view is beautiful."

He noticed how she was looking around, trying to take in the scenery from the windows of his truck. She seemed to be growing out of her earlier gloom. "Okay, we can do this."

The truck strained the last few hundred feet, but eventually they found the area with the land for sale. "Why anyone bothered to put electricity in this area is beyond me," he muttered. "Someone obviously paid big bucks to get this place ready to build on, but then changed their mind. With good reason."

When he stopped grousing about the land, he looked around, and Sophie was no longer with him. "Sophie?" he called.

No answer. "Sophie!"

"Over here!"

He followed the sound of her voice and found her standing heart-stoppingly close to the edge of a cliff.

"Look." She pointed towards the distance. The mountains dropped away, chiseled by the power of the Payette, which didn't look big at the moment, but would become much wider, deeper, and faster as spring thaws melted the snow packs.

"Come join me." She sat down on a rocky outcrop with an unobstructed view of the land to the south. "I took a few photos, but I had to remain a moment and enjoy this view. It's breathtaking."

He sat beside her. The outcrop was so small they were shoulder-to-shoulder. "It is. And it sounds like you're feeling better."

"A bit. Not that I know what I'm going to do about it, though."

He was tempted, but he didn't ask.

"Okay," she said after a while. "It's nothing compared to what you're dealing with, but I received an email that the magazine that was interested in a big travel piece I'd planned to do is closing. They're out of money. And the editor who knew and liked my work, is also out of a job. This means the reason I'm taking photos in this area is dead."

"That's definitely a big deal," he said. "No wonder you feel bad. It's got to be especially troubling since you're on the other side of the world from home."

"I don't know about that." She stared out over the landscape, her jaw tight. "I'm not sure where home is anymore. To tell the truth, I have no reason to return to Italy."

"There must be other magazines who want the story."

"There are, and I'll query them. But this editor was a friend, he knew and trusted my work, and that makes a difference. I guess the real problem is that I never expected, at age thirty-two, to be starting all over."

"I hope that's not old," he said. "Since I'm four years older."

She studied him. "And you have a fourteen-year-old? You were a young father."

"I was. I thought I was a man of the world at the time, but now, I realize I was still a kid myself."

She nodded. "It sounds as if you've done a lot more living than me."

"I doubt that," he said. "I've been a rancher. You've traveled the world."

She cocked her head and studied him awhile. "One thing a photographer learns is to spot the little things, tiny signs, that most people miss when they're busy absorbing the overall picture. With you, I see the small laugh lines edging your mouth, the hint of crow's feet by your eyes, and I can't help but think you're a man who's lived hard and fully, and who's grown stronger for it. Whereas when I look at myself, all I see is someone who's dashed around looking at other people and places through the lens of a camera. But how much have I really lived? Sometimes I wonder."

He was taken aback at the way she'd described him. He'd never heard anyone speak about him that way. The little things, the tiny signs, she had said... and then he took those in as he slowly detailed her face, from her mesmerizing eyes with long, long lashes, to her broad cheekbones, straight nose, and full lips. At that thought, he tore his gaze from her face, but it dropped to her shoulders and from there to the soft curves of her woman's body. He swallowed hard.

If he had the sense he was born with, he would have told

her she was being too hard on herself, and that the way he'd lived was nothing so special at all. And maybe, depending on how she'd reacted to his words, she would have liked him to put an arm around her, maybe even kiss her.

Wow, where in the world had those thoughts come from?

He drew back a bit from her. After all, the last thing he needed was an entanglement with a woman—especially not with one he found to be intelligent, thoughtful, and interesting. Not to mention the fact that she was just passing through the area. He wasn't a casual man. Involvement meant something to him. And he'd spent enough time being hurt by loss to allow himself to get close to someone he knew would soon leave, no matter how kissable she seemed. "You'll be fine," he said, getting to his feet. "I'm sure of it."

She nodded. "I'm keeping you from finding a place you might want to buy. I didn't mean to do that." She then reached out her hand for him to help her stand.

He took it and memories hit hard of the last time he'd held a hand with such soft skin and so delicately shaped. He pulled her to her feet. "It's okay. Sometimes, I'm still not sure what I should be doing." He glanced down at their still joined hands and reluctantly let her go. "And my biggest worry is figuring out what's best for my son."

They walked side-by-side in silence to the truck. Tray drove another fifteen minutes north of the mountains where the land flattened to a high plateau.

"How's this property?" Sophie asked after they left the truck and she snapped a few shots near the For Sale sign.

Tray studied the land, his hat tilted back and one foot on the lower rung of the fence rail that separated the property from the road. This property, he had to think long about. "It's not bad," he said finally. "But I'm afraid it's just too far from other people. A fourteen-year-old boy needs friends. I don't know that he'd find many out here."

"You're right about that," Sophie admitted.

"It's suitable land, though. I could probably even run cattle out here, if I wanted."

"If?"

He frowned. "That's another conundrum."

"Oh? Why?"

"Been there, done that." He then shrugged and headed back toward his truck. He noticed her brows knit as if puzzled by his words, before she quickly followed behind him.

CHAPTER 9

Sophie and Tray stopped for pizza and beer for dinner in Garden Valley before returning to the cabin. When they walked into the great room, she asked if he'd like coffee. "Sure, if you're making a pot," he'd said.

She took a step and jumped, startled at the sight of Bree crawling along the floor by the credenza that held a stereo player, CDs and DVDs. "What are you doing down there?" she cried. "Are you all right?"

Bree stood up, smoothed her red hair, adjusted her glasses, and then brushed dust off the knees of her jeggings, all the while attempting to look poised. "I was trying to find something."

"What did you lose?" Sophie asked as she continued on to the kitchen area and filled the coffeemaker with water, and then ground coffee.

"I, uh, I lost an earring. No, actually, the backing for an earring—a tiny gold piece."

"I have extras if you need one," Sophie said.

"No need." Bree then pointed at Elijah Donnelly's portrait

over the mantle. "Have you... either of you... ever noticed any changes in that portrait?"

"Changes?" Tray asked, looking from Bree to the painting. "It looks the same to me."

Bree flapped her arms. "Of course it does. Why shouldn't it? Just joking."

"What kind of changes?" Sophie asked.

"Nothing. Kidding! You know, ghosts and all." Bree then stomped from the room and up the stairs.

Tray looked at Sophie. "She's at least one brewski short of a six-pack, isn't she?"

Sophie shook her head. "I think this cabin is freaking her out for some reason. Maybe she'll leave soon."

"Happy day," Tray muttered. He went to some maps he'd left on a side table in the seating area. He took one of them now, unfolded it, and began to study it. "I've pretty much looked at the places within some 25 miles of this valley. Looks like I'll need to search for property farther out."

Sophie brought him a cup of coffee as soon as it was ready and took her own cup to the coffee table in front of the sofa. There, she sat with a stack of fashion magazines she'd purchased in Boise and began going through them.

But even though she turned a magazine's pages, she couldn't help but think about the man in the room with her. He'd told her a lot today that helped her understand why he seemed so driven about finding a place for himself and his son to live. Although he didn't say it, she could tell he was worried about the boy, and about their relationship. In her limited experience, she'd heard from friends with teenagers how difficult those years could be, and to raise a son alone when he still seemed to be mourning the loss of his wife had to make a tough situation even more difficult. She found it commendable that he was trying hard to make a good life for them.

Tray kept going through maps and muttering under his breath. Finally, he folded up the maps. "It's a waste of time trying to search when the cabin's internet won't cooperate. It's being more stubborn than ever tonight. Sometimes, I can get two bars, but then it drops to one and takes forever to open up the simplest website. I give up." He walked over to the couch where she sat and spent a moment staring at the fireplace. "Would it be okay with you if I built a fire?"

"I'd love that. And I'll put on some music. Time to simply relax." She put down her magazines and went to the CD player. Whoever supplied the CDs and even older tape recordings liked classical music, Broadway shows, and easy-listening ballads from years ago. Maggie once told her that the mother of the sisters who owned the cabin had been a singer and often performed in off Broadway musicals.

"I don't know why they don't just put up a satellite dish," Tray said as he got the fire started.

"Maybe the ghosts wouldn't like it," Sophie replied with a chuckle.

"Right. We can't upset the ghosts," Tray groused. "Who knows what they might do?"

"Heaven forbid they haunt us! Ah, here's a CD with some ballads I've heard of." She put it on the CD player. "Chances Are" came softly through the speakers. She listened awhile, then, as soon as Tray got the fire going, she dimmed the lights to better see its glow.

"This is lovely," she said, taking a seat on the sofa. "It's as if I can shut off all the noise of the outside world and live here in a peaceful bubble."

"You make a good point," he admitted as he sat beside her. "Like now, poor me. I'm forced to sit here in this lovely room with a beautiful woman at my side, warmth from the fireplace, and romantic music in the background. Maybe the ghosts are onto something after all."

Her eyes caught his, and everything about him seemed so much more relaxed than usual, she felt her heart warm to him. She wanted to dismiss whatever it was she was feeling, but then he turned to her and said simply, "Thank you for today. You've made something I was dreading into a pleasure."

His words touched her, and she could only whisper, "It was for me, too."

"I'm glad." His gaze captured hers as he smiled that funny little half-grin he had, and then he settled back to face the fireplace and relax in the warmth and flickering of the flames. Watching him, she felt as if something shifted inside her, something that told her there was substance and quality to Tray Bowman, and that he just might be someone special to her.

On the CD, an oldie-but-goodie began. "A Certain Smile."

CHAPTER 10

T he next morning, Saturday, when Sophie showed up for breakfast, she found Maggie in a dither because the married couple she'd expected that day had just cancelled their reservations. Sophie kept mum, but she found that good news.

Bree and Tray were already eating. Bree was enjoying an éclair, and had a second one on her plate, while Tray seemed to be wolfing down his bacon, eggs, and pancake breakfast as fast as humanly possible.

Sophie grabbed a scone and cranberry juice and sat down at the table to pour herself some coffee just as Tray got up, his breakfast finished. "Morning," he said to Sophie, and then all but fled from the room, muttering something about having a lot going on.

"Good morning," she said to his retreating figure, wondering what his fast escape was all about. Was it her? Or had some new issue arisen with his family?

Last night, she and Tray had stayed up until midnight talking. She had told him a lot about her childhood in Chicago, and a little about Italy, even touching briefly on the affair with Sergio that hadn't worked out.

Tray had fascinating stories about the Crow people, their history and beliefs, as well as life on the "rez," as he called it. He wasn't sad as he talked about his wife and her family, but seem to enjoy telling her things he'd learned from them. She hoped his sudden departure that morning didn't mean something bad had happened back in Montana.

She then faced Bree, who ignored her as she sat working the crossword puzzle she'd brought to the table.

As Sophie ate the scone, her gaze turned to Elijah Donnelly's portrait, and the deep sadness of his expression struck her. How had she never noticed it before? Was she really that oblivious to the emotions around her? Or was Elijah changing his expression the way Bree had suggested?

But Bree was a strange one, asking about the ghosts and crawling around on the floor. Sophie never saw her wear earrings, so how could she have lost the backing for one? On the other hand, Bree seemed to be constantly watching everything going on around her while keeping completely quiet herself.

Tray implied he thought she was a little crazy, but Sophie suspected Bree was only as crazy as she wanted to be.

Sophie thanked Maggie for the breakfast and hurried up to her room as her own feelings of sadness and loneliness grew stronger. What was going on with her?

She should feel quite good. She was staying at a place she loved; she had prospects for making a little money; and found herself spending time with a man she liked. That surprised her the most. She never expected to be able to like anyone of the opposite sex for months, if not years, after the way Sergio had all but torn out her heart and run it through a sausage grinder with his cheating.

At the same time, her growing attachment to Tray worried

her. He had serious family issues to deal with, and had no idea how the situation with his son and finding a home would turn out. If he couldn't find what he needed in Idaho, he might go back to Montana, once again living near the Crow reservation —near his dead wife's relatives. If Sophie wasn't careful, she could be setting herself up to face a world of hurt with him. That was the last thing she wanted to deal with again.

Besides, if she was serious about becoming a travel photographer, she had to be ready to leave her "home"—wherever it might be—at a moment's notice. No, there was no way she should get into a relationship with anyone at this point in her life, especially not someone with all the baggage Tray Bowman carried.

At the same time, she'd enjoyed last evening more than any in a long, long time, including the entire past year in Italy.

"Ghosts, where are you?" she softly spoke the words aloud. "I need you now! Can't you tell? You're supposed to be good at matchmaking. Are Tray and I a match or not? You need to sort out our relationship, if we can even have one, which I doubt. But you've got a reputation to uphold!"

Despite her attempt to "summon the spirits," her body didn't levitate, no lights flickered, no woo-woo sounds were heard. She guessed not even the Donnelly cabin ghosts wanted anything to do with her.

That was clearly the mark of a true loser.

Since it was Saturday, Sophie decided to check on the outdoor market Dr. Waterton had told her about. She had already bought photographic supplies and colorful items to set up a photo booth, so she hoped the market wasn't a complete dud.

Maybe she would see the good doctor there? She should get

to know him better, and hopefully, would find him interesting enough to help her get over her growing feelings for Tray. The thought of getting involved in another hopeless relationship was awful. No, thank you!

She changed into a short sheath dress and high heels, pulled the sides of her hair high on the back of her head, held it in place with a silver clip, and then let it cascade down her back in an array of waves and curls. Finally, she grabbed her camera bag and headed to town.

The Saturday market was easy to find. There were booths with jewelry, pottery, jams, jellies, woodwork, paintings, and the kinds of bric-à-brac usually found at markets like this throughout the country. It was still a bit chilly, but she could see the potential in the event. She imagined that once crops ripened so that a true farmers' market could join this one, it would become quite busy.

"Hey, there. Sophie!"

She turned at the sound of the voice to see Josh standing beside a massive sign introducing his new bakery. She went over to him. "What is all this?" she asked.

"I'm doing some neighborly outreach. I made a bunch of mini-scones that I'm giving away so that people will come over to my bakery to buy the real thing. And I also brought some croissants and muffins in case anyone wants to buy a full-sized treat right now."

"What a great idea!"

"How about you? Can I get you something?"

"I'm afraid I ate one of your scones for breakfast this morning. I find I enjoy them more than bacon and eggs."

"A girl after my own heart." His smile caused his eyes to crinkle and showed teeth that sparkled in the sunlight. How had she forgotten how cute he was?

"I'm going to move on," she said. "Good luck with your outreach."

"Thanks. I thought you must have already left town, but if you're sticking around a while longer, maybe we can get together again. I still owe you a dinner, after all."

"Don't worry about it. See you!" She walked away.

She kept looking for Dr. Waterton, but didn't see him. She spent time looking at some fairly pricey hand-crafted jewelry, and it took every bit of strength to remind herself she had no business buying trinkets when she didn't have a paycheck coming in.

She liked the looks of the outdoor market and was relieved her purchases for it weren't wasted. Maybe she'd even come back here the next day, Sunday, to give it a try. It wasn't as if she was otherwise engaged. As she headed back to her car, she noticed a sign across the street that read, "Middlefork Family Medicine" and below it, "Carter Waterton, M.D."

The lights were on and it looked like the office was open. Sophie crossed the street and went inside. A heavyset, middle-aged receptionist wearily gazed up at her. "Can I help you?"

"Is Dr. Waterton in?"

"He is, but he's seeing the last of his patients now. We close early on Saturdays," she said, then heaved the sigh of someone who clearly felt she was going above and beyond. "All right. Tell me the nature of your illness? Is this an emergency?"

"No, it's not an emergency. In fact, it's not anything. I'm not even sick. Just a friend." Sophie felt increasingly awkward under the receptionist's now cold-eyed scrutiny. "I just wanted to stop by and say hello." As her awkwardness grew, she said, "I think I'll just leave. Maybe I'll see him in town some point."

She began backing away when the receptionist stopped her. "Wait. Take a seat. He'll be free in just a few minutes."

Sophie debated with herself. Perhaps she was just being

silly to have even come here, but then she said, "Great. Thanks."

"Your name?"

She wondered if he'd remember it. "Sophie. Sophie Evans."

She had no sooner taken a seat when a woman and a little boy with a splint on his finger left the office, waving goodbye to the receptionist. Once they left, the receptionist hurried back to the doctor's office. In no time, Carter Waterton himself stepped into the waiting room. She'd found him attractive when she saw him in the brewpub, but here, wearing his white doctor's coat, and with his perfectly coiffed hair, he looked like he stepped off the set of *Grey's Anatomy*.

"Well, look who's here. This is such a pleasant surprise. " He flashed her a shiny, toothy grin.

She stood. "Yes, well, I went to the Saturday market that you told me about, and I was so impressed with it, I wanted to thank you for letting me know it existed."

His eyebrows rose at that, looking a bit confused. "The market?"

"You talked about a photo booth," she prompted. She noticed the receptionist taking in every word.

"Oh.... Ah! That's right! I'm glad you liked it," he said with another smile.

This wasn't working out quite as she'd hoped. How many women did he meet in bars? And how many scotch and waters had he drunk? Feeling increasing awkward, she forged ahead. "So, since you're good at street fairs and markets, I was wondering if you have any suggestions for good places to eat in the area, places close to home."

He studied her a moment. "Tell you what, how about this evening, I take you to a place that serves a great meal? I could swing by, uh, the Donnelly place, wasn't it?"

"That's right." At least he remembered that much.

"How about seven o'clock?"

She hesitated, but looking at him in that doctor's coat... "Sounds great."

"Good. Then, I'll show you the most swinging place in town. By the way, how's your line dancing?"

Oh, no, she thought, and hoped this dinner at Mama's Folly would end better than her last one had. "How about nonexistent?"

"That's about the same as mine. Good! That means you won't be disappointed. I'll see you tonight."

CHAPTER 11

That evening, Sophie went downstairs to the great room wearing a green Louis Vuitton off-the-rack dress which she'd bought when money was no object, a whole two months ago. She saw Bree going through a stack of compact disks and making a selection of classical music, and Tray was seated at the dining table shuffling papers and maps.

"Wow, looks like somebody has a date," Bree said.

Tray looked up at the comment, and Sophie noticed that his expression quickly went from stunned to a frown before he turned again to his papers.

"I'm just going into town for dinner," Sophie said.

Bree gave her a knowing grin. "With the baker, I take it?"

"No. I met the town's doctor."

"Oh!" Bree gasped. "Even better!"

Tray didn't look up, but she saw that his frown deepened. She couldn't help but think it was because of her date. He had acted as if he might be growing as attracted to her as she was to him, and realizing that, she felt oddly joyful, which she tried to suppress. But there it was.

A knock sounded on the door, and she suddenly wasn't nearly as interested in going out as she had convinced herself to be. But she hurried to the door and opened it. "Hello, Carter."

Waterton stepped into the foyer. "You look beautiful," he said, and to her surprise, gave her a light kiss on the cheek.

Sophie grabbed her coat and rushed him out of the cabin.

Before long, they were at Mama's Folly and from the moment they entered, people were greeting the town doctor and giving her a once-over. Naturally just about everyone knew him, she reasoned, although she found it strange that whenever he introduced her, he would point out that she was new in town, just visiting for a very short time, and he had promised to show her what a real country-western music, dance, and restaurant was all about... before she left... which she would do soon.

It puzzled her that he would be so insistent on making all that information clear to everyone when he was the one who'd given her the idea about a way to make some money and stay there awhile.

When the waitress appeared to take them to their table, it was the same waitress who had looked as if she would love to stab Sophie with a fork when she was there with Josh. But now, the waitress gave her such a wide-eyed "I-can't-believe-what-I'm-seeing" look, it was all Sophie could do not to laugh.

After handing them the menus, the waitress asked if they'd like a before dinner drink.

Waterton ordered a Scotch and soda, but before Sophie could say a word, the waitress said, "A whiskey sour, right?"

Sophie laughed. "Sounds good."

The waitress cocked an eyebrow and walked away.

"You've been here before, I take it?" Waterton said.

"Only once. She must have a phenomenal memory."

He looked puzzled. "No kidding."

"Oh, my," Sophie said. "Look at how nicely they line dance, all in rows."

"That's the idea," Waterton said. "My feet never seem to want to go in the right direction. And the syncopation drives me crazy."

Sophie had to admit, however, it looked like fun, and she found it took some effort to turn away from the music and dancing to listen to Carter tell her in great detail about his medical background, the experiences he'd had at the different, albeit important, hospitals he'd worked in before finding his way to his own practice there in the valley.

Even after the waitress brought their prime rib dinners to the table, Carter continued to talk about himself. She was glad he wasn't interested in her—she wasn't in the mood to give him her life story anyway. Clearly, he was proud, confident, and self-absorbed, which she supposed was a good thing, except that it reminded her too much of Sergio.

Stop, she told herself. Dr. Carter Waterton was nothing like Sergio; he simply had a lot to say about himself. Clearly, being the town doctor here was a big thing, especially in his own mind.

When he brought her back to the cabin, he asked if he could look inside, since he'd never been in there and he, like everyone else in the county, was curious about it.

She was happy to oblige. Tray was in there reading a seriously thick book, and Bree was reading a paperback mystery. "Some Enchanted Evening" from the old musical *South Pacific,* played.

Sophie quickly introduced Waterton to her fellow lodgers.

"Evening," Tray muttered, his gaze darting from Sophie to Waterton and back.

"What do you two think of the woman's voice?" Bree asked. "I'm playing an old tape recording. The singer is one of the former owners of the cabin, Roxanne Donnelly. I find her voice beautiful. She apparently sang in musicals all over the country. But she's gone now, poor thing."

"She's great," Sophie agreed.

"Is she one of the ghosts?" Carter asked with a broad smile.

"Very funny," Sophie said. "As you well know, there are no ghosts here."

"I wouldn't be so sure of that," Bree said, tucking in her chin and giving them both a knowing stare.

"Oh?" Waterton faced Bree. "It sounds as if you know something about them."

"I do," Bree said proudly. "And I'm hoping to learn a lot more. In fact, for all I know, you and Sophie are dating because of them. I mean, you two just met by chance, right?"

"Most people meet by chance," Waterton said.

Bree shrugged. "Are you sure of that?"

"Don't be silly, Bree," Sophie snapped.

"Well, it makes it easier if you don't believe the ghosts are matchmaking because of the bad things that can happen," Bree announced knowingly.

"What are you talking about?" Sophie asked.

"The rumors about the ghosts say that if the ghosts want the two of you together, but you don't follow their wishes, you'll never be able to find true love in your life."

"Where have you heard this?" Sophie asked.

"I did my research before coming here," Bree told her. "And Maggie confirmed the rumors."

Waterton looked confused. "So, I need to fall in love with whoever the ghosts want me to love, or I'm doomed to loneliness?"

Bree nodded. "So they say."

Sophie jumped in. "Thank you for bringing me back to the cabin," she said to Waterton as she took his arm and walked him back toward the front door. "I had a marvelous time."

Waterton was still gawking at Bree, but once at the door, he turned all his attention to Sophie. "It was a great evening," he said.

"Very nice," she said, as she pulled open the door for him. "Thank you."

He looked from her to the door and got the message.

"I'll call you," he said.

"Bye!" Bree called from the doorway to the great room. Behind her, Tray stood, seemingly waiting for her to move so he could go upstairs, but fiercely glaring at Waterton.

Waterton's eyes widened at the spectators, then he muttered goodbye to Sophie and left the cabin.

CHAPTER 12

On Sunday morning, Maggie had gone to church and the cold breakfast selection she had left out was sitting, uneaten, when Sophie entered the great room. Neither Tray nor Bree was around. Sophie took an early morning walk along the river and went down to the footpath.

To her delight, before long, Anna appeared. "Good morning," Sophie called to her.

"How are you, Sophie?" Anna said.

"Okay, but it's been a crazy week." As they walked, Sophie filled her in on all she'd learned about the inn's other two guests, the Italian magazine shutting down, possibly setting up a photo booth at the weekend market, and even about her date with the town doctor.

"Well, it sounds as if you're making a home for yourself here," Anna said. "Do you feel good about that?"

"Running a photo booth is hardly a career move. And the doctor seems nice, but he'll ever set my heart ablaze."

Anna chuckled. "But there's someone you're interested in, I think."

"I'm just not sure. And after all those years with Sergio, I'm don't know how much I trust my own emotions anymore. Maybe I'm simply gun shy, as our cowboy guest would probably say."

"And how is your cowboy guest?" Anna asked.

Sophie wrinkled her lips. "Ornery, bossy, and stubborn on the surface, but I think it's all bluster to hide that, once you get to know him, he's a really nice guy."

Anna laughed. "It sounds like you're getting to know him."

"It's not what you're thinking," Sophie added. "Besides, a person doesn't get over a seven-year love affair over night."

"I'd imagine not."

"Maybe never. Someday, Maggie and I might be the only people living here. The townsfolk will call us the two crazy women at the old cabin. The ones who live with the ghosts. That'll give the townspeople plenty to talk about, won't it?"

Anna rolled her eyes. "It certainly will."

At that point, they reached the place in the path after which Anna continued on by herself.

It troubled Sophie that her dear friend didn't want Sophie to see her house. All she could do was to be there as Anna's friend. If Anna ever did want to talk about her strange lifestyle, Sophie would gladly listen and even be a shoulder for her to cry on if necessary. On the other hand, Anna seemed as level-headed a person as Sophie had ever met.

The two women said goodbye, and Sophie hurried back to the cabin to shower and put on an eye-catching outfit. She was going to the Sunday market, and would see what the day would bring.

Sophie set up her photography booth in a corner of the marketplace so that she had plenty of room on each side and behind her for all the equipment, backdrop, and props she wanted to use to make her photos interesting.

A selection of cowboy hats, women's bonnets and straw hats, neckerchiefs, fake holsters and old-time pistols were there for customers to use if they wished.

To Sophie's surprise, Bree joined her and helped with the set-up and even volunteered to stay in case so many customers appeared they needed to be given numbers. Sophie couldn't imagine that would happen, but she was glad for the company.

Her biggest fear was that the photo booth would be such a disaster she'd want to chug down the photo developer and end it all.

Fortunately, she wasn't there long before a young couple took a chance with her. That seemed to break the ice as more people lined up to have their pictures taken looking like real world cowpunchers. Also, her prices were quite reasonable.

Before long, Bree wandered off to do whatever things Bree did. Sophie couldn't say she minded being left alone.

She was taking pictures of a brother and sister, ages ten and eight, when a man marched up to her. He wore a white shirt, tie, and dress slacks, had slicked-back gray hair and a stiffly erect carriage.

She scarcely glanced his way, but continued to look into her lens at the kids. "Just a moment and I'll be finished here."

"I'll wait." Something about his tone made her glance at him again to see a sneering scowl on his face. He looked like trouble.

"Smile, kids!" she called. She moved them into different positions and poses and before finishing the session.

The stranger hovered ever closer. Finally, she faced him. "Would you like your photo taken?" she asked.

He looked as if he'd bitten into a pickle. "I am Omar

Timmons, and I assuredly am not here for you to take my photo. Or anyone else's!"

She didn't appreciate his tone. She put her hands on her hips. "Then what are you here for?"

"You should know that Omar Timmins is *the* photographer in this valley. The only photographer in this valley, and I have been for fifteen years."

His foul expression suddenly made sense. "How nice to meet you. My name is Sophie Evans and I'm just passing through. I learned about the town's outdoor market and since I'm a professional photographer, I thought it might be nice for some of the people here to take home a personal memento of their visit to this charming place."

"Who gave you permission to set up this booth here?

"The mayor."

Timmons' mouth tightened into a corkscrew. "Well, I'm sorry to tell you, but Omar Timmons is in charge of all things photographic in this town, not the mayor. I am on the board of the Chamber of Commerce, and we do not allow anyone selling goods or services in our town without our permission."

"Interesting," she said, "because while I've been here, I've watched several people simply plop themselves on the ground without even a table, and start selling a few goods off of a blanket spread in front of them. From what I've seen, no one especially cares."

"Omar Timmons cares, as you would if you were doing anything but just passing through. I suspect you don't even have a proper license."

This pompous moron and the way he kept repeating his own name was getting on her nerves. "I've never heard of a license to take photographs and I've traveled the world over doing exactly this."

He puffed himself up so much he was practically on his tiptoes. "I have a photography license," he proclaimed.

"What did you do, photoshop it? Or are you trying to tell me Garden Valley is the only place in the world with such a requirement? Who put it into place? You? With your pals at the Chamber of Commerce?"

"What I'm telling you, is that people in these parts don't just move into another person's territory simply because they feel like it. If the town had a need or desire for someone to take photos during a farmers' market, which I frankly find hilarious, then Omar Timmons would be the one to satisfy that desire. Not some frivolous outsider."

Two could play at this game. She lifted her chin. "Maybe you're the one who couldn't figure out that people wanted photos. And you coming here shows only that you're jealous that someone else spotted it. If you can't even see past the end of your nose, it doesn't say much good about your ability to take decent photographs."

"You're talking big for your britches, young lady, and I, for one, don't appreciate it."

"Just as I don't appreciate you coming around here and trying to intimidate me. So, unless you're at my booth so that I can take a photograph of you, you should leave."

His cheeks mottled bright red as he glared at her. "I suggest you don't show up here next weekend, because if you do, we'll see who's right and who's wrong."

———————

As Tray sauntered over to Sophie, he watched Omar Timmons strut off like a peacock, head high and walking like he had a stick somewhere the sun didn't shine. "Should I ask what that was all about?"

"It was nothing. He's apparently a photographer who has come to regard this valley as his personal property and said I have no business being here." Although it appeared she had gotten the best of Mr. Pomposity, she looked upset.

"Well, a person does tend to find that reaction in areas like this from people who aren't used to competition and don't like it. Sometimes even the town itself wants nothing to change. But if you have good ideas, the townspeople will usually come around."

"Do you think?" she asked, hands on hips.

"I couldn't help but notice that you've had a fairly steady stream of customers today. You're providing a service that guy never thought about, so kudos for you, and it sucks to be him." He placed his hands on her shoulders, to let her know he was there to support her. "Besides, you've done everything right, so don't let him get to you."

Her eyes were bright as she looked up at him. "Thank you, Tray."

Suddenly, he was too aware of the feel of her narrow shoulders, of the scent of roses and springtime that hovered around her, of the tickle of her long hair brushing against his fingers. He quickly dropped his hands. "By the way, it appears you've got a few people behind you right now, also wanting your service."

She glanced over her shoulder and smiled at two family groups including kids who looked as if they were interested in having their photos taken. She faced Tray again with a smile on her lips. "I appreciate the pep talk. I do feel better. And when I'm done here, I'd like to take a photo of you—free of charge."

He was puzzled. "Why me?"

She hesitated, and then said simply, "Because I'd say you're my best friend here."

Her words surprised him, but he also liked hearing them,

liked the idea of the two of them being friends, in fact. Friendship, he could handle. More than that he doubted was in the
cards for them, not with her now dating the town doctor.
Besides, he still wasn't sure he was ready for getting serious
about another woman, although if he was ready, he couldn't
imagine anyone much finer than Sophie. So, in response, he
gave her a small smile, nodded, and touched the brim of his
cowboy hat. "I feel the same. And with that being the case,
seems a snapshot or two can be arranged."

CHAPTER 13

"You didn't come back for me to take your photo today," Sophie said as Tray walked into the great room that evening. She had been so tired after taking photographs for most of the day, she bought a burger to go at the Rusty Nail, and sat at the dining table to eat it. She had just finished and was having an after-dinner cup of coffee.

"No, I got caught up in something." He didn't look or sound at all happy, and she wondered what had happened. He went to the refrigerator, grabbed a beer, opened it, and took a long swallow as he leaned against the kitchen island. "Besides, you don't need a photo of me. You'll forget about me soon as you've shaken the dust of Garden Valley from your boots. Isn't that what travel photographers do? Always on to the next big photo shoot, the one that might end up as a Pulitzer or whatever kind of award it is you guys give each other."

She stared at him, shocked. His words hurt. What had brought all that on? A while ago, they were talking about being best friends. She wondered if something else had gone wrong, something with his son or family, and he was lashing out at her for no reason except that she was the one here. She decided to simply answer him. "There are the International Photography Awards, and the TPOTY—"

"Tea potty?"

"Travel Photographer of the Year."

"Of course." His tone was snide.

"Yeah, right." She shook her head, wanting to know what was wrong as she watched him drink down more of his beer. "Anyway, who cares? I'd like a photo of you for myself—a memory of the fellow who badgered me all over this country-side, and who I feared was going to get me killed on some of those mountainous roads we traveled."

He raised his eyebrows. "How could you forget any of that, photo or not?"

"You may have a point," she said dryly.

"Why, when you can take great portraits of people, do you want to be a travel photographer anyway?"

She thought about that a moment. "A couple of reasons. One is to capture the beauty around us in places that many people in this world will only be able to see because of photographs I take. And the other is to inspire people to get out there and see such places for themselves. Each day, as I grow older, I realize how short life is, and how a person's life can change in a heartbeat. That means we need to act, to discover, as much as we can while we have the time and the good health to do so. For me, doing photography and capturing what's truly important is an act of faith and of love."

"I had no idea." He looked suddenly sheepish, as if realizing his earlier grouchiness was uncalled for. "Okay, you've convinced me. Maybe next weekend I'll 'pose' for a photo. That is, as long as you don't let Omar Timmons scare you away, and if I'm still in town."

Her smile vanished, and an emptiness filled her. "Oh? Do you think you'll be leaving us so soon?"

Their gazes locked. "I've got to leave soon," he murmured, and then looked away as he said, more to himself than her, "I've got to work something out."

She was about to ask to him to talk to her, to tell her what was troubling him, when there was a knock on the front door.

"Who could that be?" Sophie said. "Maybe Bree forgot her key."

"The door isn't locked yet," Tray said.

Just then, Sophie heard a woman's voice called out, "Yoo hoo, is anybody here?"

Sophie looked at Tray and shrugged. She didn't recognize the voice. He, on the other hand, looked perplexed. "Just us ghosts," Sophie called as she stood up to go and see who was calling.

"Uh oh." Tray muttered and then hurried past her toward the foyer.

But before he reached it, a woman stepped into the great room, her eyes wide and her expression stark. "Ghosts?" she murmured. She was tiny, with platinum blonde, shoulder-length hair, wearing a pretty teal shirtwaist dress, and carrying a pie.

Tray all but froze mid-stride. "Georgina! What brings you here?"

Sophie could help but notice that the woman positively beamed as her eyes met Tray's. And Sophie also couldn't help but notice how handsome he looked in the tall, rangy way of many Western men as he stood facing the newcomer.

"Hello, again," Georgina gushed in a voice so high Sophie feared her ears might bleed. "I can't tell you how much I enjoyed our conversation this afternoon." If Georgina's eyelashes batted any faster, she might achieve lift-off. "And since I remembered you saying that huckleberry pie was your favorite, well, I had some huckleberries in the freezer from last year's crop, so I thawed them and baked this just for you." She then thrust the pie at him.

He stood there holding the pie in two hands as if it were a keg of nitroglycerine. "Well, isn't that nice of you? Thank you."

Since it was obvious why Georgina had come to the cabin, Sophie quietly eased herself onto the back porch. But she couldn't resist leaving the French doors slightly ajar and peeking inside to watch.

"Think nothing of it," Georgina said. "By the way, I've never been in this cabin before." She walked to the center of the great room and then slowly turned in a circle. "It's so much nicer than I ever expected. You know, a haunted house has some eerie connotations." But then she looked up at Tray, who towered over the tiny woman, and said, "Of course, the associations with the ghosts in this home are quite pleasant, don't you think? I mean, matchmaking is so sweet!"

"Well, frankly, I never really thought about them," Tray said nervously. "Since they're, you know, ghosts... which aren't real."

Georgina shook her head back and forth at least three times. She took the pie from him and placed it on the kitchen island. "Silly boy! Of course they're real. Everyone here knows it. You should, too. I mean, a handsome single man like you coming to an inn like this. Oh, my, but the most wonderful things can take place!"

Tray cleared his throat. "Well, I thank you for the pie."

"Oh, sure, and it was so nice of you to recommend the photographer. She seems good. Of course, only time will tell if she can develop the photos as nicely as Omar Timmons. Did you look at the artist I recommended, my cousin Dora?"

"Not yet, but I will, I'm sure." He took a few steps toward

the foyer, but Georgina ran around him to block his way. They were now out of Sophie's line of sight, and she had to shift to keep an eye on them.

"You know," Georgina now placed her hand on Tray's chest, "if you'd like to try a sliver of pie to make sure the huckleberries are as good as when first picked, we can do that."

He stopped moving. "I'm sure they are. But I must excuse myself, it's time I head upstairs and call my son."

Her face fell, and she dropped her hand. "Your son? But didn't you say something about being here alone? I had the impression you aren't married."

"Oh... well... uh..." He sucked in his breath. "My wife passed."

"Oh, poor man. I'm so sorry." This time she lunged at him and grabbed both his hands holding them up between them.

Sophie clutched the doorknob tight. It was clear Tray, her friend, was uncomfortable. He was too nice a guy to tell that woman to back off. But Sophie wasn't.

"Now I'm doubly glad I went through all the trouble of baking you that pie," Georgina cooed. "It's got a hint of orange in it. You must promise you'll think of me as you eat every tasty bite, and I just might check in on you tomorrow to see if you're doing all right, you poor dear. And your sweet motherless son, too! It makes my heart hurt just to think of you two all alone this way."

"Thank you, but..." He tried pulling his hands free, but the more he tugged, the tighter she held on. He backed up, but Georgina stepped toward him.

Sophie felt as if steam were coming out of her ears if she watched. If that woman got anymore "handsy" with Tray, she'd be in for a world of hurt!

"In fact," Georgina said with a big smile, "why don't you come to my house tomorrow night for a delicious home-cooked meal? I'll bet you haven't had one of those in some time. It'll be my pleasure."

Sophie grabbed the doorknob, about to push the door open, go inside, and get that Jezebel away from Tray, when Georgina cried out, "Yikes!" She let go of Tray and sprang backwards.

He gawked at her. "What's wrong?"

Sophie didn't move. With her limited view, she had no idea what had just happened.

"The pie." Georgina pointed a shaking finger toward the kitchen island.

Sophie watched as Tray looked over his shoulder. He seemed baffled. "Is something wrong with it?"

"No. But it was off the..., I mean, it looks like it was levita..." Georgina suddenly held her hands to her cheeks and looked ready to burst into tears. "I think I may be a little under the weather. I better go home. Right now."

Tray stood gaping as Georgina ran from the room and out the door.

Sophie was trying to see what was going on better than her limited view, but she must have pushed the door a little too hard because it suddenly swung all the way open, revealing her standing there listening.

"What were you doing?" Tray asked, flapping his arms against his sides, looking both miserable and embarrassed by his visitor.

"Is it safe? I didn't want to get between you and friend. Especially when she baked you a huckleberry pie."

"Come inside! Don't be silly."

"Silly?" Sophie entered and shut the French doors behind her. "The woman obviously has a mad crush on you, and I hate being a third wheel, so I left you alone to let nature take its course."

Tray put his hands on his hips. "That's not funny, Sophie."

She put her hands on the back of the dining room chair where she'd been sitting earlier, and let the scene replay in her head. "That was truly bizarre. I couldn't tell what caused her to rush out of here so quickly, could you?"

"Beats me. So much for my charm, I guess."

Sophie chuckled. "And were you really recommending me to strangers?"

He looked even more embarrassed as he put the pie in the refrigerator and poured his now-flat beer down the sink. "Why not? It's not often they'd have a chance at getting a real pro to take photos of them. I mean, I assumed you would do better than Omar Timmons. Of course, I might be wrong..."

"Just stop!" she said with a laugh.

"Anyway, once people here see your talent, your photographs will sell themselves. But people have to see them first."

She cocked her head, her forefinger pressed to her cheek. "So, are you telling me that on top of everything else, you're now my knight in shining armor, or maybe I should say, in a rolled-brim cowboy hat?"

"Sounds good to me."

"Oh, my. Such arrogance. And the way that woman was mooning over you, you must be John Wayne, Clint Eastwood, and Sam Elliott all rolled into one."

He folded his arms. "So you're saying I either look very old or dead."

Her gaze drifted over him, realizing how different he was from the beautiful male models she'd photographed, and yet she liked his looks far more. "Actually," she confessed, "I'm saying quite the opposite."

He gave a baffled look to Sophie, then shook his head and headed up the stairs. "Not another word! Good night. And don't eat my pie!"

CHAPTER 14

Monday morning, when Sophie showed up for breakfast, Tray wasn't at the table. Only Bree. She had filled a large bowl with honey and nut Cheerios and was loudly crunching away on it, a spoon in one hand, a pencil in the other, and a sudoku on the table beside her bowl of cereal.

"Good morning," Sophie said. "Have you seen Maggie or Tray?"

Bree glanced up at her, then back to her puzzle. "Maggie had to go into Boise this morning. She left everything set up for breakfast, other than we'd have to cook our own bacon, sausage, eggs, or pancakes. I prefer to eat cold cereal than to cook. And I'm not sure where Tray went. He said he's taking a walk, I think." She then put a heaping tablespoon of cereal in her mouth, a clear sign to Sophie that she considered their conversation ended.

"A walk? Not a drive?"

"He said a walk." She barely got out the words, her mouth was so full.

"Maybe I'll do that myself," Sophie said. She thought she heard Bree crunch out something that sounded a lot like, "Why doesn't that surprise me?"

Bree's words made no sense, but she didn't care enough to stick around and question her. Instead, she ran back upstairs for her camera and jacket, and then went out the door.

She wondered which direction Tray might have gone in. Not that she wanted to find him, but she was simply curious. He most likely hadn't turned right which led to the road toward town. To go straight would bring him to the river, but to turn left, heading north, would take him along the property owned by one of the cabin's sisters, Julia, and her husband, Jean-Philippe.

According to Maggie, Julia and Jean-Philippe were having a home built and planning to set up a ranch for horse breeding. At the moment, while the house was being built, they were in Spain where Jean-Philippe was doing some kind of study of raptors. Sophie wasn't even sure what a raptor was, except that it was some kind of bird.

Also, that was the direction Sophie and Anna often walked after meeting on the footpath. And it was there, on Julia and Jean-Philippe's property, where Anna would leave her and ask that she go no farther.

With Anna, she always obliged. But now, alone, she could walk as far as she wanted.

As she continued on along the footpath, she soon realized that Julia and her husband owned quite a bit of property. The area where the house, stables, and other outbuildings were being built was some distance from the cabin and the river. Surrounding it was a great deal of pasture land. But along the river, they had left the land in its natural state. She soon left the footpath and headed for the river.

The many trees along the river's banks were beautiful, and

she was glad they weren't being removed. She'd have to find out what kind of trees they were. She snapped photos as she went, staying as close to the river's edge as possible. At times there was a little beach area, but mostly the bank was either steep or rocky.

So far, she'd seen no signs that she'd either left Julia and Jean-Philippe's property, or that any other family lived in the area. It made her wonder just how far Anna had to walk before she reached her home.

Finally, she reached a spot where the river bank was a bit higher and steeper than usual. To keep going, she would need to climb over some rocks. She guessed that if she climbed over the outcrop, she'd probably find both the property line and Anna's house. Having gone this far, she hated the idea of giving up. She scrambled up the rocks and soon could see what was ahead of her.

First, she saw the river, next a small beach area, and then as her gaze followed the river upstream, she saw, near the water, a huge, furry, dark brown creature.

She couldn't move, but stared at it, her mind slowly registering what she was facing.

It can't be a bear! She felt herself panicking. *It can't be!*

But it was. A round, chubby, enormous bear stood between the trees and the river, as if trying to decide in which direction it wanted to go.

"Oh my God, oh my God, oh my God," she whispered. Heart pounding in her chest, she slowly retreated, quietly backing down the side of the rocks she had come up, the entire time keeping her eyes all but glued to the massive creature.

Every step seemed agonizingly slow, each movement carefully calculated so as not to startle the bear, until one of the larger rocks beneath her foot came loose and bounced loudly against the other rocks as it tumbled to the ground.

The bear turned around at the noise. Then its beady eyes met hers and held as it reared up on its hind legs.

For a reason he couldn't quite articulate, Tray didn't want to face Sophie that morning. Her teasing him about Georgina had gotten too much under his skin, not because of Georgina, but because of the way he was starting to feel about Sophie. But the fact that she thought it was funny that some other woman could be interested in him told him everything he needed to know about the possibility she would ever consider him as anything more than a "friend." But that was fine with him. After all, that was exactly what he wanted, wasn't it?

But if it was, then why, whenever he shut his eyes, was Sophie all he could see?

Foolish man, he chided himself. He needed her out of his system, especially after the latest news from Montana.

He headed to the river, a peaceful spot where he could think about what to do next and not suffer any distractions.

But to his dismay, the neighbor, Luke, was again there fishing.

"Good morning," Luke called. "You should take a rod with you next time. Maybe you'll have better luck than me."

"The fish aren't biting?" Tray asked.

"Not even a nibble." He reeled in his line, and glanced at Tray. "You're looking troubled, my friend."

Tray shrugged. His feelings weren't anything he wanted to talk to a mere stranger about. "It's nothing."

Luke went over to a felled log and sat. "And I have nothing but time, if you want to talk. Sometimes, in nature, things seem clearer than in our too muddled 'real' world."

Tray snorted. "This is true." He also took a seat on the log.

There, the two remained quiet, staring at the river, watching the water slowly flow by. As Tray breathed the clean, crisp air, listened to the cry of an osprey, and smelled the fresh scent of the pines, a peacefulness slowly settled over him.

"I received a troubling email," he said after a time, not sure why, but feeling he wanted to talk about it to the fisherman. "It was from my late wife's brother. He and my son's grandmother have been helping care for the boy. Anyway, a while back, I had to sell my ranch. It was the only way to get out from under doctor and hospital bills. Now, my brother-in-law has decided that because I sold the ranch I have no home and no job, that means the boy needs to stay with him and his family. His home is stable. Mine doesn't exist. He has a job. I don't. The damnedest part is, he's right."

"I'm sorry to hear you have such difficulties," Luke said. "But the boy is your son. He needs his father, especially having lost his mother."

"But what if that father isn't worthy of him?" Tray asked, again astonished that he would have mentioned any of this to a complete stranger. But the fisherman was remarkably easy to talk to. He'd clearly missed his calling as a father confessor of some sort.

"In whose eyes are you not worthy?" Luke questioned. "Did your wife ever suggest you weren't a good father?"

"Never. But her family is part of the Crow nation. Their home is on the reservation in Montana while my family's roots are in this valley. I was hoping to move here with my son, have him find out about my side of the family. But there are problems with that—my family isn't exactly close. Now, I'm not so sure that's the right thing for him."

Luke seemed to study Tray a moment with those sad eyes of his, and then he dropped his gaze to the ground as if in thought. After a while he faced Tray again. "It sounds, to me, as much as your brother-in-law might think he has your son's interest at heart, your son's heritage is from both the Crow nation and this part of the world. So, isn't it right for the boy to learn both sides of who he is as he's growing up? Even if your family has what you call problems, they're here. Your son deserves to know that, perhaps some day to meet them. And they deserve to know about him."

"That's one side of the argument. On the other side, my brother-in-law threatens to go to the tribal council to ask their opinion," Tray said. "I'm afraid they'll side with him."

Luke looked worried. "Perhaps a tribal council opinion will hold water in Idaho, or perhaps not. But before it goes that far, you might want to move quickly."

"I've tried. I've gone out each day trying to find land to buy with the money left from the sale of my ranch to show that my life will be stable once more. But so far, I've found nothing. I wonder if it's fair to take Brody away from school and a loving environment to travel around with me while I try to find something."

"Things will work out," Luke said. "Have faith."

"I wish I did."

"Sometimes, a path you never imagined will open up to you. When it does, it will feel right deep inside. Then, don't be afraid to act. That's the only real advice I can give."

Tray stood. "Thank you. You were right, watching the river, talking to you... it did help."

"Until next time," Luke said with a nod.

"Until next time."

As Tray headed back to the cabin, he mulled over his conversation with Luke. It was clear he needed to act quickly to get Brody with him, preferably in Idaho, but definitely out of the reach of the tribal council.

Of course, that presented another whole set of problems.

The day before, after leaving the Sunday afternoon open market in town, he'd driven once more to his sister's property. But this time, instead of the farm being empty, the driveway was filled with cars. He watched long enough to understand that the family was holding a birthday party for one of Maeve's sons.

Watching the party goers and hearing the laughter and music coming from the house and garden, he realized how little he knew about his sister's life or that of her kids. He knew she had four boys, but not their ages, birthdays, or anything else a half-way decent uncle ought to know.

Clearly, he wasn't any kind of uncle to those boys. He was nothing to them, and that was wrong.

But to unexpectedly show up at Maeve's son's birthday party was also wrong. He couldn't do that to his sister. Seeing him could upset her and bring back a lot of memories neither of them wanted to come back.

So he left.

He wondered if he'd ever have the nerve to go back there again. Yet, he knew he had to. If he didn't, this trip to Idaho would be even more of a dud than it had been already.

He walked on, scarcely seeing where he was going or paying attention to anything but the situation with Brody and Maeve.

And then he heard a scream.

Sophie quaked as the bear watched her. All she could see was its great hulking form looming larger and larger.

Godzilla seemed tiny by comparison.

Suddenly, as much as she'd heard all the advice about standing still, playing dead, making noise, or raising one's hands to look big and tall—and not having a clue how to do all that at the same time—the rock that she'd caused to fall must have loosened others because suddenly she felt herself sliding down the rocky slope. When she hit the ground, she somehow managed to stay on her feet, then turned and ran toward the cabin. She thought she was being quiet until she realized it was her own voice that was screaming for help as she went, hoping somebody, anybody, would come and save her.

Did bears eat humans? She knew they ate honey, and she thought she'd heard they ate fish, but she wasn't sure. But they definitely mauled humans. That much she knew. Especially grizzlies. Was that a grizzly? Were there grizzlies in Idaho?

Whatever it was, she didn't think she'd ever seen anything so large. She could hear its hot breath right behind her. Or was that her own panicked breathing?

All she could think of was how much she really, really didn't want to be mauled or eaten that day.

Then, up ahead, she saw Tray on the pathway running toward her. She launched herself into his arms and practically crawled atop his shoulders. "A bear!" she shrieked. "Run!"

"Calm down!" he said holding her tight. "I don't see any bear."

"Yes!" She held his neck so tight, she was nearly choking him.

"It's gone, Sophie."

She eased her hold ever so slightly. "Are you sure?" she whispered.

He held her tight against his chest, as she turned her head. No bear was on the path she'd used to run back to the cabin.

"With all that caterwauling, you probably scared him as much as he scared you," Tray said with a gentle smile in his voice.

She turned her head to look at him. The way he continued

to hold her, her face was scant inches from his. Those light green eyes were now filled with concern for her even as he'd tried to tease her to end her fears. Then she took in his straight, slightly flared nose, his high cheekbones, and his parted lips. With her body pressed so closely, even intimately, against his, she could feel her pulse beat faster, and she suspected it had little to do with the bear.

"My goodness," she whispered. She dropped her arms and pushed herself away from him. "I guess I was a bit frightened."

"I'd say so. Come on." He took her hand and helped her hurry back to the cabin.

As she looked up at Tray, a torrent of different emotions washed over her. She couldn't remember ever being so relieved to see someone, but it was the feel of his strong arms holding her, the protection he'd offered, that was like nothing she had ever experienced before.

Once they reached the cabin, Sophie threw herself onto the couch, panting hard. He filled a glass with water in the kitchen and brought it to her. "This might help," he said.

"Thanks." She gulped down half the glass. "Do you think it might have been a grizzly? I mean, when it stood up, it was so, so tall and really mean looking. I mean, *sooo mean* looking."

"Despite all that, grizzlies are mostly further north, closer to Montana, or east, near Yellowstone, not around here," he said. "I suspect it was a black bear looking for something to eat. They have them around these parts, and they aren't really dangerous as long as you don't find yourself between a mama and her cubs."

"How should I know if she had cubs? Or even if it was a she. It's not like I carefully checked it out. When its eyes met mine, I ran!"

"Well, anyway, it's good you got away. I'll get you some

bear spray in case you want to go wandering off by yourself again."

"Don't bother. Wandering off alone is the last thing I ever intend to do again." She put her hands to her forehead. "Why didn't anyone warn me?"

This time, he grinned. "Maybe they thought you'd kind of figure it out for yourself, given where you are. What were you doing out there, anyway?"

"Well, I..." She cleared her throat. "I just thought I'd take a walk. I mean, I heard you were out there, so I thought it should be safe."

His eyebrows rose. "You heard I was there?"

"Yes! Which had nothing to do with why I went!"

"It's okay. I think Maggie has some whiskey somewhere in here if you'd like some to help calm down."

"No need," she stated, her voice still shaky. "I'm calm enough, and I'm going to my room!" She ran up the stairs, not able to remember the last time she'd been so scared... or had made such a complete fool of herself.

CHAPTER 15

About an hour later, Tray knocked on Sophie's door. "Have you finished shivering from fright, yet?"

She opened the door. "That's hardly the way to get me to feel all warm and fuzzy about you being thoughtful enough to come and check on me. But I am better. A bit."

"There's no need for you to stay up here worrying about bears and such. How about we make some sandwiches, and drive out to take a look at the national forest? I'll point out the elk and moose, so you'll know not to tangle with them either. And snakes. And wolves, although they're mostly gone from this area."

"Gee, you really know how to make a girl want to go out with you." She folded her arms.

"Well, I wasn't asking you for a date. I was just feeling sorry for you hiding up here in your room when it's a sunny day out. I suspect you'll find lots of places to take really pretty pictures because the Middle Fork of the Payette goes right through that forest."

She grabbed her camera bag. "How can I pass up an offer like that?"

They packed a lunch, then headed north. Sophie managed to take a lot of great photographs, including a number of Tray wearing his cowboy hat and squinting hard at the untamed land before him. They were iconic shots, she knew, but she wanted to capture the look of a man whose eyes had a seriousness to them and his mouth firmness, as if he were a man who said only what he meant and didn't waste words or time.

She didn't mind at all that they never saw a moose or an elk or even a snake. But she was pretty sure everything he'd told her about them was true.

She noticed that, although he liked to tease, he didn't tell tall tales.

"You were wondering about raptors," he said when they were deep into the national forest. "That's one, a red-tailed hawk."

She could see the sunlight on the tail of a large bird, and it seemed as if the sun shone through its red feathers.

"They're birds of prey—carnivores, in other words," he said. "They all have hooked beaks and sharp talons, and can easily kill a mammal using either one. Eagles, hawks, and falcons are all over this area. In fact, that bird in the distance is a golden eagle. It looks like he's hunting rodents, most likely."

She could tell that, although the bird was soaring high above them, it seemed to be looking at the ground—hunting, as Tray had said. For the first time, the term "eagle eye" made sense to her. "It's a beautiful bird, and huge," she said.

"They are."

As they drove, he was able to give her an amazing amount of information about the types of trees, shrubs, and even pointed out an osprey nest, high in a tree—one of the rarer birds of prey that preferred a diet of fish.

All in all, riding with him and concentrating on nature, the birds, animals, and land around her, was an experience she'd never forget. "How did you learn all that?" she asked.

"Living out here as a boy, observing, and reading about what I saw. I like finding out about things around me. The more you know about what you're looking at, the better you can see it, if that makes sense."

"It does."

In the evening, they stopped back at the cabin to change into something nicer to go to dinner. It wasn't a date, she told herself. Just the two of them deciding to share a dinner meal... for the first time, in fact.

She didn't want to overdo dressing up to go with Tray, so she put on a pair of white slacks and a pretty, v-neck Kelley green top, and then high heels in a beige color. She wasn't sure where they were going, but when they arrived in Crouch and he pulled into a parking space, she wondered why she was surprised at all.

They went into Mama's Folly.

And once again, the same waitress as on earlier visits came by to serve her and Tray. She looked as if her eyebrows were going to be permanently attached to her hairline as she gawked from Sophie to Tray and back. "Well, well," she said. "Good evening. Welcome to Mama's Folly. Lots of folly going on in these parts, we like to say."

"I'll bet you do," Sophie said, her voice high and sickeningly sweet. Didn't that woman ever take a day off? "And before you even ask, I'll have a whiskey sour. And a menu. I can't wait to see what Mama's has to offer."

"You'll be surprised, I'm sure," the waitress said, tongue-in-cheek, then turned to Tray and gave him a bright smile. "And you, sir, what would you like?"

"I'll have a beer on tap. Whichever is a popular light brew in these parts."

"You got it, cowboy." He earned a smile, Sophie noticed. She hadn't. "I'll be right back."

Tray looked at Sophie. "Was there something going on between the two of you?"

"Whatever do you mean?"

Tray glanced at the retreating waitress. "Nothing, I guess."

Sophie chose the Idaho finger steaks—she'd been told they were a "thing" here—and fries, while Tray ordered a porterhouse, which didn't surprise her, him having been a cattleman and all.

"Do you miss your ranch?" she asked, as they sipped their drinks, waiting for their dinners to be brought out.

"I do, in fact," he admitted.

"And you've already sold it, right?"

He nodded. "There are times we all have to face up to things that aren't necessarily our first choice."

"Oh? What—"

"That's a good old song," he interrupted, as the band began to play the country classic, "Crazy."

She guessed he truly didn't want to talk about having sold his ranch, so she let the conversation move to music. The song was slow and she wished he would ask her to dance, but he didn't—which made sense since they were just a couple of friends eating dinner together, not engaging in slow dancing or anything that smacked of a date.

Before long, their dinners were served, and they had an enjoyable time talking about everything except his ranch, his family, or his reason for coming to Idaho. Whenever she tried to broach those subjects, he came up with something new to talk about.

When the meal ended, he didn't ask for any "after dinner

dance," and not even an after dinner cocktail, and they soon returned to the cabin.

When they arrived back at the cabin, Josh the baker was sitting in the great room with Maggie. As he stood up, his gaze jumped from Sophie to Tray.

"Josh," Sophie blurted.

"Hi," he said, his voice laced with hope and anticipation. "I've been waiting for you, hoping you'd come back soon." He glanced at Tray. "But, if you're busy..."

"No, she's not," Tray said, distancing himself. "I'm a just another guest here, and we kept each other company at dinner. That's all. I'm heading upstairs. Goodnight, Sophie."

Sophie's heart sank as she watched Tray walk away even as she told herself everything he'd said was right. They were both guests and had simply been keeping each other company as friends. Right?

Maggie jumped to her feet. "I'll also say goodnight." She hurried from the room as well.

Josh's eyes were wide as he studied Sophie and she guessed he'd picked up on her reaction to Tray walking away. She forced a smile. "Would you like some coffee or tea?"

"No, thanks. I was just hoping to see you now that I know you're still in town. Oh, and everything's squared away with Piper. She's over her old boyfriend."

"I'm glad to hear that," she said, sitting down on the sofa. "Has she gone back to school?"

He joined her. "Not yet. I think she's burned out. Maybe she needs to take this semester off and try again in the fall. Anyway, she's helping me at the bakery, so I'm actually glad of her visit."

"Well, that makes it sound as if the bakery is doing well."

He grinned. "It is. And I'll never forget the help you and

Maggie gave me taste-testing my pastries. I appreciate that you two had faith in me."

"I don't know if it was faith as much as having spent time in some very excellent French and Italian cafes. I know good pastries. I also know they aren't easy to make."

"High praise indeed," Josh said. "Frankly, I never dreamed I'd be baking for profit. It was just a fun thing for me to do in college."

"I'll bet it made you very popular with the girls."

He grinned. "You could say that." An eyebrow lifted. "Let's call it one talent among many."

"Ho boy!" a voice said in a decidedly snide tone.

They turned to see Bree standing in the doorway. "Don't mind me. I'm just getting a soda and an apple."

Sophie said, "This is Bree, another guest of the inn. Bree, this is Josh. He provides the baked goods each morning."

"Ah. So that's where Maggie gets them." Bree looked up at the wall clock in the kitchen area. It was a little before ten. "And here I thought bakers had to get up before dawn to bake. Guess I was wrong."

Josh frowned at her. "You should come by my shop, The Pastry Corral, on the main road in town."

She did a quick dive into the refrigerator. Apple and Mountain Dew in hand, she headed out of the room. "I've seen it."

With that, she left the room.

Josh gazed at Sophie. "Guess she's not a fan."

"Of anything, from what I've seen," Sophie said.

"Well, anyway, she's right. Bakers do have to get up early." They walked to the front door, where he turned to her. "I was wondering if you might be free tomorrow night. Mama's has a special of her Buttermilk Fried Chicken that's as close to heaven as most people ever get in this world."

Mama's... again. And immediately, her thoughts went to Tray and the possibility of spending time with him the next day. "My schedule is a bit crazy these days and I'm not quite sure how tomorrow will go. The best thing would be for you to call me tomorrow afternoon, if you haven't made other plans by then, and I'll be able to say if I'm free or not."

"Not a problem. Whenever you're free is fine with me. I'll be here to pick you up, which means I can also give you a good-night kiss," he murmured, his hands going to her waist.

She stopped him. "I don't want you to get the wrong impression about our relationship."

"Ah. I see. It's okay. I can wait for you to come around," he said with a twinkle in his eye.

She couldn't help but think back at the way the young women at Mama's had eyed him. Obviously, he'd been successful at getting women he was interested in to "come around," as he put it.

"We'll see," she said.

As he left, he said, "I'll give you a call tomorrow."

CHAPTER 16

"Good morning," Sophie sang out the words as she grabbed a Pastry Corral croissant, put it on her plate, and sat across from Tray who was eating his usual breakfast fare.

Bree was also at the table, but she was working a crossword puzzle instead of talking to anyone.

"How is everyone this morning?" Sophie said.

Bree glanced at her over her glasses. Sophie wondered if anyone ever told her the purple glasses didn't exactly go with the red tones in her hair. Separately each would have been fine, but together, they caused a glow that cast her skin in red tones.

"Fine," she said.

"Okay," Tray mumbled, then eyed her. "You seem to be in a good mood. Nice evening, was it?"

Something about his tone wasn't right. He couldn't be upset about Josh's visit, could he? After all, he was the one who all but ran up the stairs to get away from her. As she bit into the croissant, it made a flaky pastry crackling sound, and she noticed Tray all but wince. She gaped, and then she got it—a

Pastry Corral croissant, made by Josh. Tray was jealous! He did care about her! She smiled inside.

She decided it was best not to talk about her evening, and turned to Bree. "What have you been up to?"

"Nothing. I'm not even sure where to go for dinner," Bree said. "What about you two? I noticed you came in together last evening."

That caused Tray to stop eating for a moment. He glanced at Sophie and grimaced. "Sophie can tell you all about places to eat around here. She's the expert in going out to dinner, as you probably noticed."

Sophie raised her eyebrows critically at him. Snarkiness was unbecoming, especially since he was one of the people she'd gone to dinner with. She faced Bree. "There's Mama's Folly if you'd like a huge meal, music and dancing, or there's the Rusty Nail, basically a pub with burgers. That's it."

"Well then, I'm glad I went to the market and got some frozen dinners," Bree said. "I've been calling for a pizza delivery almost every night lately, but I'm sick of it."

"Right." Sophie went to take another bite of her croissant, but put it down. She seemed to have lost her appetite. Just then, her phone rang. "How weird. It's my phone. Calls usually don't come through way out here." She pulled the phone from her back pocket, and was stunned to see that not only was a call coming in, but the caller's name showed as Sergio.

She jumped to her feet, hit "accept," and put the phone to her ear. "Hello? Hello?"

The sound was garbled. "I need to take this," she mumbled to no one in particular as she hurried out the French doors to the back porch.

"Hello? Can you hear me?"

"Keep walking toward the mountains," Maggie called to her. "Out past the porch, it'll work. Mostly."

Sophie held the phone tight against her ear, loudly trying to get through to Sergio as she hurried away from the cabin. "Can you hear me yet? I'm trying to find a spot where the phone works."

"Sophia." She heard him say her name, and then everything became garbled. He always insisted her name should be Sophia, much more elegant and suited to her, he'd said, than Sophie. Right now, she didn't care how he pronounced her name, she wanted to hear his voice. She was so frustrated by the connection, she could have cried.

"Can you hear me now?" She was all but shouting.

"Yes! Yes, I can hear you," Sergio said. And she heard him, his voice as silky smooth as ever. Just hearing it brought back so many wonderful memories created before everything went south, her heartbeat went into overdrive. "I just learned what happened at the travel magazine, and I was calling to say I'm sorry. I'm so sorry, Sophia. For everything."

"You are?" She could hardly believe what she was hearing.

"Of course! I wanted to tell you, if you come back to Rome, I promise I'll do whatever I can to help you find work at another travel magazine, if that's what you want. Or, come back to my magazine. Or none at all. Whatever you want, Sophia. Just come back to me."

She steeled herself. The initial thrill of hearing the voice she'd loved for years had already passed, leaving her with the bitter memory of why she'd left him. Sergio had always been able to talk her into anything he wanted. But those times were gone. She'd learned a hard lesson with him, beginning with exactly what it meant to be a doormat. In the end, that was pretty much all she'd become to him. "It's not that easy."

"*Mi dispiace*, Sophia. You know I feel bad about how this ended. I may not be ready for everything you want, but that doesn't mean I don't love you! I miss you. I miss your insight, your suggestions. I want you back in my life. After everything we've been through together, I think we can do that. Don't you?"

She fought against her tears. Why did he do this to her? And why did she let him? "Maybe someday we can at least be friends," she whispered.

"What was that?" he asked. "This connection..."

"*I said,*" she shouted into the phone, "*now isn't the right time for me! To go back there, to see you—*"

"You're breaking up."

Yes, she wanted to scream at him that she was breaking up in many senses of the word. She spoke as loud as she could. "To see you will only make me feel worse. I can't do that! I'm dealing with a lot of changes and I have to learn to handle them alone. I'll always love the time we had together, but it's over. For me to stay here is best."

"Listen, if you won't return for love, for me, there's a practical reason for you to come back. I've got a new project coming up. An exciting one—one that would be perfect for the two of us to work on together. *Together,* I think we can make it even better than ever. It involves Sicily, *bella Sicilia,* which is working hard to increase its tourist trade. The government has asked if I know anyone willing and able to develop a photographic plan for their tourism office. Basically, a visitor's guide to the entire island, with pictures of all the best spots and write-ups, in English, of course, on what they all mean. It's a massive project with a budget equal to the task."

He paused. She said nothing, her heart sinking at what she expected was to come.

"Of course, Sophia, *cara,* I thought of you and how much it will help your career. With your insight on what American travelers would want to see in those photos, you are perfect for the job. I would help you, even let you use some of my models.

And we would work together, a fresh start, a kind of part-nership."

The phone connection had settled down enough that she'd heard every word he spoke. Every single word of the kind she used to be thrilled to hear—all his talk about them working together, being partners, developing projects that paid well, all under his name. He would get the praise, and everyone would laud her as his assistant... not another photographer, not a partner in the enterprise, but his assistant. She would do most of the work, while he would get most of the money and the credit.

"I can't hear you," she said finally. "I'm sorry."

"What do you mean? You didn't hear anything I just said? My proposal for you, with me in the background, of course, to work—"

"What? What was that? Sergio? Are you still there?"

"Yes, I'm here! I can hear you perfectly!"

"Hello? Hello? I guess the connection's gone." She ended the call and then threw her phone hard on the ground as she stood and fumed a moment. But at the same time, speaking with him, hearing his voice, filled her with memories of how much she'd once loved him. All but worshipped him, truth be told. He had been everything to her until she realized how much he was lying to her, and that those lies were slowly destroying her.

She had run from him then, and was glad she did. But facing the disappointment, the betrayal, still hurt.

As she bent over to pick up her phone, hoping she hadn't broken it, tears filled her eyes and she found herself kneeling on the ground as she let her tears fall.

"Sophie." It was Tray's voice. "Are you okay?"

She didn't want him to see her this way. She was supposed

to be a strong, modern woman, and she was, most of the time. "Go away."

He squatted down beside her. "You looked like you all but collapsed out here."

"I'm fine." She wiped her eyes, but the tears kept falling as he put an arm around her back and helped her stand. He then picked up her phone and handed it to her. She stuffed it into her back pocket, still fighting her tears.

He wrapped her in his arms. "It's okay to cry," he whispered.

For just a moment, she allowed her arms to circle him, and let herself accept the comfort he offered. Then she pulled herself together and stepped back. "I'm sorry. I'm afraid I've got your shirt wet. I didn't mean to. I didn't even mean to cry." She drew in a breath. "I should explain. That call was from, um..."

"Someone named Sergio," he offered. "I heard. If we had any neighbors out here, we all would have heard."

Her cheeks reddened. "That bad, huh? Then, I guess you know everything."

"Not really. And we've all had Sergio types in our lives. At least you got to shout at yours. In time, I suspect that'll feel plenty good."

She couldn't help but grin at his odd attempt to cheer her up. "I hope you're right. All I know is, I've spilled quite enough tears over that man. I'm angry at myself for letting him upset me again."

"It's okay."

"He needs my talent, not me." The words hurt to say, but she had to get them out. "I wonder if he ever really cared about me."

He put an arm around her shoulders and they slowly strolled away from the cabin. "He'd be a fool if he didn't," Tray said.

She allowed her arm to drape along the back of his waist and she leaned against his side as they walked. "Thank you. You're a good man. A good friend. That call... it was 'a remembrance of things past' that got to me so badly. It also convinced me I was right to leave him. What we once had is gone, completely."

His brow knitted as if he wondered if she were being truthful.

Nevertheless, they kept their arms around each other as they strolled along, enjoying the early morning mist, and eventually headed back to the cabin. She felt as if something fundamental had changed in their relationship, and they both knew it. As they entered, Sophie noticed that Bree's eyes studying the two of them were wider and rounder than she'd ever seen them, but the girl had the good sense to keep her mouth shut.

That day, Tray asked Sophie if she'd like to join him in his property-hunting adventure. She definitely did. They explored land both with and without homes to the west of them.

The following day they went so far west, they were practically in Oregon, and the day after that, they headed northwest. Tray's search for land was bringing him farther and farther afield since he was unable to find anything suitable close to Garden Valley.

Sophie learned a lot about the areas they traveled through on those long car rides, and the history, the flora and fauna, and a surprising amount about Tray as a young boy when his life was happy living in Garden Valley, as well as how much he had loved the area and wanted to come back here. But he still was unable to find the right property, and she could see was he growing increasingly upset and worried.

The exact reason for his tight timetable, however, he wouldn't say.

CHAPTER 17

The following morning, all Maggie could tell Sophie was that Tray had gotten some message from home that he needed to handle and expected to be gone all day.

She decided to drive into Boise, where she'd been thinking about finding a place to rent. Her days with Tray, learning about the area just north of the city as they drove through it, had caused her to appreciate it, but being a "city girl" made her think it would be better to find an apartment in Boise than to live alone in the middle of nowhere, especially in winter where, in a mountainous area like Garden Valley, she could get snowed in and wouldn't have a clue what to do about it.

Also, continuing to live in a bed-and-breakfast wasn't the most ideal life style. But once she looked for an apartment, she quickly discovered that rentals in the area often required year-long leases, first and last month's rent, plus huge cleaning deposits which many people said were difficult to get back in full. She had no such issues where she was.

Adding to her disappointment, she saw that Boise wasn't

the Old West any longer. It looked like any other mid-size city except that the mountains were fairly close and covered the northern and eastern horizons.

Finally, adding insult to injury, she picked up a bunch of local magazines. They confirmed what she'd feared, that the job market for magazine photographers wasn't a big one.

When Sophie got back to the cabin, Tray still hadn't returned. But Josh phoned to ask if she was free for dinner, just as he had each of the previous three afternoons. Only this time, she was home to receive the call.

She had learned about his earlier calls from Maggie, and was actually beginning to feel sorry for the guy. He was nice, and young, and she wasn't sure what to do about him. She decided to go with him this one time—he kept insisting he "owed" her for the dinner she'd paid for—and would make it clear, once more, she wasn't interested in him as a dating prospect.

The same waitress was at Mama's Folly to greet her, looking as irritated that she was with Josh as she'd looked at their first dinner.

Sophie was almost sorry Piper didn't interrupt their date because she soon realized that other than Josh being cute, aside from the times he'd spent in Europe learning to make pastries, they had nothing much to talk about.

They didn't watch the same kinds of movies or television shows—not that she even had much American TV in Italy or time to watch it. Neither had much interest in politics except to agree that it did nothing but disappoint. And their taste in music was at polar opposites.

Also, he liked line-dancing, and was clearly disappointed

that he couldn't even convince her to try it. A lot of friends of his, men and women, seemed to think nothing of plopping down at their table and talking to him. And he had a lot more to say to them than he did to her.

When they returned to the cabin, it wasn't even late. He had some beer in the back of his truck where, he said, it would stay cold. Of course it would, since the night temperature was close to freezing. He suggested he bring a couple of bottles inside.

She figured it was the least she could do, and besides, Bree was always in the great room at night, reading and listening to old tunes on the ancient stereo equipment. Besides, she couldn't help but think Bree was better suited to Josh than she was.

This time, though, Bree wasn't around.

Josh poured his very cold beer into two of the cabin's pilsner glasses and they sat on the sofa together. It didn't take long before any attempt at conversation stopped, and Josh put his arm around her.

She suspected he was good at kissing—he had all but said that to her—but she thought there should be more to a relationship than that. Nothing about him attracted her. She escaped his hold and reached for her beer.

"Yeah, a little more beer sounds good to me, too," he said, withdrawing his arm that was now dangling in the air, wrapped around nothing. But as he went to pick up his glass, it slid across the coffee table to the opposite side. "What the heck?"

She gawked, too. "One of us must have bumped the table."

He half stood as he reached for his glass, but then he abruptly stopped, spun around and looked at her with a smile. "How did you do that? I didn't even see you move."

"Do what?"

"I felt your fingers glide over the back of my neck, your breath blow against my ear. That was very sexy!"

"I beg your pardon." She couldn't believe what he'd just said. Was he making some kind of joke?

He quickly sat back down, a big grin on his face. "You aren't as uninterested in me as you pretend. I get it."

As he reached for her, she ducked under his arm and stood up, increasingly angry and put off by everything about him—including his weird joke, or whatever it was. "I'm not pretending anything!"

"Come on, you can't fool me. Or is this some kind of game you're playing?" he said as he slowly rose to his feet, his brow furrowed.

"You think *I'm* the one who's playing? Are you insane?" She darted behind the couch.

"What's going on?"

They both froze as Bree stood in the doorway.

"Bree! How good to see you," Sophie said, rushing to her side. "Josh was just leaving."

He looked from one to the other, then at his untouched beer. His eyes blinked with confusion and finally he shook his head. "You're right. It's been a long day. Goodnight, Sophie."

With that, he strode from the room.

Bree gave Sophie a confused look. "What was that all about?"

Sophie stared at Josh's beer glass, which was now back to where he had first placed it. How had it gotten there? A sudden chill rippled down her spine. What if Josh hadn't been playing games with her? What if he was being sincere in his confusion? She could scarcely breathe as she whispered to Bree, "I have no idea."

Sophie lay in bed, unable to sleep. She couldn't stop thinking about Josh's beer glass. She knew what she saw. The glass had moved. By itself. As much as she wanted to blame Josh for everything that took place that evening, she knew he hadn't bumped the table. No one had touched it. So how did Josh's glass slide across the coffee table top? It was wood, and not "slick" wood, and the bottom of the glass itself was completely dry.

Most of all, no one, especially not her, had touched him, and especially not in any sexy way, for pity's sake! At that point, she was so bored with him, she'd rather have set herself on fire.

Added to all that was Georgina's reaction the other day...

The woman had gone absolutely white at something in the great room. She had said something about her huckleberry pie. That it had levita...? Levitated? Was that what she was about to say? Had she seen it levitate?

How could that be?

Sophie had to come up with some rational explanation for all that. She was a sane, twenty-first century woman who abso-lutely knew there was no such thing as ghosts. To think other-wise would go against everything she had ever known about life.

But if the cabin didn't have a ghost, or even a poltergeist, what could be going on here?

To make matters even worse, her strange friend Anna popped into Sophie's troubled thoughts. Anna would suddenly appear when Sophie most needed to talk to her, and where she came from and where she went to both remained a mystery. Then, there was her strange style of dress, her secretive way of life.

Sophie's thoughts swirled about Anna, about who she might actually be. And one such thought frightened her badly.

No! Impossible. Clearly, Sophie thought, she was wrong and was simply overstressed. She lay back down in bed, curled up like a ball, squeezed her eyes shut, and concentrated on counting sheep backwards in hopes it would help her finally fall asleep.

CHAPTER 18

W hen Sophie saw Tray the next morning, he looked tired and drawn. "Did you go looking at land yesterday?" Sophie asked.

"Eventually. I've pretty much depleted any land close by, and ended up much farther away than I expected," he said. "I found myself in a town called Weiser and by the time I had dinner and made my way back, it was fairly late."

"Oh?" Sophie said.

"When I got back, Bree was still up. She told me about some strange goings on here last night."

"Really? I hadn't heard," she said.

He cocked his head. "That's not what I was told."

She didn't appreciate his attitude. "By the way, I heard a different woman came by yesterday while you were out and she also left you a huckleberry pie. Are you sure you were out late visiting Weiser and not one of the pie makers?"

He held his hands up to stop her. "Okay, okay. Maggie already told me about the pie." But then he cocked an eyebrow. "I didn't think you cared."

She frowned at that. "I have no idea what you're talking about," she said in the calmest voice she could muster.

He couldn't stop a small grin. "Anyway, I'm going out again today. I'll warn you, the weather's not looking good, but if you want to join me, feel free to come along."

"Even though I've never baked a pie?"

He wrinkled his lips. "I guess I can forgive you. Besides, you're not disagreeable company."

"Not disagreeable?" Her eyebrows rose, but immediately she realized she had a choice to make. She could remain in the cabin, irritated at the world, and alone. Or go with Tray, whose company, despite how much he irritated her at times, she enjoyed. It was no choice. She liked his company more than she dared to admit to herself. She stood. "What time do we leave?"

Tray drove in the opposite direction from the one he usually took, and headed eastward toward a spot on a map named Lowman. They found a gas station with a food mart and bought some water and packages of cookies, chips, and chocolates in case they got hungry as they headed eastward, going high into the mountains.

As Tray drove, he followed the road he'd marked on his map where a large spread of land was supposedly for sale, and had been available for several years. That wasn't a good sign, but Tray was growing increasingly desperate. He needed to find something soon, and so decided to check it out.

As he continued into the mountains, the road became dirt and was scarcely maintained, giving a washboard effect. He realized this wasn't an area to bring his son since it was even more remote than other places he'd seen.

The scenery around them, however, made up for the fact

that this was yet another wasted trip. It was pretty enough that it nudged him forward. At the elevation they'd reached, there was still snow on the ground, including on the road that snaked between mountains and forests. He loved landscapes like this and often lost himself simply imagining what dangers the men who carved a road through such rugged and steep land must have faced.

He was so lost in the enjoyment of nature he didn't immediately realize how long he'd been driving.

"I thought we would have reached the land for sale by now," Sophie said, although he'd noticed that she, too, seemed to enjoy the scenery.

"Out here, I can imagine the distances are guesses at most," Tray said. "And it always seems slower when you're going somewhere than when you're driving home. At least to me. Anyway, I guess I should turn around."

"Actually, I'm enjoying being here. It's almost as if we're at the top of the world," Sophie said. "So if you want to go a little further, it's fine with me."

After another ten minutes, Tray stopped the truck.

"Do you finally spot the For Sale sign?" Sophie asked.

"No, but I see something I'm pretty sure you'll want photos of. Look through those trees. I suggest you stay close to the truck." He rolled down the passenger side window so she could see better and then pointed.

She looked where he indicated. "I don't see anything... Oh, my!" A bull moose stood among the trees, reaching up for the needles and twigs on a fir. She almost missed it because its long, brown legs blended with the tree trunks around him. Only when he moved his head did she make out his form, particularly his thick, massive antlers.

The moose was enormous.

She quietly opened the door and got out of the truck, stepping a little closer to take better photos, and extended her lens for close-ups.

As she took photos, droplets of snow fell, but she cautiously continued toward the trees.

"Looks like a storm is coming, Sophie," Tray called. "We should get back to the highway. Sometimes these mountain roads turn slick with ice."

"Okay, just a couple more minutes."

"These storms move in fast," he warned.

"I'm sure everything will be fine. And we aren't that far from the highway, I don't think."

"It's a good thirty or more minutes, all downhill."

"So that'll make it even easier," she said, continuing to take photos as the moose started off in the opposite direction from her. But doing so, he moved into an open area where she could take much better photos of him, despite the snow.

Sophie was following the moose when the sky opened up with bucketfuls of heavy, wet snow. It fell so fast and so hard Tray could scarcely make out where she stood. He could no longer see the moose at all. In no time, the snow had become so thick he grew frightened for her safety and got out of the truck when he saw her running back, slipping and sliding. Relief, and something more, filled him just looking at her, a big smile on her face as she ran toward him.

As they both got back in the truck, her eyes were sparkling with delight and her cheeks and nose red from the cold. "Whoa, that weather turned crazy fast!"

"Told you." He took a moment to brush some snowflakes from her shoulders and her hair, and they both laughed as he did it. But the moment he heard her laughter, something inside him tightened, and his hand all but burned from doing something as simple as to touch her hair. He knew he was quickly getting in over his head.

He tried not to think about her nearness as he carefully turned the truck around in the narrow pathway and then headed back toward the highway. The snow was rapidly accumulating on the already frozen ground, and in a matter of minutes, the wind picked up in a way that caused the heavy flakes to churn into a thick, swirling mass. Tray ran the windshield wipers as quickly as he could, and had the defroster turned on high, but no matter what he did, his line of vision grew smaller by the moment.

They were in a whiteout. His hands tightened on the wheel as he felt the truck lurch from side to side in the wind, and his usually reliable tires were already struggling with the iciness on the road. At one point, he was forced to swerve quickly as the road dropped away in a 90° turn.

"This is bad. It's too hard to see the road," he muttered. There was a mountain on one side and a drop-off on the other. One wrong turn and they could be in big trouble. He even rolled down the window, hoping that might help, but it didn't.

"Maybe we should pull over and wait," Sophie said.

"Look for a turnoff," Tray told her. "That'd be better than sitting out on the road, especially if the whiteout continues into nightfall."

They inched along, until Sophie said, "Is that a turn off?" She, too, had rolled down her window and was trying to help.

"I see it. Let's give it a try," he said.

He turned onto what might have been a driveway of some sort. He went a short way and was about to stop when he saw some sort of building up ahead. "Do you see that?" he asked.

"Yes, but I can't tell what it is," she said. "Hopefully, it's a warm house with a friendly owner."

He continued along the narrow roadway until they saw that the structure was a barn. "I wonder if it's still being used."

"There's only one way to find out," Sophie said.

Sophie watched as Tray got out of the truck and found that the barn door was unlocked. He waved to her to join him.

Inside, other than a few stacks of hay, it was empty. But it was dry and sheltered them from the wind and snow.

"I hope we aren't stuck here too long," Sophie said, arms folded and hugging herself against the cold. The barn offered protection, but it was still freezing.

"I can make it less scary." Tray went out to the truck, and in a couple of minutes he was back with thermal blankets, a flashlight, a battery-operated lantern, water, and the junk food they'd bought at the gas station. "Living in Montana, where in an emergency, it's easy to end up in a spot where you'd have to wait a day or two to get out, I've learned to always carry some emergency survival gear."

"Thank you, Montana," she said as he spread some hay on the ground and then put a blanket over it. After she sat on the blanket, he placed another over her shoulders and then wrapped it around her to cover her legs. "That should help keep you warm," he said.

"Thank you," she murmured, although the feel of his hands going over her to make sure the blanket was in place seemed to warm her more than any blanket could do.

He did the same for himself and sat beside her. In front of them both, he placed the water and junk food they'd bought. "Squalls like this rarely last very long, but the safest thing to do is to hunker down and wait them out. If we're stuck here until nightfall, we're better off staying all night than trying to drive down the mountain in the dark, trusting only the headlights."

She gulped at that, but could see his point. "At least you're saying we don't have to worry about being stuck here for days and having to ration our candy bars."

"I'd say not. And if we get desperate, we can probably make it to the highway one way or another once the snow stops."

"I don't like your use of the word 'probably'." She hugged the blanket. "Now I know what the Donner Party felt like trying to cross over the Sierras in winter. I'll tell you now, I'm not very tasty."

He glanced at her, then looked away. "Whoever told you that was lying or blind."

She raised her eyebrows. Was he actually being risqué? If so, she liked it, but decided not to pursue the comment.

"Since we're stuck here awhile," she said, "maybe you'll answer a question I've been wondering about."

He frowned. "Maybe."

"Why are you really here and what are you truly looking for?"

He looked stunned. "But I've told you. I'm looking for land for myself and my son."

"And I know there's a lot more to it, a backstory if you will, that you aren't saying." Her tone was firm.

"Oh?"

"Sure there is. Especially after I've told you my entire sordid, miserable story, you owe me."

"I see." He seemed to think a moment, then shrugged. "It's nothing exciting, and not even sordid." She nodded, but said nothing. "I've already told you how my folks had a farm in the valley. The problems started after my mom passed away when I was twelve. Things went downhill with my dad from that time on. Finally, I left home, worked any job I could get, and kept traveling. Is this the kind of thing you want to hear?"

"Of course. It's what makes you who you are today. Go on."

"I'm not sure that's a good thing," he said through gritted his teeth. But he continued, his words fast and factual. "Anyway, I ended up in Montana, got jobs on ranches, and became good at poker and pool. At eighteen, I ended up just outside of Billings, and working on a cattle ranch. The Crow Reservation is nearby."

He stopped then, and she knew what was coming was difficult for him to speak of.

"There, I met the most beautiful woman I'd ever seen. She was like some kind of goddess, soft, and delicate. It took forever for me to get up nerve just to talk to her." He paused again. "Over time, I learned her being delicate wasn't an act. She was born with a heart condition. She'd gone through lots of surgeries as a young child to try to fix it, but it seemed one problem was no sooner remedied than another turned up. Eventually, all she could do was to learn to live quietly and not do things other kids did. She never imagined she'd fall in love and told me not to love her, that she could never grow old with me. But I didn't care. I kept seeing her. She was twenty-four when we met and I realized that if I wanted any kind of life with her, I was going to have to somehow provide the life she needed."

As Sophie watched him struggle to find words to voice his story, she realized how much she had come to care about him and all he'd been through.

"I worked, saved, used pool and poker to add to those savings and eventually got enough money for a down payment on a ranch. It took nose-to-the-grindstone work every single day, with visits to Charlene whenever I could fit them in. Finally, when I was twenty-one and Charlene twenty-seven, we married. We were happy, except that the one thing she really wanted was a child. I was scared her body couldn't handle it and I'd lose her, but she was adamant. I couldn't bear to see her unhappy or even to deny her anything, as much as we both heard the doctors warn her against pregnancy. We had Brody— a Caesarian delivery, of course—and Charlene was over the moon. I refused to go through another pregnancy, watching the strain it had put on her. She was with us until Brody was ten, and one morning, I found that she had passed away in her sleep. That was four years ago."

Sophie's heart ached at the pain in his words. He was scarcely an adult himself when his life took a turn that led to joy but also so much sadness.

"I'm so sorry," Sophie said and took his hand.

His gaze met hers with surprise that she'd done that, but he kept their hands joined as he continued.

"It was the most difficult thing I've ever been through. I knew she was on borrowed time, and doctors and others on the reservation told me that her living as long as she did, and bearing a child, was a miracle in itself. Maybe. All I knew was she was gone."

"What did you do?"

"What I learned to do after my mom died. I cut myself off from everyone, got angry, fought. Whenever I looked at Brody, I'd see his mother, and it hurt. I brought him to stay with his grandmother." He shook his head at the memory. "Then, before I knew it, he was a teenager and going to middle school. His grandma, Jane, bless her, kept telling me the boy needs his father. By then, I was working hard trying to save the ranch, but the medical bills piled up and no matter what I did, I couldn't keep my head above water. I had to sell the place. Also, Brody had to go to a high school and so he went to stay with his uncle, my wife's brother, and his cousins. Now, Brody's uncle has asked the tribal council to meet with him as a first step in his desire for custody, saying the boy is half Crow and shouldn't live with a father who has no home and no job." He shut his eyes.

She was appalled. "No, he can't do that."

"But he can. I just learned that in less than three weeks there'll be a council meeting about my son."

"And so you need to get Brody back with you as soon as possible."

"If I want to keep him with me, yes."

"Do you?"

"Of course! But at the same time, I can't help but wonder if his uncle is right. It's almost like a re-run of my life with my father. He was awful to live with after my mom passed. Maybe I was, too. Maybe Brody is better off without me."

"No, I'm sure he isn't. You're a good man, Tray, and you're trying to make things right. I can see that, and your brother-in-law should see it as well."

"It was so wrong of me not to think about how Brody was handling being left by both his parents. I regret it every single day now, even as I'm afraid it might be too late to undo the damage it's done to my relationship with him."

"He'll understand," Sophie said. "If not now, when he's older."

"I hope," he said.

She reached for the blanket, trying to hold it closer. He pushed aside his own blanket and opened his arms. "Come here. I can see you're shivering."

She scooted right next to him and he adjusted their blankets to wrap around the both of them together. "I've been told I throw off a lot of body heat, so this way might be warmer."

"You're one hot guy," she said with a smile as she snuggled against his side and rested her head on his shoulder. "You do feel warm, and so good," she said, draping her arm across his chest.

As he held her, her heart raced with the full realization of his nearness. It was as if an electric current passed through her, igniting what had long been a desire for him. No, he's a friend and all wrong for me, she told herself, even as her body betrayed her.

She looked up at him.

As their eyes met and held, his hold on her loosened, as if realizing they could reach a point of no return. "Sophie, I..."

"Don't say it," she whispered. She placed her fingers against his lips stopping his words of protest. But then, feeling his warm breath, she couldn't stop herself from letting her fingers trace his firm jaw, then lift to his hair.

She felt his arms again tighten as his head moved ever closer to hers. The heat of his gaze drew her as she, too, moved closer until, finally, their lips met. Heat exploded between them as they allowed feelings too long denied.

But as the intensity of their kisses and their desire grew, Sophie forced herself to pull away from him.

"We can't," she said, all but breathless. She couldn't allow what she wanted to happen between them. She knew how much it would complicate their relationship. He was still getting over his wife's death, and she had her own relationship demons to deal with. It wasn't fair to either of them to take this burgeoning feeling they had for each other—the "friendship" as they called it—to another level.

He kept his strong hand on her arm, whether to pull her closer or to hold her back she had no idea, and it seemed he didn't know either. Finally, he pressed his forehead to her hair and whispered, "You're right."

She shifted a bit away from him and they lay down on the blanket. He did the same, both on their backs, both staring up into the darkness, scarcely able to see the rafters of the barn with the lantern's light. Outside, the storm howled, and through the barn's one window, she could see that night was falling.

To her surprise, he reached for her. "We can still keep each other warm," he said. "I promise I won't try anything more, tempting though you are."

She smiled as she scooted close and curled up against him.

"I know. And you're pretty tempting yourself, if you don't mind my saying."

"Good to know," he murmured.

Finally, emotionally spent, in the chilliness of the deserted barn, wrapped in Tray's arms, she slept.

CHAPTER 19

"What the hell!"

Sophie opened her eyes to see an old man standing in the doorway of the barn.

Tray stood up at the stranger's voice. She kept the blanket over her.

"Sorry," Tray said, his voice calm, reasonable, and friendly but she could hear an edge to it—almost a warning in case the stranger wasn't inclined to be equally friendly. "Is this your barn? We got caught in a whiteout and needed shelter."

"The snow's stopped. I saw the truck half-covered with snow and was afraid I'd find someone frozen to death in it. Looks like you two found a way to stay warm."

Tray hesitated to answer, then said only, "Seems so. We'll be on our way now."

"You do that." The man walked out and shut the barn door.

Tray glanced down at her. "You okay?"

"Of course." She reached for him, and he took her hand and helped her to her feet. He scarcely glanced her way.

"Tray?" she asked.

"The old coot is probably waiting to come in. We need to get out of here."

His voice was cold. She knew something was wrong, but she didn't know what.

"What's going on?"

"Nothing." He stood before her, a hard expression on his face.

Finally, he slid his hands in the pockets of his jeans. "Look, Sophie, last night was crazy. Nice, but most likely because of a weird circumstance, the storm, the danger, the silence. I'm sure nothing that... that almost happened... meant anything to you. And of course, it meant nothing to me."

She listened, and all she could do was hold herself together. It had meant a lot to her, more than she ever imagined possible. Now, hearing his words, her embarrassment was suffocating. "Of course," she said. "My feelings exactly."

He nodded, then turned away, and began to fold the blankets. "Good," he murmured. "I'd hate it if last night got in the way of our friendship."

She found it impossible to look at him. Had she been so wrong about him, about them? She didn't think so, except she'd been wrong about Sergio. Why not now as well?

"Right, we wouldn't want that to happen."

As she thought of all he'd told her about his situation, what made her think a former Montana rancher with a teenage son would have a serious interest in someone like her?

It was silly of her to even think in such terms.

"You ready?" he asked.

"Of course." Without looking at him, she helped to pick up their gear and carry everything out to the truck. The morning was sunny, and once they got the snow off the truck and themselves off this mountain, they would have an easy ride back to the cabin.

Driving back to the cabin, Tray had time to think. Maybe too much time. He had never felt as torn as when he woke up that morning. At first, looking at Sophie asleep beside him, their arms and legs still intertwined for warmth, he was reminded of the early days of his marriage, when Charlene was healthy enough for him to kiss her awake and make gentle love to her.

And in that instant, he felt like the lowest piece of scum that ever lived as a sense of betrayal to Charlene washed over him. How could he conceive of being that way with another woman? But here, he'd done just that.

Foolish, foolish man, he told himself.

Even putting Sophie in such a position with him was wrong. She was obviously still so completely in love with her former boyfriend that a mere phone call from him had her collapse in tears. Having seen that, he understood why she'd gone out with the baker and the doctor. She was simply hoping to find someone to help her forget the one she really loved.

He was nothing but her third attempt to forget the one who'd caused her to travel halfway around the world. Plus, she talked all the time about leaving, going to the next place, town, wherever, to take photos. Being a travel photographer was her profession, and she told him how passionate she was about it.

For a little while there, he'd thought he might have found true love a second time in his life. He had liked the feeling, he had to admit, and thought it meant he was finally getting over his grief at losing Charlene. There might even be a light, a love, at the end of the tunnel.

But it wasn't Sophie. If a woman with her background, her talent, and her career experience, would fall in love enough with the likes of him to want to give all that up, she should find a good shrink.

He didn't have a home or a business. Maybe soon, not even a kid. He had nothing.

In the light of day, he could face how wrong they truly were for each other, no matter how strongly he felt about her.

He glanced at her. She looked unhappy, thoughtful. He reached over and gave her knee a quick squeeze. "It'll be okay, Sophie."

She turned to him, surprised, and then touched his hand briefly as she whispered, "I know." He thought he heard a hint of sadness in her voice, but it was probably just a reflection of his thoughts.

Before he knew it, they were down the mountain and back on the highway, and soon walking into the cabin.

All he wanted to do was to hurry to his room and try to forget everything that had happened. But instead, he faced an older man in the foyer signing Maggie's guest book.

"Hello, there," the fellow said as Tray looked him over. Sports jacket, round horn-rimmed glasses, gray hair combed back and flowing. And if the guy didn't stop ogling Sophie, he'd also have a bloody nose messing up the cute little bow tie he wore.

"Here are a two of our guests now," Maggie said to the newcomer. "This is Tray, who has the Mountain View room next to yours, and Sophie, who has the River View room. And this is Malcolm Beauregard. Professor Beauregard will stay with us awhile."

"Oh, well, welcome," Sophie said, holding out her hand to him.

Beauregard's jowly face lit up and he took her hand in both of his and continued to hold it as he said, "It's such a pleasure to meet you, my dear."

Sophie's eyebrows rose at the enthusiastic greeting and then she pulled her hand free.

"Enjoy your stay," Tray muttered, and then headed up the stairs before he said something to the "Professor" that he shouldn't. Some people didn't have the sense they were born with.

And at that moment, he included himself in that description.

CHAPTER 20

Sophie didn't want to see anyone the next morning and waited until breakfast was nearly over before going downstairs. Bree was still at the table finishing a sudoku, but then left without a word other than "hi." Maggie was cleaning up the kitchen. The latest guest, Professor Beauregard, wasn't around either.

"Are you feeling okay today, Sophie?" Maggie asked.

"I'm fine, but not very hungry. I'd just like a slice of toast, please."

"You've got it," Maggie said.

"Has Tray gone out already?" she asked.

"He has. He left about a half hour ago. Did something happen between you two? He was even quieter than usual."

"No," Sophie said. "Other than having to spend the night in a barn because the snow was coming down too furiously to drive in, nothing happened. I guess we've both got a lot on our minds."

"Okay," Maggie said. "That's good, I guess."

Sophie knew why Maggie had asked about her health. The

day before, after she and Tray returned to the cabin, Sophie had gone to her room and stayed there, not wanting to see or talk to anyone. Tray's words about their closeness, their kisses, meaning nothing to him—and thinking they meant nothing to her—hurt more than she would have expected, and she felt completely confused.

Did that mean she was getting over Sergio that quickly? Was she that fickle? But if she was honest with herself, she'd been unhappy with Sergio for over a year before she got up the strength to walk away. It was more the idea of him, of the way she'd once seen him and once felt about him, that was the most difficult to set aside.

Was her interest in Tray nothing but a rebound, or was it genuine, perhaps because he was simply causing her to be real? Causing her to feel honest emotions as a woman facing an interesting, down-to-earth man, and not as a wide-eyed ingenue swooning over an idol?

She believed this was no rebound, and her feelings about Tray were true. But she also knew he didn't feel the same. Every time he mentioned Charlene's name, she could hear the love he had for her.

He wasn't ready to move on. Maybe some day he would be. But not yet, and definitely not while his life and his relationship with his son were in such turmoil.

After finishing her toast and coffee, Sophie took her camera and went down to the path where she often met Anna. She desperately needed to talk to her friend that morning.

As if in answer to her prayer, before long, Anna appeared.

"Please tell me what's wrong with me," Sophie cried as soon as Anna was near enough to hear her.

"Relax, my friend," Anna said. "Let's take a seat on that small rise overlooking the river, and you can tell me what has you so upset."

Once seated, Sophie couldn't figure out where to begin her tale without sounding like a love-hungry idiot with no control over her emotions. But maybe that's what she was, and she'd never realized it before. "I'm sure you're sick of hearing how I came here because of my breakup with Sergio, and how I swore off men for a good long time. I mean, the last thing I ever wanted or expected was to meet someone I'd have feelings for."

"It's your cowboy, isn't it?" Anna asked.

Sophie's lips wrinkled. "Is it that obvious?"

Anna gave her a gentle smile. "When you talked about him, your face was always bright and joyful. And it seems your conversations were sometimes fun and other times meaningful. That was never the case when you talked about the two other fellas you've gone out to dinner with."

Sophie drew in her breath. She needed to be completely honest about her relationship with Tray, but if Anna lived as sheltered and, perhaps, righteous a life as Sophie imagined, she wasn't sure how Anna would react. Finally, she blurted out the truth. "We were snowed in and spent the night together in a barn. Nothing happened beyond some kisses, but it could have. A part of me wishes it had. I've fallen hard. I think I'm in love with him, which I know is crazy. I've only known him a short time, but I can't deny how I feel when we're together."

"That's all right," Anna said. "You never know when true love will find you. When I met my husband, it was love at first sight. Truly. We lived far apart, and my family was completely against us."

"What did you do?" Sophie asked.

"We eloped. What else?" Anna said with a laugh.

Sophie smiled with her. "You're lucky you were both on the same page. I thought Tray felt the way I did. He'd given every sign. But the next morning he said our kisses, the feelings I thought we shared, meant nothing to him, and he suspected they meant nothing to me as well! He said we were good friends and nothing more."

"Oh, no," Anna murmured.

"There must be something wrong with me. Why is it that when the wrong man comes along, he's the one I throw myself at?"

"I can't imagine Tray doesn't feel about you the way you do about him," Anna said. "I think if he were lying to you all along, you'd have known it."

"I don't know anymore. It makes me wonder if I have any discernment at all."

Anna cocked her head to the side as she studied Sophie. "When he told you he suspected your—how should I put it?—your physical reaction to each other meant nothing to you, did you tell him he was wrong?"

"How could I? It would have made me ridiculous."

"Or it might have made him rethink everything. Have you considered he might have been trying to protect his heart as much as you are protecting yours?"

"He has no reason to protect himself from me," Sophie said.

"Doesn't he? To me, you're a well-traveled, well-educated woman of the world with a profession. Didn't you say he had a ranch but lost it?"

Sophie was puzzled. "I don't think I said that, but it is true."

"Oh." Anna looked a bit flustered. "Who knows where I heard it, then? But anyway, he could well be thinking there's no way you could be in love with him. And you talk about leaving here to do your travel photography. All the while, he's searching for a job that will tie him to the land. Perhaps, from his viewpoint, you're a person he doesn't dare fall for. He's already suffered a lot of loss in his life."

"That could be true," Sophie said, pondering Anna's words.

"If you love him, don't give up on him. Or on yourself. Let

him know how you feel." Anna stood. "I hope I've helped at least a little. I need to get home now."

Sophie stood as well. "You're always a help to me. Thank you."

She would have loved to give Anna a hug—she liked the way people always hugged and kissed on the cheek in Italy—but she'd learned early on that Anna didn't want to be touched. So, she merely nodded her thanks and then watched as Anna walked down the footpath to the spot where it curved and she vanished from view.

In the afternoon, feeling better after baring her soul to Anna, Sophie headed into Crouch to walk around a bit. As she passed a beauty salon, she glanced in the window and saw that the hairdresser was just finishing up with a client. It appeared no one else was in there waiting. She had been due to get her highlights touched up around the time she left Italy. She ran her fingers through her long, wild tresses. Maybe getting it done would help take her mind off what to do about her hopeless feelings for Tray, for an hour at least.

Sophie waited until the salon's customer walked out of the shop. Seeing the woman leave with a hairstyle that was at least thirty years old gave Sophie pause, but she hoped it was the customer's decision and not the stylist's.

She opened the door and stuck her head in. "Are you free to do something with my hair?"

The hairdresser, a young woman wearing a pink smock, glanced at the clock on the wall. "I've got an hour before my next appointment. Come on in. What are you thinking?"

"I need my highlights touched up. It's been a few months."

"Have a seat." She walked Sophie to a chair. "My name's

Wanda. Let's see what's going on here." Wanda combed through Sophie's long, curly mane. "You aren't going to ask me to cut much off, are you? I mean, you've got a few split ends that can go, your highlights need attention, and I have a nice conditioner for you, but most women would kill for hair like yours."

Relief filled Sophie at those words. "That's exactly what I want."

Wanda was chatty and welcomed Sophie's questions about the weekend market and the long-term possibility for the success of her photo booth.

"I think lots of people who come up here on weekends who would find it all kinds of fun to dress up as if they were in the old West and have some photos taken," Wanda said. "As long as they aren't too spendy, of course. I mean, the world doesn't start and end with iPhone photos, does it?"

"My world certainly doesn't," Sophie said.

"Then go for it. You said the one time you tried worked out all right, and it'll soon be a lot warmer here. That's when the crowds show up. You'll do fine, believe me. And with that pretty smile of yours, not to mention the way your hair will look when I'm finished, you'll have a lineup of fellas wanting to have you take their pictures. If nothing else so they can show you what they can do with a six-shooter," she said with a chuckle, which Sophie took to be some obscure country saying that she didn't exactly understand.

"Also, this weekend is our Founder's Day celebration, so already, the crowd will be a lot bigger."

"I saw signs about that," Sophie said, "but I didn't know what they meant."

"Can't say I'm surprised. Publicity isn't our strong suit."

As Wanda chatted on, Sophie would have been able to pick up a lot of the local gossip if she had any idea who the people

were that Wanda was talking about. But as the stories continued, Sophie found them humorous enough that soon, she didn't
even care if she knew the people involved or not.

Maybe, Sophie thought, she'd even find out the reason Tray
wanted to move back here.

"Do you know the Bowman family?" she asked. "I understand they live, or used to live, in this area."

"I think Maeve Sheridan's maiden name was Bowman.
Nice woman. But I can't think of anyone else who might have
that name."

"Is she young? Old?"

"Somewhere in her thirties, I'd say. Husband, four kids.
Why?"

Tray had mentioned having a sister. Could this Maeve be
her? It made sense she might still live here. But if so, why
hadn't he talked about her? Or about visiting her? No, it was
probably just a coincidence that he shared the name with that
woman. "It's nothing. I know someone with that name who
once lived around here. Tray Bowman. Do you know him?"

"Afraid not. But then, I tend to meet mostly women."

"Right. Anyway, it's not really important," Sophie said. Not
important at all, she thought. After all, she and Tray were just
friends.

CHAPTER 21

Sophie sat in the great room that evening, her hair freshly styled hair with renewed highlights, hoping that Tray might show up. The more she thought about it, the more Anna might have been right about why he said what he did.

Bree also sat in the great room reading a book. The woman bothered Sophie. She was young and should do something other than skulking around the cabin all day and night. Why wasn't she out exploring the area? Although, after she heard how Sophie and Tray got snowed in, she acted more nervous than ever about driving around the area if the weather was at all iffy.

"Well, hello again."

Sophie looked up to see Professor Beauregard enter the great room. "Hello," she said. "Have you met Bree, who's also staying here?"

"No, I haven't." He looked over at her.

Bree scarcely glanced up from her book. "Hey."

Beauregard sat on the sofa near Sophie. "What do people do for dinner around here?"

"If you want to stay in town," Sophie said, "you have a total of two choices."

"Don't think you're going to find great cuisine in this town," Bree muttered without looking up from her book. "Ain't gonna happen."

Beauregard smiled in Sophie's direction. "I wasn't expecting greatness, but I do like satisfaction." He lifted an eyebrow, making his glance nothing less than a leer.

Good God, Sophie thought.

"If you aren't doing anything, maybe you can show me one of these places?" Beauregard said to her. "My treat."

Sophie glanced at Bree and hoped the woman had the sense to play along. "Actually, I'm sorry, but Bree and I were going to get something together." She faced Bree and gave her a dagger-like stare.

Bree's eyes widened at suddenly finding herself included in their conversation. And Sophie's glare couldn't have been any clearer. She put her book down. "That's right. We were."

"Well, you don't mind if I join you, do you?" Beauregard asked. "I mean, I don't know anyone else here, and it's no fun to eat alone. And it's still my treat!"

"I don't..." Sophie began, but to her surprise, Bree stood up.

"Sounds good to me," Bree said, "as long as Sophie agrees. I haven't been to any restaurant in town yet."

Sophie checked the time. It was already a little past seven and still no sign of Tray.

"Okay," she said, disappointed.

"Can we go to Mama's Folly?" Bree asked. "I hear it's great."

"Cute name," Beauregard said. He faced Sophie. "What do you think?"

Sophie sighed. "Why not?"

"We'll take my car," Beauregard said as they grabbed warm coats. He then led them out to a BMW.

"You rented this?" Bree asked.

"No. I drove over from Seattle. I teach at the University of Washington there. American History."

"What brought you to a place like this?"

"The Donnelly Inn has a certain reputation I found quite irresistible," he said with a smile as he navigated the short distance to the center of town. "And considering that I'm going to dinner with not one but two lovely, single women, it just may live up to everything I've heard."

"Interesting," Bree murmured. Sophie noticed her interest was always sparked by any mention of ghosts, but she never said why. Once Sophie asked, and Bree's answer was a simple, "Isn't everyone interested in ghosts?"

"You can park here," Sophie said to Beauregard when she noticed that the spots closer to Mama's were all taken.

They went inside, and like magic, the same waitress showed up yet again to take them to their table. As she looked from Sophie to Beauregard, who was now holding Sophie's arm, her eyebrows rose while her lips downturned. "You have got to be kidding me."

"Nope," Sophie replied, despite the rudeness of the comment. "We'll need a table for three, please."

"Interesting," the waitress muttered as she led them to a spot by the windows. "Would anyone like to start with cocktails? A whiskey sour, perhaps?"

"That sounds good," Beauregard said.

"I'll have one as well," Bree told her.

The waitress then eyed Sophie.

"Make mine a Pendleton," Sophie said. "Double. And straight."

"Good idea." The waitress muttered, then marched off.

They all ordered chicken-fried steak. Sophie was glad she didn't have to do much talking because it turned out Beauregard was filled with questions about the area, and then often answered them himself because of his knowledge of history, which made for a strange conversation.

"Hey there," a familiar voice said. Sophie looked up to see Josh.

"Hello," Sophie said, sarcastically thinking this evening couldn't get any better. She wished she was at the cabin with a microwaved Lean Cuisine.

"What's up?" Josh looked from her to Beauregard to Bree, who sat up a little straighter.

"Josh, you remember Bree, I'm sure, and this is a new guest at the Donnelly Cabin, Professor Beauregard." She turned to them. "This is Josh, owner of The Pastry Corral. He creates the delicious pastries we have each morning."

They greeted each other.

"Say, if this is just a group of Donnelly Cabin friends," Josh said, "mind if I join you?"

"Not at all," Bree said. "We just gave our orders. Chicken-fried steak is on special tonight."

"And every night," Josh said, as he caught the waitress's eye. She quickly came over, smiling at Josh in a way she never did to anyone else.

"Hey, Mindy, how's it going?" he asked.

"Oh, it's getting more and more interesting," she said with a glance at Sophie.

Josh's brow rose a bit. "Could you add a chicken-fried steak to the orders for this table? I'm joining these newcomers to our fair town."

"Anything for you, Josh," she said with a smile. "Drink?"

"I'll take a Corona-rita."

"You got it."

The small talk that passed for conversation before Josh joined them grew even more deadly as the Professor had a new person with whom to pontificate. Sophie was glad when the food arrived, so they could at least talk about that.

As they sat back enjoying the after-dinner coffees, the country-western band started up, and Sophie feigned interest in the lyrics, effectively shutting out Beauregard.

When the band began "Achy-Breaky Heart," Bree stood. "Okay, I didn't want to say anything, but you people can*not* just sit here while that song is playing. I think it's older than I am, but you've *got* to dance to it. Don't any of you know how to line-dance?"

Sophie gawked at her as if she'd just sprouted wings.

"I do," Josh said.

"Well, come on, if you dare," Bree said, heading toward the dance floor.

"Did little sprout just challenge me?" Josh asked to Sophie.

"I'm afraid so."

He jumped up and hurried after Bree, taking a spot by her side.

Beauregard faced Sophie. "Alone at last," he said with a chuckle, and she had to wonder if he realized she was half his age. "This is something else," he continued. "It's like another world. Or stepping back in time to the ages I've always studied. Quite remarkable. Did you know Lewis and Clark's journey to the Pacific went through the northern part of this state?"

As he droned on and on, his words gave her an idea of how to start her travel piece about the Donnelly cabin and other places a person could stay in the West, places that would bring them back to another time, when the world was quite different. She liked that and smiled. Unfortunately, Beauregard mistook her smile and leaned closer.

Sophie was more than ready to return to the cabin, but one line dance led to another, and finally, when the band began a slow dance, Josh and Bree returned to the table.

"That looked like fun," Sophie said, relieved they could finally leave.

"It is," Bree said.

"And so are slower dances." Josh held out his hand to Sophie.

She debated for about half a second and stood up. She couldn't help but notice Beauregard's face fall as she took Josh's hand. He quickly turned to Bree. "Would you like—?"

"Not on your life," she said.

As Sophie stepped into Josh's arms, where she really didn't care to be but felt it would be rude to refuse him, she decided she could learn a thing or two from Bree.

CHAPTER 22

On Saturday morning, Bree and Maggie went with Sophie to help her set up the photo booth for the Founder's Day celebration. She had a folding table that held all the costume products from hats to boas that people might want to use for their pictures. Beside it was a dark red velvet curtain hanging on tall rods that she used as a backdrop. Cute and colorful Western memorabilia was strewn around the area to entice people to stop and check out the booth.

Everything was easy to break down and fold up to fit in Sophie's VW.

Throughout the morning, Sophie kept a lookout for Omar Timmons to appear and send her away, probably in handcuffs given how he'd been talking. But as the day went on, she was growing a little more assured that Timmons was all hat and no cattle, to use one of Tray's weird ranch expressions.

Tray... he left the cabin early the day before and she was already in bed when she heard the door to his room open and shut that night. She had thrown herself into getting everything ready for her photo booth, doing her best not to think about him. But, of course, he was pretty much all she thought about. Still, she didn't know if he was busy, or trying to avoid her. She missed his company, a lot, but told herself it was for the best to stay away from him. Best for both of them.

A short while after the market opened for business, Sophie saw a young mother with her baby looking over the photo booth. The child looked about six months old, which Sophie had learned was a very cute age for taking photos.

Everything about the woman made Sophie pretty sure she didn't have extra money for anything as frivolous as Western costume photos, but the thought of not being able to capture the adorable child in a photo made Sophie surprisingly sad. But then, everything about babies made her a little sad these days. She hadn't really thought about kids while she was with Sergio and enjoying a fun, somewhat jet-setting life style, along with a steady relationship. Not until their breakup did she realize how much she did want children. She'd always assumed she and Sergio would have them eventually... until she accepted he meant it when he said he wasn't interested. At least, not yet, and most definitely, not with her.

"Hello, there," she said as she walked over to where the woman was standing. "I'm trying to take pictures of people all ages for my portfolio, and I've taken no photos of babies yet. How old is your child?"

The mother proudly said, "She's seven months old today, but I'm afraid I don't have money for pictures."

"I'd like to take some photos at no charge to you." Sophie noticed the woman's cautious frown, and understood it. She needed to reassure her. "You'd be doing me a favor. Of course, I'd send you copies, but I'd like to put them in my portfolio to show potential customers that I can take eye-catching photographs of very young children. Your daughter would be perfect for that since she's so lovely."

Seeing the mother's worry continuing, Sophie quickly added, "And it goes without saying, although I'll say it, that I wouldn't reproduce the photo without your permission, and I'd never publish the names or addresses of you or your child."

"I see." The woman still sounded a bit skeptical.

"They would be simply for my portfolio."

"You're sure?"

"Absolutely."

The mother heaved a happy smile. "Okay, then. I'd really love to have some pictures of my little girl at this age. She is pretty, I think."

"She definitely is. I can tell you that with a photographer's eye," Sophie said. And she wasn't lying. Although she never told a soul, she'd taken more photos of kids that weren't exactly model material than she cared to think about.

She took several pictures of the baby alone, with the mother making faces to get the child to smile, and then several more photos of mother and child, some angelic, and others simply warm, fun, and loving.

During the photo shoot, Sophie noticed Tray standing a bit in the distance watching her and smiling in a way that warmed her heart. He didn't say a word to her, but as the day wore on, she saw him talking with people in the crowd, looking over her way, and a short while later, the ones he'd been talking to would want their photos taken. She hoped he wasn't going too overboard in his praise of her, but at the same time, she appreciated that he was helping her get a few more customers.

She'd never had to think much about money while in Italy, and never even realized how much money she'd wasted in the past when she had both a steady paycheck and Sergio to rely on. None of that made her proud. A lot of things she'd done in her life didn't make her proud. But now, she was finding she did have a backbone, and that she would and could make it on her own.

During a lull in her photo taking, she noticed an attractive woman eying Tray. At least she wasn't carrying a pie, Sophie thought. Somehow, the woman, a tall blonde and not wearing a wedding ring, engaged Tray in a discussion about the watercolors on display at the booth where they stood.

Sophie didn't know Tray was such an art critic, but clearly he was enjoying talking to the blonde about the paintings. In fact, he looked positively at ease chitchatting with that busybody stranger, and even seem to be putting on the charm since she kept smiling and nodding at whatever it was he was saying. And as the woman moved closer to him, he made no effort to move away.

Might he be starting to put aside some of the grief he bore? To open himself up to attention from women? It would be good for him if he did, she knew, from having watched some acquaintances go through similar situations.

On the other hand, just who was this interloper who was now flirting outrageously with Tray? Even worse, Tray seemed to be increasingly enjoying the attention. Sophie felt herself growing more irritated with each smile the blonde gave him. And the way the blonde laughed and threw her head back with almost every comment Tray made was sickening to see. Tray had a good sense of humor, but he wasn't *that* funny.

She knew she was being pricked with a jealousy pin, but she couldn't stop herself from feeling it, or from feeling how much it hurt!

When that pushy Georgina brought a pie to Tray at the cabin, that was one thing. He obviously wasn't interested in her, and Sophie was ready to help him get rid of her. But this blonde bombshell was another matter. Sophie fumed. Tray was her man, and the Garden Valley hussy could lay off.

And that was when the Blondie put her hand on Tray's arm and kept it there.

Next thing Sophie knew, she was marching over to them. Tray's brows rose as he watched her approach.

"Hello," she said when she reached them. She faced the woman. "My name's Sophie, and I'm running the photo booth over there. Tray has been doing a great job talking me up to people. I hope he's not taking up too much of your time." She smiled up at Tray and stood next to him, close to him.

"Oh?" the woman said, her eyes darting from one to the other. "Are you two--?"

"Uh oh," Tray suddenly said, completely ignoring the question as he moved even closer to Sophie and placed his hand on her back. "There's your buddy."

Sophie, on the other hand, was zeroed in on the other woman and said, "Yes, we are."

"I'm not sure what's going on here," the blonde said, "but I think I need to be someplace else." She then hurried off.

"Sophie," Tray said. "Look."

Sophie didn't know what he was referring to until she followed his gaze to see Omar Timmons marching into the area. Two men carrying supplies followed him.

"What in the world is he up to?" Sophie muttered.

As Sophie watched, hands on hips and teeth clenched so tight her jaw ached, Timmons set up a photo stand right across from hers and filled it with Disney princess costumes, from Ariel to Moana to lots and lots of others that Sophie wasn't around enough little girls to even have any idea who they were.

But the little girls in the area certainly knew.

Sophie stormed back to her booth with Tray staying at her side. There, she watched terrifyingly bossy little girls drag their hapless parents to Timmons' booth and loudly declare that they wanted to be a princess and have their pictures taken.

They acted more like evil stepmothers than princesses.

"I don't believe him!" Sophie said to Tray. "How did he know to do this?"

Clearly, a lot more little girls wanted their pictures taken as a princess than little boys wanted photos of themselves as cowboys. In fact, very few little boys wanted their photos taken as anything.

Tray hooked his thumbs to the pockets of his jeans and grinned. "Probably taking pictures at birthday parties and schools. I guess you aren't around kids much."

"I'm not. Oh, my God!" Sophie wailed as she saw two couples with daughters heading her way, but then make an abrupt turn to Timmons' booth. "Now what am I going to do? He's taking all my business! Who in the world knew that little girls, not parents, figured out which photographs the whole family took?"

"Don't worry," Tray said. "Things will change soon. The little kids will start getting tired and cranky. They'll go home, and a whole different crowd will be here. You'll see."

"Do you really think so, or are you just trying to placate me?"

He gave her that half-smile he did so well. "I'd never attempt to placate you, sweetness." With that, he walked away.

As Tray suggested, as Founder's Day continued into evening, the number of kids lessened, and country-western and rock bands brought a whole different crowd to the market.

At one point, Dr. Waterton came over to Sophie's booth and, to her amazement, he began suggesting hats, scarves, flowers, jewelry, and other costume supplies for women to wear while taking a photo. Few of the single ladies there were able to resist his suggestions and ending up sitting in front of her camera, probably much to their own surprise. Even those with boyfriends and spouses rarely could resist the good doctor's charms.

The more Sophie worked with Dr. Carter Waterton, the more grateful she was for his help.

On Sunday morning, Tray couldn't bear the thought of listening to Sophie talk about the Founder's Day celebration. He'd watched Waterman join her last evening. It was bad enough seeing so many women gaga over the guy with his chalk-white smile and flashing eyes, but to find Sophie among his admirers was more than he could handle.

But why shouldn't she be? He was definitely her type. At least he was a step up from the baker-boy-about-town she'd been seeing. He was sure the doctor would be there again that day. Maybe the baker as well. Maybe they'd fight a duel over her. Wouldn't that beat all?

Well, good for her. If she needed all that attention to get over her Italian lover, fine. More power to her. Although, he had to admit, she looked more than a mite jealous when she came over and got the pretty blonde talking to him to skedaddle. Maybe Sophie wasn't as immune to him as he thought she was.

He didn't want breakfast, which caused Maggie to ask if he was ill. Instead, he grabbed a couple of biscuits and went down to the river. The small beach area was mercifully empty, the way he hoped it would be.

He sat on the felled log and stared out at the water, breathing deeply. Ever so slowly, he felt himself relaxing and the tension beginning to leave his body.

The one thing Sophie had definitely done for him was to let him know he wasn't dead inside.

For years, he'd felt as if he'd died along with Charlene until Sophie somehow badgered him into driving her around the countryside. And then he got to know her and like her. A lot.

Every square inch of his body felt alive when she was near, and when she wasn't, he felt as if he was missing some vital part of his being. It was all but scary how much he wanted to be with her, especially knowing this wasn't going anywhere.

Behind him, he heard a light cough and turned to see Luke standing nearby.

"I didn't hear you," Tray said.

Luke grinned. "Sand is quiet, that's for sure. May I join you?" He pointed to the log.

"Have a seat. Not fishing today?" Tray asked.

"Not today. But tell me, I heard a rumor that a couple of women brought you pies. Is that true?"

"Oh, my God." Tray grimaced. "Are people actually talking about that?"

"So it seems. My mother knows someone connected to the Donnelly house. But good for you. Getting yourself out there, right?"

Tray shook his head. "It means nothing. I tell you, after my wife passed, an unbroken string of single, divorced, and widowed women brought over so many pies, casseroles, and cookies for me and my son, I was afraid I'd need to buy a freezer. But then they figured out that I wasn't interested no matter how much food they shoveled my way, and the nonsense stopped."

"Well, there is the nonsense, as you call it, but I suspect a lot just wanted to help. They realized you had a lot of changes to deal with. Sometimes simply having someone to talk to makes everything a lot easier."

"That's true," Tray said. "But I'm not one to talk about

private things. I'm surprised, frankly, that I've told you so much!"

"I tend to have that effect on people, although I don't know why," Luke said with a wry smile. "Does it help to talk to Sophie?"

"Sophie?" Tray was surprised by the question. "Do you know about Sophie, too? I never mentioned her to you."

Luke blanched and then coughed. His cough was still quite nasty. "I guess my mother is telling stories she shouldn't. Sorry!"

"Do I know your mother? Is she a friend of Maggie's?"

"I doubt you've met her. I'm sorry. I shouldn't have brought up Sophie."

"It's okay. She and I are just friends."

"Oh?" Luke's voice was skeptical. "Are you sure?"

Tray stiffened. "Of course! And it's pretty clear she's not seriously interested in a guy like me."

"Has she told you that?"

Tray couldn't remember her specifically saying that, but she hadn't disagreed when he brought it up.

"Let me just tell you this," Luke said. "I don't have anyone special anymore. Like you, I had someone once, but I lost her. My friend, I've never found anyone else. But if I had been lucky enough to, I would've done whatever I could to keep her. So, if Sophie means a lot to you, don't let her slip away."

The intensity of Luke's words shook Tray to the core, as well as his admission that he'd once lost someone he had loved. Tray wondered if that was what made him so sympathetic to all Tray was going through.

He also wondered how their simple conversation had turned so sharply serious. Tray scarcely knew the man, yet he had to admit Luke's advice was good.

He faced Luke. "You're still a young man. There's plenty of time for you to meet someone else."

Luke's mouth tightened and he shook his head. "Not like-ly." Then he said goodbye and continued on his way.

As he went, Tray noticed a folded piece of paper fall from his pocket. "Hey, wait! Luke!" Tray called.

He bent to pick up the paper, but it got caught up in a gust of wind and tumbled in the direction of the river. Tray chased after it, afraid it might be important. He managed to step on it and pick it up just before the wind carried it into the water. "Luke, I caught it!"

He turned around. "Luke?"

He didn't see the fisherman and ran down the path he thought Luke had taken, but no one was there. He wasn't sure what to do and unfolded the paper, thinking it might be nothing important at all.

To his surprise, it was a flyer about a new piece of property just placed on sale down near Horseshoe Bend. An odd piece of property, but the more he read about it, the more curiously intriguing he found the ad to be. Why, he wondered, would Luke know or care about such a place?

Bree again went with Sophie to help with the photo booth. Sophie was glad for the young woman's sake more than for any help Bree gave her. She liked seeing Bree getting out and meeting people, not staying cooped up in the cabin reading, working puzzles, and listening to internet podcasts using the expensive satellite internet system she had somehow managed to set up in her room. When Sophie asked Bree about it, Bree's response was simply, "It keeps me in touch with my parents." To Sophie's mind, that reeked of a lie.

Bree honestly made no sense to her, and wouldn't give Sophie any insight to her, so she stopped asking, figuring if Bree wanted to talk to her, she would. Although it seemed to her Bree was quite happy being a loner—except that she did perk up a bit whenever Josh was around. But Josh, unfortunately, paid no more attention to her than he did to Maggie or even Professor Beauregard.

At the Founder's Day celebration, everyone had said Sunday would be a much bigger day than Saturday because more people were off work. In addition, several outdoor bands and a number of food trucks would be driving up from Boise to add to the festivities.

To Sophie's delight, Dr. Waterton again spent the morning at her booth, attracting customers like bees to honey. But at one o'clock, he left to go to a party with some big wigs at a hospital in Boise. He explained that he needed to keep a connection to them. But before leaving, he looked into Sophie's eyes, holding both her hands, as he told her how much he regretted leaving her alone there.

She had to admit the man was handsome, and if she hadn't spent years taking photos of exceptionally beautiful people who had nothing else to offer the world beyond their looks, her heart might have been doing a polka over all his attention. But it wasn't. In fact, it didn't even beat faster around him.

She couldn't help but think back on some of the best-looking male models she'd met. They had nurtured an appealing softness, the latest fad, by wearing perfectly fitted expensive clothes over low BMI bodies, having haircuts that cost in the hundreds of dollars, and leaving the exact length of closely clipped beard on their faces. Even Sergio had moisturized every day, wanting to maintain a youthful freshness as long as humanly possible.

Sophie had to chuckle at the thought of Tray ever walking around with moisturizing cream or, God forbid, a facial.

Yet, something about Tray appealed to her on a deeper level than any of those models or even the handsome Dr. Waterton. And, she had to admit, that fact was disturbing. Cowboys were about as far from what she had always considered her "type" as was a pro-wrestler covered in garish tattoos.

At least, that's what she had thought until she met Tray.

To her dismay, Tray didn't show up at all that day.

As evening approached, Bree came over and stood beside her. "I see the good doctor had to take off. Is he coming back?"

"I doubt it. He's a busy man. I'm lucky he was able to spend as much time as he did with me helping to raise money for Founder's Day."

Bree lifted her eyebrows. "Come on, now. You don't really think it's Founder's Day that was on his mind, do you?"

CHAPTER 23

Sophie got up early Monday morning, dressed, and then listened for Tray's door to open and shut. When she heard his footsteps going downstairs, she waited two minutes and then went down to breakfast herself.

Maggie was chatting with him about the day's weather, which was definitely warming up, and Sophie could smell the aroma of her cooking.

"Good morning, Sophie," Maggie called out. "Can I cook up a Denver omelet for you?"

Tray looked up at Sophie, but when their eyes met, he quickly dropped his gaze and poured himself some coffee.

"What a surprise," she said to Maggie. "I'd love one."

"Just trying to change things around here," Maggie said. "I think it's time. You could have a pastry while I cook your omelet."

"No thanks. I've had my fill of those."

She noticed Tray's mouth tighten.

Maggie put Tray's omelet on the table with a waffle on the side.

"Any luck with the land hunting?" Sophie asked him.

"Not yet."

"That's too bad," she murmured.

Maggie soon had Sophie's omelet ready. She quietly ate.

Tray put down his fork and lifted his gaze to hers. "How did the photo booth work out? You seemed busy whenever I went by there."

She nodded, surprised to learn he was there on Sunday but hadn't stopped by to say hello. "It went much better than I ever expected, despite Omar Timmons' attempt at sabotaging it. You were quite correct that as the day wore on, both days, there were fewer and fewer little girls and their families at the event, and an adult crowd started arriving. The later it got, the more the crowd had to drink, which seemed to make more of them think they were in love and wanted photos taken with the man or woman of their dreams. I stuck around until closing time, and it paid off."

"Yeah, I can imagine people do stupid things when they think they've found someone they can care about. In the light of day, I wonder how many of them will feel nothing but remorse."

He dropped his gaze to his plate and went back to eating. She was speechless. Was he taking about himself? Remorse? Was that what he felt? And why?

She couldn't sit there across from him and say nothing, but she also didn't know what to say to make this right.

She left her breakfast, grabbed a jacket and went down to the river.

———

Sophie paced back-and-forth until, finally, she—as she'd come to expect, almost like magic—she spotted Anna headed her way. She waited until Anna reached her, then they fell into step together.

"You've been busy, Sophie," Anna said.

"I have. But my topsy-turvy life has gotten even stranger."

"What do you mean?"

"I don't understand what's going on, Anna. If I was smart, I'd pack my bags and leave. But I don't know where to go. Maybe to a ghost town and I could write about it. At least there, I wouldn't meet someone who totally confuses me."

"Ah, you're talking about Tray again," Anna said knowingly.

"He told me he feels nothing but remorse about us!"

"Do you really believe that?"

"It's what he said."

"Did he? Or do you think that's what he said?"

"I just don't know anymore! Maybe I did overreact. Or not."

Anna said nothing as they continued walking, and then asked, "Who do you talk to the most, other than me?"

Sophie sighed. "Tray."

"Who's been there when you need someone? Anyone?"

"Bree helped at the photo booth," Sophie said.

"Oh, so Bree is more help to you than Tray?"

"No, I couldn't say that. But it doesn't matter. Tray and I are completely wrong for each other."

"Is that your head talking, or your heart?"

She stopped walking. "It doesn't matter how I feel. He's not interested in me."

Anna said nothing for awhile, and then asked, "Have you ever thought there could be something else going on? Something he's not saying?"

Sophie stopped walking. "As a matter of fact, I think he is

holding something back. For all I know, he's got a fiancée back in Montana!"

Anna shook her head. "You know he doesn't. But if he is holding something back, maybe you should try to find out what that is."

"I'd love to get him to tell me, but he keeps so much inside, it's hard." Sophie all but wailed as she spoke those words.

"What if he's the one for you? The true love the cabin's ghosts found for you. Isn't it worth facing things that are 'hard' if, in the end, you and Tray can be together?"

"The cabin's ghosts? Surely, you know I don't believe in such things. In fact, sometimes I think..." Sophie stopped herself, appalled at the strange and scary thought that came to mind.

"You think what?" Anna asked.

"Sometimes, it seems you must be an imaginary friend since I've never met anyone who understands me as well as you do. Is that crazy?"

Anna gave her a small laugh and shook her head. "Yes, I'm afraid it is. Believe me, I'm not imaginary. My husband and son would have something to say about that if I was!"

"Why haven't I seen them, or your house?"

"I told you, we're very private people. That's all. But I've enjoyed our talks, Sophie, whether you believe I'm a person or not. All I can tell you, is to think about my words," Anna said. "Think carefully. And here, I've got to leave."

They had reached the point in the path where Anna continued on alone.

Sophie stopped and watched Anna walk away as ever, but she was struck with the sudden feeling that this might be the last time they would meet. "I'll see you again soon," she called, alarmed at the sense she could lose Anna's thoughtful companionship.

But she was met with only silence.

CHAPTER 24

When Sophie returned to the cabin, expecting to be alone, she was shocked to find Tray in the kitchen getting himself a glass of water. "Oh, thirsty, I see," she said.

"It happens," he said, and then put the glass in the dishwasher.

She couldn't think of a better time to confront him. Although her knees felt trembly, she forced herself to march up to him before he could escape upstairs, or out, or wherever he chose to go to avoid her.

"Tray, it's time to talk." Her voice shook with emotion.

All she saw was bewilderment. "I don't think we have anything to talk about."

Sophie looked at him intently.

He gave her a puzzled look.

"We have everything to talk about," she said. The hurt she had been carrying threatened to overwhelm her, and a lump rose in her throat. "I need answers."

His shoulders slumped, and he shut his eyes a moment.

"You haven't done anything wrong, Sophie. I'm the problem. It's all on me."

"I thought we might have something," she whispered. "I care about you, Tray. Am I wrong to feel that way?"

He looked defeated. "No, not you. I'm the one who's stuck. I can't seem to find what I'm looking for. And the way it's going, I'm going to lose everything. My ranch is gone. My son may soon be. And if I had you, which of course I don't, you'd probably end up running *back* to Italy!"

"That's not true," she cried. As she looked into his eyes, she remembered her conversation with Anna about something he wasn't telling her. "From what I see, this isn't about only the land. There's something else stopping you from moving forward. Maybe if you told me what that was, I could offer some help."

"Help? Based on what? Your great experience with ranching or farming?" His voice was angry, but his eyes looked tortured and sad. He paced, waving his arms in frustration. "The last thing I need is help from you. You know even less about this land than your city boy doctor. Or that Italian guy who wants you to go back. You think I haven't noticed? You think I'm blind? Oh, I almost forgot your baker boy. How could I forget him when you swoon over his pastries every morning!"

She stared at him in shock. And then her heart skipped a beat. Swooning over pastries? Railing about other men. A mixture of surprise, elation, and confusion filled her.

The realization that he'd been hiding the depth of his feelings for her caused a rush of emotions, from disbelief to hopefulness to a tinge of regret for not having seen it earlier.

"I don't care about the baker or the doctor and I'm well over Sergio," she said as she gripped both his arms, deciding to lay it all out for him. "How can I make you understand that *you're* the one I have feelings for? Only you."

He looked hopeful, but then he shook his head, his lips tight, and stepped back, freeing himself from her hold. "If so, I'm sorry for you."

This was hopeless. "Me, too," she whispered. She was tempted to give up, to walk away, but she remembered how Anna had urged her to get him to talk to her, and even though it would be difficult, he was worth it.

Anna was right.

"Can we go outside?" she asked him. Her heart raced as she looked into eyes that were sadder, more vulnerable, than she'd ever seen them.

"Fine," he said, his voice a mere breath.

They went to the back porch and sat on the cushioned bench, Sophie on one side and Tray on the other. "What's going on, Tray?" she asked.

Silence stretched between them.

Then he sat hunched forward, his elbows on his thighs, and he stared at the wooden floor as if pondering where to begin. Finally, he spoke, his voice strained with emotion. "None of this has been easy. It's not easy to turn your life upside down when you don't know what the reaction is going to be."

He was a proud man, so Sophie knew how hard it must have been for him to admit that. "You mean Brody's reaction?"

His jaw tightened, and it took a while before he said, "Yes. His, Charlene's family, and my sister's."

Sophie remembered the hairdresser mentioning a woman with the Bowman family name. "Is she in Garden Valley?"

"She is. She's a couple years older than me and we were really close growing up. My dad was never an easy man to get along with, but when he drank too much he got mean—a meanness he tended to take out on his son. Maeve, my sister, tried to stop him, but she was a kid, too. Finally, I felt I either had to leave or end up fighting with him, and when I say fight, I mean the kind that could end with one of us dead. Things were really bad, Sophie."

"I'm so sorry," she whispered.

He made no reaction, but simply continued. "Maeve was furious when I left home, leaving her to deal with him. I hated to do it, but I knew he would never hurt Maeve. At least I was right about that. Anyway, after I settled in Montana, I never heard from my sister until she called to tell me Dad was dying. She said I should come home to see him before it was too late. But it happened at the same time as Charlene was eight months along with Brody. The doctor was monitoring her—he wanted to give the baby as much time as possible in the womb, but also to perform a Caesarian before any more strain happened to Charlene's heart. Clearly, I couldn't have her travel, and I wouldn't leave her. And, frankly, I didn't see a death-bed reunion as solving anything, so I didn't go.

"My last call from Maeve was when she told me Dad had died and when the funeral was. Again, I didn't go. I sent flowers, and she sent them back. I've never heard from her since. I can't say I blame her. I did wrong. I did nothing when she needed me. I failed her like I have everyone who's been close to me. It's best you keep away from me, Sophie, because I know I'll just disappoint you, too."

Sophie was chilled. She understood Tray's decision, but also Maeve's hurt, especially if he didn't tell her what was going on—which she suspected he didn't. "Your position, given what was going on with your wife, was difficult," she said. "But if you explain—"

He snorted. "Difficult. Yeah. I don't know if she'll want to hear any explanations. The whole family has a stubborn streak, and we tend to clam up instead of talk when confronted. Maybe I should leave well enough alone."

Sophie asked, "Have you tried to see her?"

"I made it as far as her house a couple of times, but nothing more. I know she's married with four boys, ages thirteen to five. They're Brody's cousins, and I'd like him to meet them. But I don't know how Maeve will react. If she throws me out... I can't lie, Soph, it'll tear me up."

She struggled to find words of comfort, but all she choked out was, "I see."

He said nothing, and she realize how trite her words sounded. Her feelings went beyond words and she moved to his side and put her arms around him, expecting him to push her away.

Instead, his arms circled her as well. She held him close, hoping he would accept the comfort she offered.

They remained that way for awhile before she drew back. "Maybe it's time to try to see her again."

"I know I should," he said. "But sometimes, not knowing what a result will be is better than facing a negative outcome."

"I understand that," she murmured. "But what if the situation with Maeve is weighing on you more than you realize and is getting in the way of you finding land you'll be happy with?"

He shook his head. "I don't know."

"Being back here is probably awakening more memories, bad as well as good, than you realize."

"I do know that's true. Almost every night I dream of people long gone, people who lived here when I was a kid. My mom, grandparents, even my dad, back when we got along fine."

She took his hands. "If you want to try to see Maeve, I'll go with you. You've stood by me time and again since we've met. Now, I'd like to be there for you."

"This is a family problem." His voice turned harsh. "And I don't remember you being a part of this family."

He was doing it again, hiding his feelings with anger, with

lashing out and trying to act cold and aloof. The big phony. But she could tell that deep down he was scared, scared that his relationship with his sister was irrevocably broken, a sister he'd once revered and loved, a sister that was the only one he had left in his family besides his son.

"I know I'm not family," she said. "But that doesn't mean I don't want to be with you."

"It's not that easy." His fake anger vanished, and he now sounded only sad.

"I can see that," she said. "And maybe she won't speak to you and will order you off her property. Or maybe she'll want to talk. You won't know until you face her. So come on. Cowboy up."

He smirked. "Where did you hear that old expression?"

She said nothing.

He got up and paced, not saying a word, but simply strode back and forth, back and forth across the wooden deck.

Please, she kept thinking, please let him get this settled one way or the other.

Finally, he stopped and faced her. "Okay, pardner," he said. "Much as I don't really like the plan, let's saddle up and get this over with."

Although Tray had said "saddle up," Sophie was glad they took his truck.

She planned to wait in the truck, saying a lot of prayers that he didn't come flying out of his sister's home in a couple of minutes. If that happened, she wasn't sure what it would mean for him. Would he stay in this area, as he'd just said, or move on, or even decide to remain in Montana?

And what would it mean for the two of them?

Every instinct told her he was a good person whose feelings ran deep, including the way he felt about her. His life experiences, sad and troubling as they were, had made him the way he was—a man she liked and respected and didn't want to lose —but who also had a lot of hidden scars.

As long as his future was unsettled, she realized, so was hers because despite all her best intentions not to get involved, her heart was involved. And she hoped her future had Tray in it.

Some ten minutes later, they reached his sister's home on the flatlands south of the Middle Fork of the Payette. "What is this land used for?" she asked.

"It's good farm land. It's too early in the year for planting, but you can see the blossoms on the trees already, and if you come back here in late summer and you'll see lots of different crops being grown."

Tray slowed down as they approached an older ranch house. It seemed to have a good amount of land around it, but Sophie had no idea how much there actually was. The two-car garage door was open, and a truck was inside, so someone must be home. It was a school day so Tray shouldn't have kids or his sister's husband interfering with his meeting.

But Tray didn't turn into the driveway. He kept going right past it. Sophie could sense his growing apprehension along with his desire to hang a U-turn and head back to the cabin as fast as the road would take him.

"Park," she demanded. "Right here, right now. You don't have to pull into the driveway. I'll sit here and wait. You go ahead."

He glanced at her, stunned at her giving orders. But then he did as she said and shut off the engine. "You're going to abandon me now?"

A CERTAIN SMILE

185

"The last thing you need is me standing there watching the two of you."

"So much for your moral support," he said, arms folded.

She placed her hand on his arm. "You know you have my support and my prayers. Just remember to talk to her. Talk, okay? Be truthful and open your heart. And also let her know how much you've regretted the split with her and that you still care about her."

He cocked one eyebrow as he slightly shook his head. "Easy for you to say."

"I know you can do this." Her heart full, she leaned toward him and gave him a kiss on the cheek.

He turned toward her and as their eyes met, she felt herself drawn to him so powerfully she knew any suggestion of "just friendship" with him would never work. It was all or nothing. She couldn't resist the pull she felt, and couldn't stop herself from whispering his name.

His fingers slid between the locks of her hair, holding her still as his lips met hers. He took her breath away. It was as if they were one, lost in the moment, lost in each other.

But then he moved back and placed his hand on the door handle.

"You do know how to encourage a guy," he murmured and gave her that half grin, that certain smile, she'd learned to love. His voice sent shivers down her spine.

She gave him a little push. "Get out of here," she said, hearing a slight quaver in her voice. "It's time to meet your sister."

"Yes, ma'am." He grabbed his hat from the backseat, left the truck, and she watched him fitting it securely as he walked up the driveway and then knocked on the door.

Nothing happened.

"Come on, open the door," she whispered, her heart racing with both anticipation and anxiety.

He backed away. The wait was excruciating. He then moved forward and knocked again.

Damn, she thought. Her stomach churned.

She saw Tray's shoulders slump, and then he turned and walked to the few steps that led off the porch to the driveway. The sight broke her heart.

But just then, the front door opened, and she saw a tall woman in the doorway. Tray spun around, facing her as she stepped onto the porch. The two had the same dark brown hair color.

Sophie felt a surge of hope.

Even from a distance, Sophie could see that neither said a word but simply stared at each other for a long moment. Please, she thought, please don't go back inside and shut the door on him. Please give him a chance.

Tray took off his hat and gave his sister a slight nod.

Maeve turned and walked into the house, but then she opened the door wide and held it for him to enter. It was a small gesture, but Sophie knew it meant the world to Tray.

Tears pricked at the corners of her eyes as she watched him enter the house and shut the door behind him.

CHAPTER 25

Sophie awoke with a start at the sound of the truck door opening. She sat up.

"Sorry about the time," Tray said as he got into the driver's seat and started the engine. The clock on the dash told her some forty-five minutes had passed. "I didn't expect it would be that long."

"It's okay. What happened?" she asked.

"It was a good start." He heaved a sigh of relief, then shook his head and gazed at Sophie, his eyes filled with incredulity. "She thought I'd become some sort of cattle baron in Montana, and that I considered myself too high and mighty to deal with my poor relatives back in Idaho. I have no idea where she got that impression, and she had no idea about my wife's health. It was an eye-opener for us both. The bottom line is she'd like you and me to have dinner at her place in two days, if you don't mind."

"She invited me?" Sophie asked. "Why? I should think the two of you have a lot to talk about."

"We do, but it'll come slow. And I kind of let it slip that a friend was the one who finally gave me the push I needed to pay her a visit." He grinned. "She wants to meet that friend."

Sophie was surprised but pleased, and especially pleased to see him looking genuinely happy.

"Okay," she said. "I'll join you if you do one thing."

"Oh?"

"Add the word 'girl' before you say 'friend' next time you talk to her about me. It makes a world of difference."

A full smile slowly spread across his face. "I can do that."

She couldn't help but to throw her arms around him and hold him tight for a long moment.

The ride back to the cabin was mercifully short. Tray clearly had a lot on his mind, and he said little. Sophie also had thoughts churning, but her thoughts had nothing to do with Tray's sister... only about him.

"Want some coffee?" she asked Tray as they entered the cabin.

"That sounds good," he said.

Her arm was around his waist, and his arm across her shoulders holding her close as they walked into the great room, but then Sophie stopped, unbelieving who was there.

Sergio stood up from the sofa. He wore a light gray casual Armani suit, slim fitted, with a white dress shirt, no tie, and the top three buttons unbuttoned—a very Sergio look. His gold Rolex glistened, as did the pomade that kept his black hair with just the right amount of waves falling in just the right way to look both casual but styled. His dark eyes in a thin face with a pronounced Roman nose and full lips were as perfect as ever.

Sophie let go of Tray and stepped toward Sergio. "I don't believe this!"

"Sophia, *bella! Cara mia, vieni qui!*" He opened his arms and when she didn't go to him, he strode across the room to her, put his arms around her waist and lifted her off her feet, spinning around and around.

Her hands grip to shoulders, and without thinking she reverted to Italian. *"Lasciami!"*

He put her down as she'd ordered, but as her feet touched the ground, his lips met hers even as she pushed him away.

She felt Tray's hand on her arm as he faced Sergio. "What's going on here?" His voice was every bit as cold and hard as his eyes. Then he turned to her. "Are you okay, Sophie?"

Sergio said nothing, but stared at her. She looked up at Tray. "It's okay. I need to talk to him. Alone."

Tray's lips tightened. "You sure?"

She nodded.

"Okay." He left the room.

She and Sergio said nothing until the front door opened and shut.

"So, your new friend has gone," Sergio said. "I guess I should have introduced myself, but I was so happy to see you again, you were all I could think of. I've missed you so much."

She was flustered and angry. "How did you get here?" she asked. "And why? I don't understand."

"Let's sit," Sergio said commonly. "I'm so tired, *cara*. I think I used everything but a stage coach to find this Donnelly Cabin. I know my visit is unexpected, but I must talk to you." He waved his arm toward the sofa. *"Prego,"* he murmured, his way of asking that she please join him there, facing the fireplace.

She sat stiffly, some distance from him.

His dark eyes traveled from her to the walls, the fireplace, the old pewter pieces on the mantle and Elijah Donnelly's portrait, Elijah's mouth appeared tight and prim as he stared down at them. "I can't believe you're staying in a place like this," Sergio said finally. "This... all this old stuff, this town... it's like you're in some movie. It isn't *you*. I know the real you. I've seen your work in Milan and Rome. Your beautiful, clever, passionate work. This place... I could scarcely find it on a map!"

She saw the disappointment in his eyes at how far she'd fallen. But had she? In his world, yes, but what about her own? What about where she belonged? "How did you find me?" she asked.

"I talked to your mother. I explained to her what's going on." His eyes left hers and he smiled as if remembering a pleasant conversation. "Your mother is a good woman. I think I won her over as we talked. At first, she was, *come se dice?* Abrupt. Short with me. She thought I broke your heart. I convinced her it was you who broke mine."

Sophie couldn't speak, so surprised she was to hear him say such a thing.

"I miss you so much, Sophia." His voice, everything about him, pleaded with her. "I didn't realize how important you are to me. But as soon as you were gone, I knew. Come back with me. Please."

She rubbed her forehead, still trying to process that he was here, that he'd traveled all this way to be with her. But also to gather strength to say what she needed. "You know," she said finally, her voice soft and low, "when I first arrived here, I would have given everything I possess to have heard you say those words. But now, I've had time to think, and I'm not going back with you."

"You cannot like it here," he declared. "It does not compare to Roma, Firenze, Milano. You must return there. It's where you belong. With me."

She couldn't help but smile. That was the way he'd always talked to her, telling her what she must do, what she could or could not want or like or enjoy. And for years, she was too awestruck to stand up to him. She was never seen as his equal, not in his mind... and not even in her own.

"But I do like it here, Sergio," she said, her voice soft. "I feel more real than I have in a long time. More like *me*." She waited a moment, finding it hard to look into his eyes, remembering how much she'd once loved them, even though she wanted to explain herself to him. "I'm glad I had that time in Italy with you. I adored Italy, and I loved you so very much. You were like a dream come true to me. But I don't want a dream anymore. I want what's real. And I've found that here."

His beautiful lips pursed. Everything about him was beautiful. She remembered lying next to him in bed and studying his features, one after the other, and how very exceptional they were. He was simply a gorgeous man, and all hers. Until he wasn't.

"No, *bella,* this is not enough for you! Come with me to Boise for dinner tonight. We can find a decent restaurant, I hope, and talk the way we used to do."

If she went with him to Boise, he would pour on the charm —and he knew how to be very charming, indeed. He would certainly bring back memories of how it had felt when she loved him, when she believed they were on top of the world, and that he felt the same way about her.

But she also knew it had been nothing but a lovely fantasy. Even early on, she had sensed there was something missing in her relationship with him. Maybe because it had all happened too easily. He had said the words she wanted to hear as if he could read her mind and then had memorized a script. She gave up everything she'd worked for in New York City to follow him, unquestioningly, to Italy. It paid off in a material sense, but at the same time, she had lost herself.

At times, while they were together, she would become overwhelmingly sad. He'd ask why, and she couldn't answer, or she'd give him a silly answer such as saying she was homesick.

But she wasn't.

Now she knew what her tears had been all about. Her outward happiness was like a gorgeous bouquet of cut flowers. It might look beautiful for a while, but soon it would wither and die because it had nothing to keep it alive. At the same time, a simple cluster of perennials off in the corner of a garden might never be especially showy, but could survive freezing blizzards and blistering heat as long as its roots remained strong.

For him to travel all this way to bring her back to Italy with him, only made her realize how badly she'd been taken in by him. If this was strictly about his love for her, he would have said something while she was still in Italy. He would have begged her not to leave.

But he hadn't. In fact, he'd been silent until he was presented the opportunity to oversee a big travel promotion, in English no less.

Years ago, when she was young and foolish, she had acted that way. But now, more than ever, she realized the importance of having someone who could be both a friend and a lover, and could be counted on to be truthful with her. Even when it hurt.

She had learned a lot from her mistakes, but she now believed she had a better idea of what love felt like. Never again would she settle for anything less.

She didn't know how or if her relationship with Tray would progress, or if they would have a future, but simply knowing him, feeling what he made her feel... for that she would always be grateful.

She walked to the French doors, her back to Sergio. "I think it's time for you to leave." And then she went out to the porch, shutting the door behind her.

———

Tray was disgusted with himself at how he had hotfooted it out of the cabin when one of Sophie's many boyfriends showed up. She'd asked him to leave, but still...

And, to think, Sophie had just told him she wanted to be his "girlfriend," not just his "friend." In his world, that meant something.

Everything about her old boyfriend bothered him. The guy was too slick by half. Tray decided to go back in there to face this Italian playboy *and* to let Sophie know it was time for her to decide. Which one of them did she truly want?

He opened the door to the cabin, expecting to hear voices, but heard none. He hadn't seen Sergio leave, so obviously they had to be in there together... and weren't talking.

He felt as if he were dying inside as one probable reason he didn't hear the two conversing came to mind.

Confrontation time. He stiffened his spine and marched toward the great room, his gaze fixed in the direction of the couch, the most likely spot to find two lovers. But the only one he saw sitting there was Sergio. Alone.

Tray stopped, still in the doorway.

As Sergio faced the fireplace, his arms folded, he called out. "I refuse to believe you want me to leave, Sophia."

Where was Sophie? Tray didn't see her.

"Come here, now!" Sergio demanded.

Tray still didn't see Sophie. But then, to his complete astonishment, the vase of wildflowers that Maggie kept on the side credenza where the CDs and stereo equipment were stored, suddenly lifted in the air. Tray gaped, took a step backward, and rubbed his eyes. Surely he couldn't be seeing what he was seeing.

The vase looked as if were suspended by an invisible thread. Tray's heart pounded as he tried to make sense of it.

Was he hallucinating? Had his confused emotions over Sophie finally caused his mind to snap?

The vase slowly made its way across the room towards Sergio. The man hadn't noticed it at first, but suddenly he turned his head, let out a little squeak, and clutched the back of the sofa, his knuckles white as he tried to steady himself. The vase floated ever closer to him.

He sprang to his feet, eyes big as saucers, and flung himself to the side of the sofa farthest from the vase. But, then, as bizarrely as it had started, the vase floated back to its original position on the credenza and settled there.

Tray gawked at the vase and Sergio in disbelief, his mind reeling. What in the world had he—and Sergio—just witnessed? It had to be a trick of some sort, being played by someone in this house.

And then he remembered having seen Bree crawling around on the floor in just that area. A lost earring, she had said. But why would Bree do such a thing? And why to Sergio? Surely, she didn't know Sergio was coming to Idaho—did she? None of this made any sense.

"Sophia..." Sergio called, his voice high and trembling.

She opened the French doors and came back into the great room. Tray sighed with relief that she was okay.

"I'm sorry," she said to Sergio. "I can't go anywhere with you. Not tonight. Not ever."

"Can't?" Sergio ranted, running both hands through his silky, wavy black locks. His eyes still nervously darted from her to the peripatetic vase to her again. But it only seemed to add to his fury. *"Can't?* Who are you to not listen to me? I made you. Without me, you were nothing, and never would be! What's wrong with you? And with this place? This, this cabin! You're coming with me!"

She looked both shocked and angry at his outburst. "Stop it, Sergio! This isn't helping."

He strode towards her, and this time when he spoke, his voice was soft. "I won't ask again, Sophia!"

She turned her back to him.

"You aren't yourself!" he shouted and grabbed her arm.

Tray saw red. He forced himself to count to three, but if that fellow didn't take his hand off Sophie's arm, he might not have a hand when Tray finished with him.

But before he even reached "two," the same vase of flowers suddenly rose into the air and sped across the room towards Sergio.

Tray gawked.

Sergio shrieked, let go of Sophie's arm and back-pedaled toward the kitchen.

Sophia gasped and ran toward the French doors.

The vase didn't stop, but rose higher and higher, nearing the ceiling as it tracked Sergio. As soon as it was directly overhead, it turned upside down, dumping flowers and water all over him.

Sophie stood with her hands covering her mouth, her eyes wide.

Sergio gawked at her, his mouth hanging open, complete shock on his face. His hair and shirt were soaked through, and water dripped off him onto the hardwood floor. For a moment, the two stood in silence, as if trying to process what had just happened.

The vase was now back on the credenza, but the flowers lay at Sergio's feet.

"*How did you do that?*" he bellowed.

"I didn't do a thing," she whispered.

Sergio's hands clenched in fists, his words an incoherent sputter, while his face grew redder and darker until it was nearly purple. Finally, he flung his arms into the air, and then grabbed his jacket and stormed from the cabin, slamming the door so hard the whole place shook.

Tray decided to give Sophie a moment to process all this, and quietly stepped outside the cabin. He, too, was shaken and needed to make sense out of everything he'd just seen. There was no way what he thought he saw could have possibly been anything other than a trick of some kind. Wasn't it?

But who would have done such a thing? And who would have known to set it up for Sergio? And, worst of all, if no one could have done it, what exactly was going on here?

CHAPTER 26

As if in a trance, Sophie added water to the vase, picked up the wildflowers on the floor, and put them back in it. Then she grabbed a large towel and began to wipe up the water.

Doing that told her she hadn't hallucinated anything. And it caused her to think about other things that she had seen, that she had tried to ignore. Unnatural happenings for which there was no explanation, except one.

Anna knew how much Sergio had hurt her and knew that Sophie wanted nothing more to do with him. Anna would have helped her get rid of him. But for her to think that way about her friend... was that a sign of madness or reality?

As she stood there, Tray came back into the cabin. He stepped into the great room and stopped, feet apart, watching her. She quickly stood, and placed the now wet towel in the kitchen sink.

"I'm glad you're here and all right," he said, a worried look on his face. "Your visitor seemed angry."

"I guess he didn't like my response," she said softly.

"Good." His gaze latched onto hers and he crossed the room to stand before her. "Although I can't help but think you might be wrong about the guy. Coming all this way could mean he really loves you. And, clearly, you once loved him a lot."

She took his hands in hers. "Whatever might have been with Sergio is over now. I had thought so before, but seeing him only confirmed that for me."

"You're sure? I mean, it wasn't that long ago you broke up, and I saw your reaction just talking to him on the phone."

She nodded. "I'm sure. Sometimes change comes faster than one ever imagines it might. You go along with your life one way, and then, *wham!* something happens and you do a one-eighty. That's how I'm feeling. But you still don't trust me."

"It's not that." He wore that worried look he had so often. "I can see all the changes that you've made in your life just recently. Seeing Sergio, his clothes, everything about him, told me a lot. Dealing with all that, and adding me to the mix might be too much. That's why, whatever we think we have, we've got to take it slow. Okay? You need time. And, maybe, so do I."

She pondered his words a moment, then nodded. "Okay. Slow. I get it."

As if to change the subject, he walked away from her, over to the spot she had just wiped up. "It, uh, looks like the floor is a little damp over there. Do you want to talk about what happened?"

He couldn't know what she had seen in this room, could he? And if he didn't see it, and she tried to explain, he'd think she'd been seeing things. She took the coward's way out. "It was nothing, just a little spilled beer. It doesn't matter." She heard herself speaking faster and faster and decided the best thing to do was to bring up what else was on her mind.

She bit her bottom lip. "There is something else."

"Go on."

"Do you think there's a possibility this cabin really is haunted?"

She was expecting him to laugh, or at least to grin, that crazy half grin he usually gave her. Instead, his eyes looked wary for a moment, and then, suddenly determined. She felt he was about to say something momentous.

But just as quickly, his expression changed once more. "I know I've met some curious characters out and about, but no ghosts... I don't think."

She drew in a shuddering breath. "I guess I can say the same."

His gaze darted to the vase—why, she wondered, did he keep looking at it?—and then to the kitchen, and finally to Elijah Donnelly's portrait. "Do you know if Maggie has a lady friend she gossips with?"

Sophie's brow furrowed. "She knows people in town, that's for sure. And I know she visits with her niece Mallory who lives on the other side of town with her husband. But I don't know how much of a gossip she might be. Why?"

"It's nothing." His jaws tightened as if in thought. "Anyway, we've both had a busy, stressful evening. Stress can make you see or think strange, sometimes very strange, things. I can't help but suspect we both need to get some sleep."

"You think so?"

"Absolutely. Tomorrow will be better."

CHAPTER 27

Sophie spent the next day alone developing the proofs of the photographs she'd taken at the weekend market. While she was doing that, Maggie knocked on the dark room, a.k.a. laundry room, door. "Sorry to bother you, but there's a woman in the great room who asked to speak to you."

"To me? Did she give a name?"

"She said her name is Nanette."

"Oh? I don't know anyone by that name, but I'll be right there."

Nanette stood as Sophie entered the great room. The woman seemed to be about her age, blond, and wearing a business suit. Sophie braced herself to hear a sales pitch. "Hello. I'm Sophie Evans."

Nanette's lips pursed. "This is awkward," she said. "I understand you're new in town. At first, I suspected you were a tourist, simply passing through the way so many people do these days. Lately, however, I'm being told you might stay here longer. Perhaps quite a while longer."

Sophie's brows knitted as she tried to think of why in the

world her plans were of any interest to this woman. "Are you a representative from some company?" she asked. "If you're selling something, come out with it, because I really doubt I'll be interested."

"I'm not selling anything."

Sophie frowned. "Are you from some religious group hoping to get me to join your church? I know there are a lot of Jehovah's Witnesses and Mormons in the area—"

"Latter-Day Saints, or simply LDS, is the proper term," Nanette said. "But my reason for being here is quite different."

"And it is?"

"I'm engaged to Carter Waterton."

Now that, Sophie thought, was not on her radar. "I see."

Nanette raised her head. "Carter is a handsome, warm individual who cares deeply about people. Sometimes new women friends misinterpret his friendliness."

Sophie wanted to say she certainly hadn't misinterpreted anything, but she kept her mouth shut about it and continued to stare at Nanette.

"Several friends saw you to at the Founder's Day Celebration this weekend and were concerned you might end up hurt."

"Bless their hearts," Sophie said, remembering one of her southern girlfriend's favorite expressions. "They are truly thoughtful, aren't they?"

Nanette squared her shoulders. "As a matter of fact, they are. Well, that's settled. I'm sure you have a better understanding of the situation now. After all, you don't want the entire town laughing at you, do you?"

"Heaven forfend!" Sophie said, dripping with sarcasm.

"What?" Nanette looked at her.

"I would be so, so upset to hear that all of Crouch was laughing at me. It's enough to make one positively suicidal. So it's really kind of you to come by and save me such embarrassment!" Sophie walked to the front door and opened it. "I take it you don't live in Garden Valley."

"My goodness, no. I live in the city."

"Boise?"

"Of course. I know Carter loves it here, but we've agreed that, at some point, when we start our family, for instance, he'll be looking at his bottom line. He's very smart that way."

Sophie nodded. "I'm sure. And I do appreciate you coming by."

"Well, we never know who'll show up in our town. And all of us work together to make sure our sweet doctor doesn't end up with some mongrel looking to be re-homed."

Sophie's eyes turned icy. "And speaking of mongrels, you just might want to put a real strong leash on that man. I don't know how else you're going to stop him from straying."

She quickly shut the door as Nanette left. She simply couldn't take it.

The nerve of Waterton making a play for her at the same time as he was engaged to someone else. She didn't appreciate Nanette's visit, but she was plenty irritated at Carter as well.

Did she have a sign on her forehead that said "Loser" or something, causing men on two continents to not take her seriously?

She marched back into the great room, hands on hips and glared at Elijah Donnelly's portrait. "If the ghosts around here are supposed to be match-makers, let me tell you, you're doing a piss-poor job of it!"

———————

After Nanette left, Sophie entered the great room and sat at the dining table where natural light was best for viewing her photos. She was engrossed with thoughts of how to enhance them before presenting proofs to her customers when Maggie walked into the room. With her was with a newcomer of medium height, a tad overweight, and with light brown hair cut so short you could see through to his scalp. He was probably somewhere in his forties. With his brown slacks, a white shirt, v-neck blue sweater, and Nike running shoes, his outfit screamed city-slicker.

"This is our great room," Maggie said, giving the fellow a tour. "Feel free to use it any time." She then gave him her usual spiel about the inn's amenities.

The man nodded, looking a bit overwhelmed.

"This is one of our guests," Maggie said. "Sophie, meet Gerald Whalley. He'll be staying with us a few days now that Professor Beauregard has gone."

"So happy to be here," Whalley said. "I'm sure it'll be a great place to stay. My wife divorced me six months ago, and, well, it does get a bit lonely, you know."

"I'm sure it does, Mr. Whalley," Sophie said.

Whalley looked at her, his eyes smiling. "Have you seen the ghosts yet?"

Sophie gaped at him. And then she looked at Maggie whose expression went from calm, to stunned by Sophie's hesitation, to appearing completely appalled that Sophie didn't immediately deny that anything supernatural existed. "No, no ghosts," Sophie said finally, then forced a laugh. "Everyone knows there is no such thing, of course! This cabin is no different than any other place in town."

Just then, the front door flew open with a bang, causing them all to jump.

"Oh, my!" Maggie said. "That door requires a bit of a push to make sure it latches. My bad for not double checking!"

She dashed off to the foyer to shut the door.

He faced Sophie, his mouth gaping. "It wasn't the least bit windy outside."

"Must have been a sudden gust," she murmured.

Whalley's expression turned suddenly hopeful. "Maybe, even if the ghosts don't exist, the cabin still helps people fall in love."

Sophie felt bad dashing his dreams. "Who knows?" she said, and couldn't help but think of Tray. Did the cabin and its ghosts have something to do with the suddenness and strength of her feelings for him? Did that mean those feelings were any less real than they might otherwise have been? "It's truly hard to say, Mr. Whalley. You might meet someone here who becomes very special to you. Who's to know why it happens? Or, for that matter, why it happens anytime two people find each other? Is it destiny, fate, or simply chance?"

Whalley nodded. "That's true enough. I met my wife, ex-wife, in a grocery store over a discussion of how to tell if a cantaloupe is sweet or not." He grimaced at the memory. "If we hadn't both wanted cantaloupes that day, who knows how my life would have turned out?"

She hesitated, then said, "Exactly. And it's a lovely inn no matter what happens," Sophie said. "Plus, you will meet many people. Who knows? Maybe the ghosts were just waiting for you to arrive. Don't give up hope, Mr. Whalley."

He smiled at her. "Thank you, Sophie. I'm glad to hear that."

"Shall I show you to your room, now?" Maggie asked him.

The two left the great room, Sophie went back to her photographs, wondering what was keeping Tray away for so long.

That evening, Sophie went to the Rusty Nail alone. To her surprise, not long after, Carter Waterton showed up with a couple of his male friends, all wearing suits and ties, as if they had been to a business meeting of some sort. But he left them for her table.

"Sophie, what are you doing here alone?" he asked.

"Having dinner," she said, gesturing toward the bacon and avocado burger in front of her.

"Mind if I join you? A beautiful woman like you shouldn't have to eat alone. The men of this town have a reputation to uphold!"

"Do they now? They have an interesting reputation, that's for sure," she said as he sat.

He gestured for the waitress and ordered the same burger as Sophie was eating.

"So, how have you been?" he asked. "It looks as if your photo booth project is quite the hit."

"It did surprisingly well at the Founder's Day celebration, that's for sure. And how are you doing? I met Nanette today, by the way. We had a very interesting conversation."

He froze. "Oh?"

"Um hmm."

He looked at her with sad puppy-dog eyes. "Nanette's been wanting to get married since high school. But I don't. And I have no desire to live in the city. I'm a country doctor and love it here. She'd hate it, but she refuses to accept that we aren't getting married."

"That's not at all what Nanette says."

"She won't listen." He flung his arms wide. "I want to see other women. I want to find with someone else what I don't have with Nanette! Can you understand that?"

"I can," she said as the waitress brought him his burger.

Once they were alone again, she added, "Just don't think I'm a candidate for your 'someone else,' because I'm not."

"Oh? You're seeing someone? Do you want to elaborate?"

"Not really. It's private."

He nodded. "Can we at least be friends?"

"Of course."

He smiled. "Good, because I wanted to tell you about an older Italian movie I watched last night. I don't know anyone in town who watches such things, and I thought you might. Have you ever heard of the director, Frederico Fellini?"

"Certainly! His work was fascinating."

"I agree, and his movies seem so modern!"

"Avant-garde, that's for sure."

They talked a bit about foreign films of the twentieth century. Even in Italy, it was hard to find anyone who still watched them.

Their dinners finished, Waterton insisted on following Sophie back to the cabin after dinner, to make sure she arrived safely. When they entered the great room, they saw Josh playing cards with Bree, and Tray reading one of his thick ranching tomes, this one about llamas.

"See, I told you she was fine," Bree said to Josh.

But Josh slowly rose to his feet, his expression all but dumbfounded as he looked at Sophie and Waterton together. "I was worried about you, Sophie. I felt bad about the way our last date ended, and I came over to apologize. But it looks like you've already moved on."

She folded her arms and frowned at him. "Moved on? From what?"

His jaw dropped and he turned to Bree. "Thanks for the card game. Good night." He then strode from the cabin, head high.

Bree stood. "Josh!" she called and hurried after him.

"What was that all about?" Waterton asked Sophie.

"Yes, Sophie," Tray said, leaning back in his chair, a smirk on his face. "What was that all about? Bree and I had to practically hold that poor boy's hand he was so upset not to find you here. He couldn't believe you'd go out alone, and we assured him you didn't have a date tonight. Guess we were wrong."

"You weren't wrong at all. We happened to meet at the Rusty Nail," Sophie said.

"Ah, I see. Well, whatever, since you're here, together, I hate to be in the way of your non-date, so I'll just say goodnight."

"Wait, Tray!" Sophie called.

"Ah!" Waterton said, watching Tray leave and Sophie's reaction. "Now, I see what's going on. It's you and the lodger—"

"You see nothing!" She folded her arms, steamed at the way Tray had acted. "There's nothing between us!"

"Oh? Could have fooled me." Waterton stepped closer. "But if your words and true, and since I'm not engaged to anyone—"

She sat on an easy chair. "Forget about it, Doc."

"We're two sophisticated adults..." He attempted to step toward her, but his tie stuck out directly in front of him, and then turned sideways. He turned with it. He tried to grab it but the tie swiveled this way and that, avoiding his hand. All the while, the tie led him quickly around the room, and he ended up running as he tried to stop himself from being dragged like— Sophie suddenly realized—like a dog who didn't know how to heel on a leash.

Sophie gaped, remembering her comment to Nanette. She'd never seen anything like the way Waterton was being led, running and at times spinning in a circle, around the great room.

"Carter?" she cried. "Carter, stop!" As he zoomed by, she

tried to take hold of his arms, but missed. He then circled the room even faster, at one point leaping over the coffee table. He all but turned into the ballet dancer, Baryshnikov, as he spun and jumped.

All by itself, the cabin's front door opened, and Waterton's tie pulled him outside.

Then the door slammed shut behind him.

Sophie dropped onto the sofa.

She couldn't help but glance up at Elijah's portrait. For a second there, it looked as if he rolled his eyes at her, but then she heard laughter behind her—a woman's laugh. Her friend Anna's laugh.

Her blood ran cold as she jumped to her feet and turned around.

No one was there.

When she again faced Elijah, he looked as dour and serious as ever.

"My God," she whispered. And then, stricken by what she was thinking, frightened and horrified that she would even contemplate such an affront to everything she had ever believed about life, death, and the possibility of a hereafter, she ran up to her bedroom and locked the door.

CHAPTER 28

"It wasn't a date!" Sophie all but yelled her answer at breakfast the next morning when Bree asked her how her date with Dr. Waterton went.

Tray had all but choked on his waffle when Bree asked that question.

"Well, maybe not," Bree said, adjusting her glasses higher on her nose, "since I heard his car drive off not very long after Josh and I left you two alone. Josh finally got the message, by the way, that you aren't into him."

"Finally." Sophie took a deep breath. If she were to tell Tray and Bree what had happened to Dr. Waterton last night, they surely would have told her she'd drunk way too much at the Rusty Nail. If she also told them what had happened with Sergio, they would have told her she'd been so angry at the way he was talking to her, she must have blacked out with rage. And worst of all, if she told them what she suspected was going on in this cabin, they would have driven her to a psych ward in Boise. So she had no choice but to keep everything to herself.

One thing that was clear about last night, she wouldn't be having dinner with Carter Waterton again.

"Since he was kind enough to see you all the way back to the cabin," Tray said, arms folded as he looked at her with a mixture of a smirk and a scowl on his face, "I would have thought you'd at least offer the good doctor a cup of coffee, if not a beer."

"Well, aren't you the Miss Manners of the dating set," Sophie sniped. "I think it was kind of him to join me for dinner, rather than leave me to eat alone, like *some* people I could name."

"I see. Well, maybe *some* people had things to do that took longer than expected," Tray added. "Anyway, he certainly left quickly. It wasn't anything we said, was it?"

"He was simply being a gentleman," Sophie said. "Something in very short supply these days!"

"Oh, I'm sure that's all that's why he was here," Tray said.

Sophie threw a biscuit at him, but he caught it in midair. "Thanks," he said with a grin, and then split and buttered it.

She tried to stay angry at him, but it was impossible. "Are we still on for tonight?" she asked.

Bree gawked. "Are you dating Tray, too?"

"Oh, my God!" Sophie cried, reverting to clutching her head and then waving her arms the way she'd seen lots of women in Italy do. "Where I go and who I go with is not everyone's business. But yes, I've been invited to his sister's house for dinner, if you must know."

"Oh?" Bree's eyes widened. "Nobody's asking me, but meeting the family seems fairly significant."

"It's not that way," Sophie said.

Tray's lips tightened. "Right. Not at all."

"Sheesh." Bree stood up, taking a chocolate chip muffin

with her as she headed for the stairs to go back to her room. "Pardon me for living."

When they were alone, Tray turned to Sophie. "Would you like to bail on tonight's dinner? It's okay, if you do."

"Not in the least."

"Okay."

"Want company today?" she asked hopefully.

"Actually, I'm zeroing in on something totally different. I'll let you know if it pans out."

"Oh? Interesting."

"It might be. About six this evening, I'll be ready to go to my sister's, okay?"

"I'll be ready."

Tray's breath caught at the sight of Sophie coming down the stairs of the cabin that evening. She was wearing a simple but stunning teal blue dress with a scoop-neckline and silver jewelry. But it was the sparkle of her eyes the most captivated him, and her smile that left him momentarily speechless. He had been looking forward to this dinner with Maeve's family, but deep down, he knew going there with Sophie would make it even more special.

When they reached the house, Maeve's husband, Ron Sherwin, opened the door. He eyed Tray cautiously as he introduced himself and explained that Maeve was in the kitchen. The three shook hands.

Tray couldn't help but feel nervous. He wanted to make a good impression not only on Ron but also on the way Sophie regarded him. They'd never been together with other people in this type of setting.

Maeve's four boys, Parker, Liam, Aiden, and Hudson, also

looked nervous and shy as they met their new uncle and his friend, but when they learned they had a cousin living in Montana who was six months older than Parker, and that he not only knew how to ride horses but also how to rope calves, they asked lots of questions and wanted to meet him right away.

Maeve soon joined them. Tray was relieved that she greeted him warmly and genuinely welcomed Sophie to join them. He had worried that she might think about the harsh and thoughtless words they'd said to each other in the past, and be upset with him because of them, but thankfully, that hadn't happened. Soon, they moved into the dining room where a pork roast dinner with mashed potatoes and gravy, mixed green vegetables, and a salad waited.

"This looks delicious," Sophie said as they all sat.

As the food was passed and plates filled, Ron faced Tray, his expression wary. "What brings you back to this area after so many years?"

"It's home," Tray said. "Our great-grandparents on our father's side first settled here. I enjoyed Montana for a while, but after my wife passed, it lost its appeal. That was when I realized I wanted to come home, to show this area to Brody, and to have him meet this side of his family."

"We'd like to meet him," Maeve said. "Are you thinking of getting a cattle ranch again?"

"Not unless I have no choice," Tray admitted. "I liked it early on, but it's a tough life." That led to a long discussion of other types of ranches and farms. The more Tray was hearing about alpacas, he thought they might be a much more peaceful way to make a living than herding cattle, but he had to admit, after having been a cattleman, he wasn't especially thrilled with the idea. Ron seemed to warm to him as the discussion continued.

Throughout it all, Tray found himself watching Sophie's

reaction to everything being said. He told himself it was because he valued her opinions, and had nothing to do with the way he loved the sound of her laughter, the way she brushed her hair behind her ear, or the way she looked at him with those mesmerizing eyes. As the dinner progressed, he felt a connection between them that went beyond words, and he liked it.

But most of all, as Tray sat at the dining room table and looked at the faces around him, he couldn't help but think that this was what family felt like, and what it might be like if he and Brody were to move here. When his eyes met Sophie's, he also couldn't help but think how perfect it would be if she were always there with him.

CHAPTER 29

S ophie sensed Maeve looking questioningly at her throughout dinner, so when Maeve gathered up the dinner dishes, Sophie jumped up to help her, and soon the women were in the kitchen together, loading the dishwasher and cleaning the pots and pans.

"Have you known my brother long?" Maeve asked.

"Not at all. We met at the Donnelly cabin a few weeks ago."

Maeve looked surprised. "You seem close for such a short time."

"I think we are," Sophie said, "which is a surprise since Tray is about the most tight-lipped man I've ever met. To get him to talk about himself is like pulling teeth, but once he opens up, he speaks from the heart, which is something I value. I haven't had a lot of that kind of honesty in my life."

"Not in Italy?"

"Oh, please! I was doing fashion photography there, which means I was constantly around beautiful but extremely vain people. And, after our delicious meal tonight, let me add that most of them were perpetually hungry and forever denying themselves the wonderful foods all around them." She chuckled at the memory. "It did not make for an especially fun or easy-going group."

Maeve joined in her laughter. "I can well imagine." But then Maeve's expression changed. "Are you sure you don't miss it? I mean, the excitement of a foreign city, being around all that glamor? It must be hard to give up."

With those words, Sophie understood what had been bothering Maeve. She feared Sophie wasn't a person to stick around a place like Garden Valley or a man like Tray. Maeve was still looking out for her kid brother, just as Tray said she used to do. Sophie felt relieved that despite the years lost between them, Maeve clearly cared about Tray, just as he did about her.

"It was fun while it lasted, or mostly fun," Sophie said. "But as I look around, for example, at your family, I see there's more to life than excitement and glamor."

"Oh, shoot me now!" Maeve cried.

Sophie gasped. "Oh, no! You know I didn't mean it that way!"

Maeve then laughed, and Sophie joined in for a quick moment. But then, Sophie met Maeve's eyes—green like her brother's—as she spoke. "Someone once said 'Life is what happens when you're busy making other plans.' In a sense, I've been so busy planning the next location for a big photoshoot, the next exciting display or show or trip to wherever the magazine wanted to send me, often with little notice, that I scarcely realized how much time was ticking away. And one day, I remember it precisely, I was sitting in the Santa Maria Novella train station in Florence waiting for the next express to Rome, and out of the blue, I wondered what I was really doing there. By that I mean, to what purpose? What did it mean in my life, and what I wanted for this life? That was when I realized how quickly the years were slipping away from me while I was allowing others to run this life of mine, to tell me where to go and what to do. I scarcely knew who I was anymore."

"That sounds a bit scary," Maeve said.

"Believe me, it was a wake-up call," Sophie admitted. "I talked to my boyfriend—the fellow I'd always assumed I'd marry one day—and discovered he had no interest in changing the way we were living. It was enough for him. He loved it. He was content, satisfied, and couldn't begin to understand why I wasn't."

"Men don't have issues as they age the way we women do, that's for sure."

Sophie nodded. "The strange part is that I wasn't even thinking about kids back then. They're scarcely discussed among people in the fashion world. The few with children are almost looked upon as aberrations. But I stayed with Sergio— that's his name—even though I was feeling increasingly unhappy. I kept hoping my increased misery was just a passing phase, that I'd get over it, or Sergio would change. And then I learned he'd been with other women—much younger women."

"I'm sorry. That must have hurt."

"As a knife through the heart. He swore it meant nothing, that he loved me. But it meant a lot to me. Maybe those affairs were 'nothing' in his eyes. Sergio even thought I was being very 'American Puritanical' as he put it. But I recognized that one day his feelings about one of those other women could easily change. I saw the writing on the wall, as they say, and it wasn't pretty. Not about me and the way I was living, and definitely not about Sergio. Finally, I left."

"Good for you! Although it must have been difficult."

"Yes, and no. Hard because so many hopes evaporated, but also, it was a relief. Now, being in this peaceful world, I've had a lot of time to think about what I want to do with my life, what

I most enjoy, and even who I am. I feel this time has been good for me. And the best part has been getting to know Tray."

"I'm glad to hear that."

Sophie smiled. "He's... he's quite wonderful. But I believe he still loves and misses his wife too much for anything serious, and the situation with his son makes it all even more complicated. I don't know if things will get better for us over time or if we'll each go our own separate way."

Maeve studied Sophie. "Or, it could be that he fears a woman like you could never be satisfied with the life he lives. You appreciate the quiet now, but it sounds like you've lived among so many wealthy and important people, how long before you find farm or ranch life completely boring?"

"I know he thinks that. He's said it. But I can't imagine being around Tray would ever bore me," Sophie admitted.

As Maeve finished scrubbing the last pot, she said, "Just talking to Tray the other day and again this evening, I see he's become a much finer man than I imagined would be the case for my wild, scruffy, always fighting little brother when he tore out of here at age seventeen and never came back. I don't know if he realizes how far he's come from those days."

"He was only seventeen?"

Maeve nodded. "That's right. He had a rough time, first living here with our dad, and then losing his wife at such a young age... I can see how much he cares about you, but I don't want to see him get hurt again."

Sophie took the pot and began to dry it. "I don't either, believe me."

"I'm glad to hear that," Maeve said. "All I can say is, if you have doubts, break it off with him before he falls for you even more than he already has. In the long run, that'll make it easier on him. And on you both."

The dishes taken care of, it was time for dessert. Sophie

went into the dining room and took a seat beside Tray. Maeve soon followed, proudly carrying a homemade pie.

"I remembered, Tray, how much you always loved Mom's huckleberry pies," Maeve said as she placed it on the table. "I'll bet this is something you don't see very often."

It was all Tray and Sophie could do to keep a straight face.

Tray's heart was full as he hugged his two youngest nephews and high-fived the older boys when the time came to leave Maeve and Ron's home. The boys told him they looked forward to seeing him again.

He shook hands with Ron, and then he and Maeve stared at each other a moment until she took a step toward him and he gave her what, as kids, they used to call a bear hug. As he did, he whispered thanks to her for welcoming him into her family. Her eyes were bright with unshed tears as they said goodbye and she had him promise to come back soon.

Even Sophie had a silly smile on her face as he led her to his truck.

"Were you bored to death?" Tray asked as he started the engine.

"I enjoyed the evening. I like your sister and her family."

"You two seemed to have a lot to talk about when you went off to the kitchen. I was wondering if I would have to go in and rescue you."

"No, we had a good talk. An enjoyable talk. And it's clear she still loves you. You have nothing to worry about there."

"Well, that's good to hear. But anything she told you about me, remember I was just a kid when I last saw her."

"Oh, I definitely heard some stories."

"What?!"

She chuckled and soon they were back at the cabin.

But when she opened the door, Josh and Bree were in the great room playing Gin Rummy. "Hey, there," Josh said, standing. "I brought some burgers over from the Rusty Nail to have for dinner with you and Bree. We ate ours, but yours is in the fridge, if you want it. Although"—his gaze jumped from her to Tray—"I guess you've already eaten."

"I have. But thanks," Sophie said, then turned to Tray and hooked her arm with his. She all but dragged Tray to the kitchen area and opened the cupboard where she saw Maggie kept bottles of whiskey, bourbon, and vodka.

"Since Josh is playing cards with Bree, let's leave them alone. I'd like to head out back so we can talk. Would you like a drink of some kind?"

"I'll pass on the drink, but sure. Let's talk."

Josh kept staring at Sophie and Tray with a confused expression, as if wondering why they were now together when he last saw Sophie with the town doctor.

"Your turn to pick a card, Josh," Bree said. "Josh?"

Sophie and Tray went out to the back porch. Sophie sat on the cushioned bench and patted the seat next to her, indicating she wanted him to take it. He glanced at the other two chairs and then sat beside her.

"So," she said, getting right to the point. "What do you think about staying here now that you've spent time with Maeve?"

He seemed to ponder his response a moment. "I feel good about it. We talked a lot about my old man and family issues. I never realized he acted pretty rotten with a lot of people. I always thought he'd singled me out for the privilege, but apparently not. That helped. Maybe I'm not quite the scum of the earth he taught me I was."

"No," she said. "Believe me, you aren't at all."

Green eyes captured hers. "Good to hear," he murmured and let his arm circle her shoulders, drawing her to his side.

"I know you and Ron were talking a lot about the kinds of ranches that were in the area," she said.

"We did. He said when I find it, I'll know."

She nodded. "Yes, I'm sure you will. As will I."

"What do you mean?"

"Nothing. It's what Maeve and I were talking about. Girl talk, I'll call it."

"Girl talk, interesting," he said with his funny half-grin. "I suspect you two weren't talking about land."

"No, we weren't," she murmured, her eyes searching his.

Her breathing seemed to quicken as their gazes locked.

She could see how much he wanted her, as she did him. Slowly, he bent his head closer to hers when the French doors opened. Josh stuck his head out so he could see them. "I'm leaving now. Just thought I'd say goodnight."

They sprang apart and said goodbye to him. When Tray turned again to Sophie, his look was resigned. "It's been a long day. I should retire as well. I've got an early appointment with a realtor about a place I saw. It's different. If my meeting in the morning with him works out, I'd like you to look at the place with me, if you have the time."

"Of course! I'd love to. How exciting!"

"Or, a waste of time. We'll see."

She gazed up at him. "Thank you again for letting me join you tonight. I had a wonderful time."

He nodded. "Me, too." Then he gave her a quick kiss before he stood to go upstairs. "Good night..., girlfriend."

CHAPTER 30

Sophie was in the dark room working on her photos a little before noon the next day when she heard a knock on the door. Her heart skipped a beat, hoping it was Tray. He'd been on her mind all morning, knowing he was going off to see a realtor about some property, and wondering if things were finally working out for him.

She wasn't developing film at the moment, and so immediately opened the door. One look at Tray's expression, and she knew he had something to tell her.

"I've found a piece of property," he said. "Want to go see it?"

Now it begins or ends, she thought. For him to find property was a breakthrough that could change everything. But in a good or bad way, she had no idea. "I'd love to." Her words were breathless. "Is it in the Valley?"

"It's actually down near Horseshoe Bend, about thirty minutes away, which is a good location, considering what it is."

His excitement was infectious even though his words made little sense. "Now you've got me curious. Let's go."

Soon, they were in his truck, heading south. Tray refused to tell her about the property, only saying he needed her honest first impression. That made no sense to Sophie since she knew nothing about land. But he'd asked her to be honest, and she could do that.

A half hour later, Tray turned off the highway.

"This road is paved," Sophie said with a pleasantly surprised chuckle after all the rocky, narrow dirt roads they'd traveled on.

"It is. You'll see why in a moment. Keep in mind, I found out about this place completely by accident. I was talking to a fisherman friend down by the river near the cabin. Anyway, as he was leaving, a paper fell out of his pocket. It was a flyer about this property. I tried to give it back to him but couldn't find him, so I left it, weighted down with rocks on the sand in case he went back looking for it. I also asked the realtor if he was working with a guy named Luke—I wouldn't want to mess up a deal if he was. But he said no. And here we are."

They were now riding alongside a white fence and soon reached a wide gateway, with the gates open. The arch over the gateway said, "The Christmas Farm."

There, Tray stopped the truck. "This is it."

Sophie's jaw dropped. "I don't understand. You're thinking of buying a Christmas farm? What in the world is that?"

"Come and see."

They got out of the truck and a fellow who had been sitting in an SUV on the property, got out and walked up to them. "I'm glad you decided to take a second look," he said.

Tray shook his hand. "This is my girlfriend, Sophie Evans. Sophie, this is Pete Lowdenger. He's the realtor for this property."

The two shook hands. "Pleased to meet you," she said,

giving a quick glance at Tray as she realized how serious he was about the property. "But what is this place?"

"It's a Christmas tree farm," the realtor said with a big smile. "It provides fresh trees for the tree lots in the cities to the south, and it's a place people can come to and cut their own trees."

She gawked at Tray. *This isn't good. Has he lost his mind?* "A tree farm? Really?"

"Hey, I said I was open to anything." Tray was actually smiling at her stunned reaction. "This isn't anything I ever thought about, but at the same time, it makes a crazy kind of sense."

Crazy all right. "It does?" Sophie could hear the skepticism in her voice. She wondered how she was going to tell him this idea was insane.

"What's special," the realtor added, "is that this place has a license as an events venue. The owner bought the license, which is transferable, plus he drew up plans and already paid for the permits for an events center building. It would be a place to hold weddings, especially for people who want winter weddings in a snowy wonderland kind of place. And with all the Christmasy trees around, it could be quite nice."

"Maybe," Sophie murmured. At least that might bring in some income during the *eleven months* of the year when people weren't buying Christmas trees. She shuddered at the thought. This seemed worse than a money pit to her.

"As I was showing Tray, the tree sales themselves pay for the place each year. Any weddings or other events held out here would be pure gravy. The current owner made enough off of tree sales he planned to use the profit for the events center building construction. Unfortunately, he became ill and didn't live to put his plan into action. Also, he knew his kids didn't want to move back here to run the farm, so his only request was that they not sell to a developer who would bulldoze the land and build houses. He hoped they could try to find someone who wanted to continue with his vision for the place. So, on the very day the property came on the market, when your friend here showed up wanting to see the place, it was like a miracle."

"I can imagine," Sophie said, feeling stranger by the minute.

The realtor chuckled. "I remember telling him a tree farm can be time consuming, although"—and here he gave a tip of his head toward Tray—"trees aren't nearly as demanding as cattle."

Sophie turned to Tray, feeling the need to gently express her reservations now, before this went much further. "I worry, though, that it's so limited. I mean, what if Christmas trees go out of fashion? Fewer people even believe in what Christmas means anymore."

"I know what you're saying," Tray told her. "But I'd like you to see the trees and where the owners wanted to build this events venue."

Sophie's opinion began as a hard sell, and a hard "No," but the more she saw of the property and especially the plans for the events center, a lovely wooden building, not some modern-looking monstrosity, the more impressed she became.

"I'd never bothered to look at property in this area because it's too hilly for what I was thinking about," Tray said. "But for trees and parties, this is a great location. It's close to a town, and to schools, close to a lot of customers—the Boise area, the most populated in the state, is only some forty minutes away, while Maeve's house is less than a half-hour north."

"Yes, but you... a party planner?" she said. The idea, frankly, was mind-boggling.

Tray shook his head. "Not likely. But me, a land and events center owner who rents space to people who plan parties and put on events, that, I can do."

She took his arm as the realtor showed them details of the events venue plans. The concept was outstanding, and not terribly costly. She could immediately see a few tweaks that would add value without costing any more money. "If you get this place," she said to Tray, "you're going to have to tell people they have no choice but to use the photographer who's a friend of the owner, and not bring their own photographer along."

He raised his eyebrows. "Oh, I will, will I?"

"Of course." She could scarcely believe what she was about to say, but it was the truth. "I'm loving this, Tray. I really am."

"Want to check out the farmhouse?"

"Thought you'd never ask."

The house had been built in the 1930s, but the previous owner had upgraded the kitchen, bathrooms, electricity, and even the plumbing. There was still some work to be done, but the house kept most of the charm of the original farmhouse, including a wide, covered front porch with four pillars, and a steeply sloped roof on the second floor with dormer windows. The inside had fireplaces in the living room and upstairs in the master bedroom.

"It's a warm home," she said. "It looks like it's made for a family."

"It's much bigger than my ranch house in Montana. Me and Brody will rattle around in it I suspect."

"You might think about a live-in housekeeper. That little carriage house in the back is set up for guests, so a housekeeper could use it and come inside to share the kitchen—much the way Maggie does at the Donnelly cabin."

"A live-in woman like that would be a big help with Brody."

"Right, until the single women in the area learn that you're out here without a wife. You're going to be literally swimming in huckleberry pies. If you remain single, that is."

His mouth downturned and the way he looked at her made

her know he wasn't thinking in general terms as he said, "Well,
I suspect the last thing a woman wants is a man who doesn't
know how he's going to take care of himself, let alone her—and
who has a teenage son besides."

"You'd be surprised," she said.

He made no reply at first, but then he nodded. "Well, I'm
glad to hear your reaction to all this. I thought I might have
slipped my trolley or something when I was feeling so positive
about the place."

"It looks like a real find. You're right to check it out. But"—
she hesitated—"is it affordable?"

"Barely," he replied. "But I've carefully guarded what I
have left from the ranch sale after paying bills, and fortunately,
hilly land like this is more affordable than rich farmland.
Anyway, I've got a good tax guy in Montana giving advice on
how to do the actual purchase since I'm going from a business
to a business. The events venue will be a stretch, but I think it's
worth it."

"That's a relief."

He nodded. "I'll have to hire a CPA to go through the
books, and an arborist to check out all the trees. I don't want to
buy this and then find out the trees are rotting and the business
might have made money last year, but the ten years before were
all losses."

"It's kind of scary, isn't it?"

"It is," he said. "I mean, even if it checks out, it could end
up a huge mistake. And then, there's Brody's reaction to these
changes."

She didn't know what to say and put her arm around his
waist. "True. But that's pretty much anything in life, isn't it?"

"Let's do one last walk around," he said, his arm over her
shoulders, "and then I'll talk with the realtor about having an

arborist check on the trees and others on the business prospects."

"You think you might really want to do this, then?" she asked.

He looked over the hills encompassing The Christmas Farm, and the many fir trees covering them. "Lord, help me, I just might."

———————

Tray quickly managed to get expert opinions on the state of the trees, the house, the creating an events center, and most of all on whether a Christmas tree farm could actually be a profitable business endeavor. He also learned that the prior owner had a core staff of five men who worked for him during the busy Christmas season, and two of them who worked year-round checking on the trees, clearing stumps, making sure no diseases took hold, growing new trees from seeds, and so on. All of them would like to continue to work at the farm with the new owner.

The bottom line told him that the Christmas tree farm had been a well-run, much-loved operation, and the heirs were happy to learn their father's legacy might continue on if Tray bought the property.

He had Sophie join them as he showed the property to Maeve, Ron, and their boys. Ron worked in Horseshoe Bend and he knew all about The Christmas Farm. He told Tray about many people from the area—himself, Maeve, and the boys included—who made it a family day to go out there and cut down a tree to bring home.

All of that was well-and-good. But Tray's biggest challenge was coming up the next day, when he would go back to Montana to pick up Brody. It had taken him two-and-a-half weeks to settle on wanting to buy The Christmas Farm, and he knew that until the last paper was signed, working out the finances could cause the whole thing to belly up. So far, a bank in Boise as well as his accountant in Montana were fairly certain that hitches which might show up, if any, could be overcome.

He had three days before the tribal council meeting with Brody's uncle. Tray needed to be in Montana, to show everyone in Charlene's family that he was working hard to provide a stable and loving environment for his son, and then to take the boy back to Idaho with him.

CHAPTER 31

Tray had told Sophie he expected to be in Montana for a minimum of four days as he met with his in-laws and tried to assure them he would do what he felt was best for Brody. She suspected it wouldn't be easy.

She also couldn't help but wonder how Brody would react to her. Fourteen was a difficult age. He wasn't a little boy anymore who could be charmed with toys and trips to the zoo. If he was anything like his father, he'd already have strong opinions. If one of those opinions was that she shouldn't be with Tray, that she wasn't good enough, or that Brody simply hated the idea of Tray being in love with anyone but his mother, she didn't know how she should handle that. Or, how Tray would handle it, especially since he wrestled with his own feelings about moving on after Charlene's death.

At one time in her life, she would have simply gone to Tray and stayed with him, no matter what. In fact, she would have followed him to the ends of the earth if he'd asked her—just as she'd done with Sergio. But those days were over.

Her main lesson from Sergio was that she couldn't place

her happiness in someone else's hands. She had to take charge of her life and to be strong in her own right before she could hope to be a part of anyone else's. If she were to be with Tray, it would have to be as an equal partner to him, never as a tag-along.

After a week passed since Tray left, her worries about what was happening in Montana grew. He was lousy at texting. She'd send him long texts, and the few replies she'd received told her nothing. "I'm here. All is okay." Or, "Coming along." Or, "Hope this wraps up soon." The most positive one stated simply, "Tribal council meeting dropped."

She'd spent the last weekend at her photo booth, and it brought in good money—enough to let her continue to live at the cabin and not have to go into her savings. If she could also pick up some free-lance magazine assignments, she'd do fairly well. But much more than the photo booth, the travel article she had once planned to write about Western towns and inter-esting places in them beckoned her.

That was where her heart was—to take photos of a place that meant something special to her. She'd received two posi-tive responses to see the final product, one from a popular travel magazine in Japan and another in Australia. Both coun-tries had large travel agencies with tours to the US.

Now that the weather had warmed up considerably, she made a list of places to visit. One day, she drove to nearby Idaho City, once the center of the 1862 gold rush and the largest town in the Pacific Northwest, and now home to only about five hundred people. From it, she traveled all around the area, including where she and Tray had been snowed in. Not too far away, she found and photographed the ghost towns of Placerville and Pioneerville.

Another day, she traveled southwest from Boise deep into the Owyhee Mountains. In the once-flourishing mining town of Silver City, she learned enough to write an entire article on it alone, and took some fantastic photos. From there, she visited the nearby ghost town named De Lamar, with its stories about sea captain Joseph De Lamar having spent a fortune mining for silver.

She was loving this, and could hardly wait to head north to Bonanza and Custer, which everyone she encountered said she needed to see. And she hadn't even touched on visiting Montana or Wyoming, which she might save for future articles since she already had more than enough material.

But each night, when she arrived back at the cabin hoping Tray had returned, she'd learned he hadn't.

Finally, on the eighth day since Tray left, she learned from Maggie that he had shown up briefly at the inn that afternoon, and had his son with him.

"A fine-looking boy," Maggie said. "I would have let him stay here with Tray, but Tray said the boy was looking forward to meeting his cousins, so he took him to his sister's house where he'll stay. I don't know if Tray will return here tonight or not. All he said was that tomorrow, he plans to take Brody to see the property he's buying."

"Okay, thanks," she said, relieved he was back, but nervous about facing his son.

"And he did ask if you were here," Maggie said. "I told him you went off somewhere with your camera."

Sophie smiled. "Thanks. I wish he'd have let me know he was coming home! I'd have waited for him."

"Oh, men! When it comes to making plans and letting others know about them, sometimes I wonder that they can put two-and-two together," Maggie said with a chuckle.

"True enough," Sophie said. Still, that night, she lay awake for well over an hour, hoping to hear Tray's footsteps or the door to his room. But she didn't, and eventually, she fell asleep.

Sophie stayed at the inn the next day working on photos from the latest weekend market. She was now developing photos in sepia as well as color having discovered that most of her customers wanted photos with the brownish, old-fashioned tinge. The whole time she worked, of course, she kept hoping to hear Tray's voice.

That evening, she and Bree ordered pizza delivery for dinner. Sophie clearly didn't want to leave the inn, but stuck around, walking in circles and looking out the window in the foyer for Tray's truck. Finally, unable to stand watching Sophie do nothing but nervously pace, Bree called Josh to come over and join her, Sophie and Maggie at a game of pinochle. Earlier in the week, the foursome discovered they all enjoyed a good game of it, and all played fairly cut-throat, with Sophie and Maggie on one team, and Josh and Bree on the other.

Sophie had asked Bree if she was developing feeling for Josh, but Bree brushed her off. "He's such a playboy! You can't imagine all the women around town who have their eye on him. I think he hangs out around here just to take a break from all the attention. No way would I ever waste my time with a guy like that. And he certainly has no interest in me."

Sophie couldn't tell if Bree was being honest or saving face. She decided to opt for honesty.

They were in a fierce battle when the front door opened and in walked Tray and Brody.

Sophie's eyes met with Tray's. She stood as a rush of happiness surged through her, causing a huge smile. He smiled back and neither said a word.

With effort, she tore her gaze from him to Brody. The boy was already tall, and at the age where boys tended to be all arms and legs as they grew in bursts of height and usually needed time for their weight to catch up. His hair was thick and jet black, his face slightly olive toned and well-tanned, while his eyes were the same light green as his father's. He was quite a handsome boy.

"Well, hello, stranger!" Maggie cried, getting up. "Come on in. Let me get the lemonade I made this afternoon. And I've also got beer and something a little stronger, Tray, if you'd like."

It took Tray a moment to divert his gaze from Sophie to Maggie. He put his hand on Brody's shoulder and moved forward. "Beer is fine. Lemonade, Brody?"

"Sure," the boy said, as Maggie hurried to the kitchen area.

"I'd like you to meet my friends," Tray told him. "This is Sophie, and that's Bree, and Josh. Josh owns the bakery in town." Bree and Josh had remained sitting.

"Hi," Brody said, his voice soft as he looked over the three. He all but dismissed Bree and Josh, but his eyes lingered on Sophie. He was clearly old enough to pick up the emotions between her and his father, but the slight wrinkling of his brow showed him to be puzzled by them.

"Nice to meet you," Sophie said, moving closer. "I've heard many good things about you."

Bree and Josh murmured hellos as well.

"Here you go," Maggie said, putting their drinks on the island. "Anyone else want to freshen your drinks?"

"Not me." Josh put his cards down and got up from the table. "In fact, I should be going. I'll see you folks tomorrow, maybe. Good to meet you, Brody."

"It's late for me, too," Bree said, emulating Josh. "Good night."

Maggie quickly did the same.

"Would you like to go out back?" Sophie suggested. "It's a warm, lovely night."

"Sure, although we can't stay very long. Maeve likes to get the boys to bed early on school nights," Tray said.

"Of course."

"But I could come back later," he said softly as they walked onto the porch and sat.

There was so much she wanted to say to Tray, but not with his son listening. "No need tonight—I suspect you're exhausted after all you've been through. Rest, and later on you can tell me all about your trip, I can hardly wait to hear it."

"Okay," he said, and he definitely sounded weary. "Although you already know the punchline," he murmured, giving a nod in Brody's direction.

"I'm so glad," she said, and then turned to Brody. "Have you seen the Christmas tree farm yet?"

Brody glanced from her to his father then back, as if surprised she was actually talking to him and that he should answer. He said, "Yeah."

"What did you think?"

He again looked at his father who waited to hear his response. He faced Sophie once more and shrugged. "I don't know."

Tray looked embarrassed. "It's a big change for him."

"I'm sure," Sophie said, her eyes holding Tray's a moment. "For you, too."

He nodded, but didn't say anything more.

"I hope it'll be a nice change," she added, turning once more to Brody, "once everything doesn't feel so strange and new."

Brody gulped down his lemonade and loudly set the glass on the side table. "Yeah, but it's no cattle ranch."

Tray's jaw tightened. "No. And I explained why."

"I liked our ranch," Brody said, completely ignoring Sophie now. "And everything there."

"I know you did."

"Then we should go back to Montana."

Tray shook his head, his eyes heavy with disappointment and weariness.

"I arrived here just a couple of months ago myself," Sophie said to Brody. "I took one look at this tiny town and thought I'd be on my way as soon as possible. But every day I find new reasons to stay. And I've come to really like it."

"Yeah, but coming here was your choice." Brody said defiantly, arms folded.

"Be nice," Tray told him.

"It's okay," Sophie said. "He's being honest, and that's a good thing. All I can suggest, Brody, is give the place a chance. It might become your choice to want to stay as well."

Brody's lips tightened the way his father's tended to do. "I know. But Montana's my home."

Tray glanced at Sophie and shook his head, then stood. "We should get going," he said.

"Right." She walked with them to the front door and then placed her hand on his arm. "I'm glad you stopped by. I've missed you."

Brody was already getting into the truck as Tray faced her. For a long moment, he said nothing. "I've missed you, too," he murmured, then gave her a hug and a quick kiss, knowing Brody was watching them. "See you soon."

"Okay," she murmured.

He then hurried to the truck. She shut the door, then picked up the glasses they'd all used, put away the playing cards, and shut the lights in the great room. Slowly, disappointment weighing on her shoulders, she glanced at Elijah's portrait, sadly shook her head, and then went upstairs to bed.

CHAPTER 32

The next afternoon, Sophie drove into town to go to the grocery store. She decided to buy a couple of steaks and potatoes just in case Tray stopped by as he said he might so they could talk. She could cook up some dinner for them so they could stay at the inn and not be bothered by other people.

As she got out of her VW, she saw Brody and Parker, Maeve's oldest son, ride by on their bikes. She waved and watched with surprise as they made a U-turn, rode over to her, and stopped.

"That's quite the car," Parker said with a grin eyeing the Beetle. With his reddish-brown hair and blue eyes, he took after his father more than Maeve, and he seemed to be perpetually smiling with a bit of an impish quality. "Is it yours?"

Brody gave Parker a light jab to the ribs with his elbow. "He doesn't mean any disrespect, Miss Sophie."

"I know," she told Brody. "But he can stop laughing at my car." She had to smile, and that little exchange told her a lot about both boys. "It's a fun car for city driving," she said to both boys, "and definitely not practical for this area. There's no way I'd want to drive it in winter, especially on icy mountain roads."

"I can see that," Parker said.

"But, tell me, what are you two doing out here?" Sophie asked.

"My Mom said since Brody is new and can't go to school here yet, I could take the day off and show him the town," Parker said proudly.

"Very nice." Sophie then turned to Brody. "What do you think of it?"

"It's a lot smaller than Billings, but I guess it's not completely terrible," Brody said.

"I've heard it's got a good ice cream shop," Sophie said, hands on hips. "Is that right, Parker?"

"It sure does. Miss Sandy's, right down the street."

"I haven't tried it yet," Sophie said. "Since today's actually kind of warm, I could go for a sundae. I'd love some company if you two would like to join me."

The boys looked at each other. "Sure, thanks."

Soon, they were sitting in the ice cream shop with enormous sundaes in front of them. The ice cream was as good as she'd been told.

"It's nice you two are so close in age," Sophie said.

"Yeah, Parker's okay for a kid," Brody said with a laugh. "I'm six months older, so he's just in eighth grade and I'm in ninth."

"Hah!" Parker gave Brody's shoulder a light punch. "Even though he's a smart ass—oops, please don't tell my mom I said that, Miss Sophie—it's fun showing this 'old' guy around. And I was telling him all about the ghosts at the Donnelly cabin. I don't think he believes me. Have you seen them?"

How to answer? "Not exactly."

"What's that mean?" Parker picked up on her hesitancy.

"Let's just say, I've seen things that are hard to explain. No ghosts, though. I don't think."

"That's what I've heard," Parker said in hushed tones. "That people don't see ghosts, or if they do, they don't say so. But they see things moving around in weird ways. It's sooo spooky."

"Really?" Sophie hadn't heard any of that. Not that she'd asked, of course.

Brody grimaced. "You two are putting me on. But if it was up to me, I'd stay someplace modern."

Sophie was surprised. "I thought you were a ranch kid, and into horses and, well, anything not modern."

"That's what my dad thinks, too. But it's not me."

"So, does that mean the tree farm isn't the sort of place you'd like to live in either?"

"No way."

Her heart sank. "I see."

He frowned as he took in her reaction. "Actually, what I'm trying to say is, it's not for me. But my dad likes it, so that's fine. My grandma told me I need to be here to help him right now, but if I really hate it here, to remember that in a few years I'll go to college. I guess I can deal with a tree farm until then."

"I see." The level of maturity of the boy surprised her, but then she realized that having gone through all he did probably caused him to grow up fast and learn to depend on himself, not others. A good lesson, she'd come to realize.

"Do you know what you want to study?"

He shrugged. "I keep changing. When I'm being practical, I'd like to study law, but when I think of my mom, I'd like to be a doctor, maybe even a cardiologist. The problem is, it'd be sad when my patients don't make it."

"I'd imagine, but hopefully, saving others makes up for it," she said, realizing how, when she was fourteen, she'd never had to think about such life and death matters.

"Anyway, right now, maybe most of all, I'd like to become a vet. Not for pets, but for cattle, sheep, horses, and even goats. Even though some of them have to become food, still, while they're alive, they deserve to be kept healthy and if they get hurt or sick, they should be treated."

The seriousness of the boy weighed on Sophie as she realized more than ever the sadness that must have hung over so much of his childhood. She couldn't help but be impressed by him. "Those are all wonderful choices, and I'm sure you'll make the right one. You know, when your father was trying to find a property for you two to live on, everyone, including Parker's parents, suggested he go with what felt right deep inside—in his heart, his gut, or what some people say is God talking to them. But at some point, you'll have a special feeling, and you'll know what's right for you."

"Like a Christmas tree farm?" Brody said with a grin.

Sophie had to smile back at him, glad to see him smiling in her direction. "Exactly! Who knew, right?"

Brody shook his head. "Not me, that's for sure."

"It's actually a neat place," Parker said. "And Uncle Tray said I can work there for extra money if I want."

They then concentrated on their quickly melting sundaes, but after a while Brody turned to Sophie. "Actually, there's something I need to tell you."

Sophie froze hearing those words, and couldn't help but worry about what was coming, although he looked more sheepish than angry or upset. "Okay," she murmured.

Brody looked at Parker a moment. Parker nodded. And then Brody said to Sophie, "You know my dad likes you a whole lot, right?"

She was surprised to hear him say that. "I know we're good friends."

"Yeah, that's what he told my Aunt Maeve. But we just looked at each other, 'cause we know he *really* likes you, and we don't mean as friends."

Since he brought it up, she had to ask him something, despite worrying about his answer. Her voice soft, she asked, "What would you think of your dad being with someone?"

Again, Brody turned to Parker, who just shrugged. Both boys seemed a little embarrassed by the question, but Brody answered. "We already talked about it, and that's why I wanted to talk to you. I heard my dad telling Aunt Maeve he's worried about me. But he doesn't have to be. I mean, I saw how he was after Mom died. He was really, really sad, and has been for a long time. So, I think if he can be with you, and you make him happy, I'd be cool with it."

"Thank you," she whispered, and slowly, she was able to smile. "I'm glad to hear that."

"Besides, as Grandma said when I talked to her on the phone about it, if I don't like you, I'll be going off to college soon, so it won't matter all that much."

She raised her eyebrows. "I see. Wise grandma, right?"

He chuckled. "That she is. But I think I'll like you okay."

"I'm glad to hear that. I think I already like you, too."

Brody looked uncomfortable again, but then said, "I don't know if I should say this, but my mom used to tell me my dad doesn't realize he's a pretty good guy. She even had to propose to him because he was so afraid she'd say no, he didn't ask. I think, if he doesn't say much about how he feels, that's why. I can tell he sees you as pretty special."

"I'm not, though."

"Actually, I think you're okay. Parker does, too. Anyway, we should get going. I've got a town to see before it's time for Parker's baseball practice."

Their sundaes finished, they all stood. "Thank you, Brody. And Parker. I appreciate all you've said. You two have explained a lot."

"Thanks for the ice cream!" both boys said as they hurried from the shop to their bikes and soon headed off to see more of the town.

CHAPTER 33

The next morning after breakfast, Sophie walked down to the river.

She hadn't seen Anna for many days, despite going down to the footpath where they'd often met. Especially while Tray was in Montana, she'd often gone there hoping for a conversation. But Anna never returned.

Sophie couldn't help but think back to hearing Anna's laughter—or what she had thought was Anna's laughter—after the silliness of Carter Waterton running in circles around the great room. Had she figured out who Anna really was? And did that mean she would never see her again?

She went over to the rise looking out on the river where they'd had their last conversation and sat. Sometimes, simply watching the water flow by was helpful.

"Maggie told me I might find you here."

Her heart leaped at the sound of Tray's voice. "Hello!"

He climbed the small rise and sat beside her. "I came over to check out of the cabin. I'll be staying in a make-shift room in the loft at my sister's, so no sense paying for a room here.

Things are moving fast with the tree farm, so if there are no snags, it'll be mine in a couple more weeks."

"That's good news," she said. "I'm glad for you."

"I heard you had a pleasant visit with Brody and Parker yesterday," he added.

A warm glow at the memory filled her. "I enjoyed it a lot. They're good boys and I think Brody will handle this change well."

"He's surprisingly tough and level-headed for his age. I'm lucky."

"You are." She drew back to look at him, at the proud expression on his face. "I can't help but think how, when we met, you were such a loner and so troubled you didn't even want to talk, and now you've got a great family around you."

"You helped me, you know," he murmured.

"No. I was there, but it's your strength that did it."

He didn't answer, but faced the river as if pondering her words.

"How did you find this spot?" he asked.

"I used to meet a friend here, a neighbor named Anna. But she hasn't come around lately."

"A neighbor? Hmm. I wonder if she's the mother of my friend Luke. He also lives somewhere around here."

Sophie hesitated, then said, "Unless Luke is about three years old, Anna's not his mother. She's only in her early twenties. But I enjoy talking to her a lot. For one so young, she gives good advice."

"Luke is more like thirty or so. He's a good listener, but he's different from most people. I can't put my finger on it, though. I wonder if the two of them know each other? Or if their homes are near each other? I've driven and walked around out here, and didn't see any house nearby, let alone two."

Sophie felt her pulse speed up hearing about the mysterious Luke. "Anna would walk northward on this path with me only so far, and then she insisted on going ahead alone. I never learned where her house is, either."

"Well, I can't leave without solving this little mystery. Let's take a walk."

She wondered if she dared tell him what she suspected about Anna, but quickly decided against it. She hesitated to look for a house that might not exist. "I don't know. The last time I went that way, I encountered a bear!"

"Probably a teddy bear," he said with a smirk.

"Funny." He gave her his hand to help stand, and then continued to hold it as they walked footpath. She gave up resisting and went along.

When they reached the point where Anna would leave her, they kept going. But before long, the path simply ended. They looked for signs that people, Anna, walked over grassy areas, but found none.

"This is strange," Tray said. "Do you think your friend was just joking about living out here, and then hurried back down the path after you left?"

"I don't think she ever joked."

"Did you ask people in town about her? Did you show them her picture?"

"She wouldn't let me take one of her."

"Why not?"

"She doesn't like photos."

"Yet, you, a photographer, kept her as a friend?"

"Crazy, I know. But I liked her."

He looked intently at her. "You think she's an okay person, then?"

"Of course."

His lips tightened, but he said no more about Anna. They stood at the end of the path and looked around, then walked down to the river. A couple of elk grazed on the opposite bank, and overhead, an osprey swooped, eyeing fish in the river.

"Let's keep on going," he said. "From what I've been told, this used to all be Donnelly land, and now it's owned by one of the cabin's owners plus her husband."

"Yes. Maggie told me the story when I first moved here. It's Julia's and Jean-Philippe's house being built up on the bluff a bit closer to the main road. I've never gone up there, but it looks like it might have a great view of the river."

"Want to head up that way?" Tray asked. "Maybe from there, we'll be able to see Anna and Luke's homes. If we could find even one it wouldn't be quite so mysterious."

"That's a good idea," Sophie murmured. "Also, did you ever ask Maggie if she knows your friend?"

"I did. She said she didn't know him, but he told me his mother knows her or someone else connected to the house. It's all strange. He could be wrong. I mean, I only talked to the guy three times. He might have been confused, or who knows what?"

As they headed up the hill, Tray stopped. "What could that be?" He was looking at an area with a low, wrought-iron fence around what appeared to be headstones.

"It looks like a gravesite," Sophie said.

"Let's check it out," Tray said as they headed toward the fenced area. The land was bare except for three headstones. They seemed old, and yet had no moss or other growth, as if someone had cleaned them.

The went to the nearest headstone.

"Oh, no," Sophie murmured as she read, Elijah Donnelly, 1864-1892, "Beloved husband of Hannah and father of Lucas."

The two of them stared, open mouthed, at the names.

"Hannah and Lucas," Sophie whispered.

Tray frowned, but didn't say a word as they moved to the

second headstone which was the largest. He read aloud, "Hannah Louise Donnelly, beloved wife of Elijah and mother of Lucas, 1868-1891."

"She was twenty-three when she died," Sophie said and looked at Tray. "That's the same age as my friend, Anna. And Anna is no more than a variation of the name Hannah—the names are basically the same."

Tray took Sophie's hand again as they walked to the third marker, which was the plainest and smallest, as if the third person had been all but forgotten by relatives or friends at the time of his death. "This grave is for Lucas Truscott Donnelly, 1891-1923. Forever in our hearts," Tray whispered. "It's Luke's grave. Hannah was his mother."

"My God, Tray." She fought back tears. "This must be where she came after she left me, after she gave me advice."

"Luke was thirty-one when he died. So young."

Sophie nodded. "Maggie told me he'd died of tuberculosis. He caught it fighting in France during World War I."

Tray shut his eyes a moment, then whispered, "It makes sense. My friend, Luke, had a terrible deep, raspy cough. Despite that, he always had time for me. To give advice." He put his arm around Sophie's shoulders. "Thank you, Luke, for helping me get to know this wonderful woman. I'll never forget you."

"And Hannah," Sophie said. "I miss you. I miss our talks, your guidance. Thank you for choosing me to help. Thank you for helping me learn what's important."

They stood a long while in silence, and then turned and slowly walked back to the cabin, each lost in their own thoughts until they reached the small beach area with a felled log.

"That's where Luke and I would sit and talk—mostly about you, it seemed, now that I think back on it," Tray said.

"And you said it was his paper that led you to The Christmas Farm."

"It was."

"So it was destiny, with a little help," Sophie said with a smile.

"I'd say you're right," Tray admitted. "Although, you realize, we can't really tell anybody about this."

"Not unless we want to be shunned as irrational," she agreed.

"Or worse," he said.

"As my buddy Hamlet said after his own encounter with a ghost, 'There are more things in heaven and earth, Horatio, than are dreamt of in your philosophy.' I'm thinking Shakespeare knew more than people suspected." Then she eyed him. "You do believe this. You aren't just humoring me, are you?"

"I never told you, but those weeks back, when Georgina brought me a huckleberry pie and was becoming, well, let's say, kind of amorous, her dang pie began to levitate."

"What?" Sophie stared at him. "You saw it happen?"

"Not actually. But you should have seen her eyes. She all but said it, and when I turned to see what she was gawking at, I kind of saw the pie settle back into place. Of course, I dismissed it right away. But then, I'm not kidding, I know old Elijah was grinning so hard I'm surprised he didn't split the canvas. Instead of admitting what I'd seen, I told myself it was just the light. Not real."

She shook her head. "Maybe it was just the light."

He took her hand once more. "It gets worse," he murmured. "When that Sergio fellow was here, even though you asked for privacy, I got so pissed off, or jealous, truth be told, I went back to the cabin to have it out with him and with you. And, God help me, I saw the vase float by itself above his head and flip over, dousing him with water and wildflowers."

She was stunned. "You saw that? But you didn't say a word —and kept asking me why the floor was damp and everything!"

"I couldn't let myself believe it. Not any of it. Not until now, because if you're crazy, then so am I."

"Thank you for telling me, Tray."

He stared at her. "It's kind of weird, though, isn't it?"

She nodded. "It makes me uneasy."

"Me, too," he murmured. "Anyway, I'd better get going. I promised Maeve I'd be back there to help clear a space in her garage. Tomorrow, a truckload of my stuff from Montana is supposed to arrive. We'll store everything at her place until I have my tree farm. Times are kind of busy right now."

She nodded, feeling increasingly awkward. "I can well imagine."

He took her hand as they walked back toward the cabin, but soon they let go of each other. When they reached the cabin, he stopped. "I don't need to go inside," he said. His voice was breathless and hesitant. "I packed up my few belongings when I told Maggie I was leaving. They're already in my truck."

"Ah, I see." She folded her hands. "The cabin won't be the same without you here."

"But I'll still come by to see you," he said.

"That's good," she whispered unsure what to say or what to do. Everything suddenly felt so wrong, so unnatural. She wanted him to care for her because of his feelings, not because of some supernatural conversations. Even thinking such a thing made her angry, but also very, very sad. "I'm glad this all worked out for you. Let me know if you need help with anything, okay?"

He frowned, looking every bit as uncertain as she felt. "Okay, sure."

"Goodbye, Tray."

He studied her. "I'll be back, Sophie."

She nodded, but stepped back, away from him, and said nothing as he headed for his truck.

Sophie couldn't sleep that night. Whenever she shut her eyes she thought of Tray and Anna. As much as it upset her to think that her feelings for Tray might have been due to some supernatural manipulation, when she thought of Anna's actual words, everything was said in terms of possibilities, maybe this and maybe that. She was never told anything directly. Maybe, she wasn't so much manipulated as merely guided by Anna—guided to what her heart actually wanted.

It was a soothing thought, and the first one she'd had since finding the gravestones with the names and dates so clearly etched. Finally, her tumultuous thoughts eased a little, and she was able to fall asleep.

Tray couldn't sleep at all. As much as he was excited about how things were going with Brody and the tree farm, all he could think about was Sophie and how upset she'd looked when they found the gravesite.

He'd seen many unexplainable things living with Charlene and getting to know her family and hearing about traditional Crow customs, or Apsáalooke, as they called themselves. It meant "large beaked bird," and living in the Garden Valley area, known for its many raptors, he couldn't help but believe the name meant all of them, not simply black crows. He didn't believe, at first, when Charlene would talk to him about being visited by her grandfather, for instance, although the man had been dead for ten years at the time. But after a while, he heard so many visitations and so many actual events that happened because of those visits, he wasn't as shocked as he might have been by what was going on in the cabin.

But even knowing all that, he couldn't sleep. He expected Sophie was having an equally difficult time.

Finally, he gave up, dressed, and drove back to the cabin.

All the lights were off when he got there, and the front door was locked. Since he'd checked out, he no longer had a key.

He picked up some pebbles and tossed them at Sophie's second story bedroom window. Unfortunately, he didn't throw them hard enough and they hit the wall instead of the window. He felt like a teenager trying to meet his first love and not wanting her parents to know he was there as he picked up another few pebbles and tried again.

This time his toss reached the windows. But no Sophie. He tried two more times before he saw her come to the window and look out. She looked stunned to see him, then raised her hand in a "wait" gesture. Less than a minute later, she opened the front door and let him in. Her hair was loose and wild, and she wore a pajamas, but she looked as beautiful as ever to him, maybe more so.

"I couldn't sleep with the way I'd left you today," he whispered. "I have to talk to you."

"I feel the same," she said. "Come inside."

They sat together on the sofa and both looked up at Elijah Donnelly's photo.

Finally, Tray spoke. "Let me tell you what's been on my mind. First of all, I like thinking that the ghosts seem to want us to be together. I feel that way, too, more than anything."

"Yes—"

"Wait, please. There's a big problem with that." He swallowed hard a couple of times before he continued. "Anyone can see you're wasting your time sitting around this old cabin. You're talented. I went online—yeah, I know, a weird thing for me to do. But I looked you up and saw your fashion photos, and your awards. You should have told me about them. Looking at those photos, I'm proud to know you. And I could see that, if you're tired of the fashion scene, with your travel photos you could be out there setting the world on fire."

"You're kind to say that," she whispered.

"It's not kindness, it's truth. I remember you talking about why you want to be a travel photographer. You have a passion for it, you love it. I can't expect you to change and I wouldn't want you to. That doesn't mean I don't want you with me, it means that, even though I've fallen in love with you, I know it would be wrong to ask you to stay. I expect you'll find all kinds of magazines that want your articles, and you'll probably put them into books before much longer as well. That's what makes you who you are."

She drew in her breath as if recognizing the truth of his words, and also the heartbreak. "Have camera, will travel, right?"

"So they say."

"The only problem is, I love you, Tray," she said. "And I've been happy here."

His heart swelled hearing her speak of love, and he confessed, "I've been happier with you than I've been for a long, long time."

Her eyes searched his. "I wish I knew how to make this right."

"Me, too," he whispered.

They sat in silence. "I can't help but think," she said, her voice sad, "that maybe the best thing for me to do is to simply move on quickly. To leave this behind and get on with my life.

As much as I've liked staying here at the inn, I'm also kind of hiding from reality."

He studied her, and everything she'd said confirmed his feelings that he shouldn't ask her, beg her, to stay with him. "I get it and I'm not surprised to hear you say that."

"You're not?"

"From the time I first met you, I had the feeling this wasn't a place you'd stay. Why do you think I tried so hard to keep away from you—to not take you along every single day I went out looking for land? Why I kept thinking, almost hoping, that you'd start dating some other guy in town so I could put you out of my mind for good. As much as I wanted you with me, I believed the closer I got to you, the more it would hurt to say goodbye. And it does. It hurts a lot."

She bowed her head a moment as if absorbing his words. "I'm not Catholic, but I remember in Italy hearing that their patron saint, Padre Pio, was said to have the ability to bi-locate when he was alive. There are many tales of him having been seen and talking to people in two places very far apart at the exact same time. I never believed those stories, just like I never believed in ghosts. But now, I have to confess, they might be true. If so, I wish I could do that because I'd definitely stay here with you, while also having my life traveling and taking photos I love."

Her words were what he'd feared she would say. She loved him, but her dream career was within reach, and she needed to pursue it. "I understand. I wish you could do this bi-locate thing as well. You'll come back to visit, I hope?"

"Of course. In time."

At that, he took her in his arms and held her a long, long time. When he finally let her go, he saw tears in her eyes.

"You'll let me know before you leave?" he whispered.

She shook her head. "It'll be too hard. Just say goodbye now, and walk out the door. That'll be easiest for me."

He nodded, and did as she asked. With his voice scarcely more than a whisper, he said, "Goodbye, Sophie."

Sophie stood without moving for a long, long while. She heard the truck engine start and the spin of the tires on the gravel driveway as Tray left.

She allowed her tears to fall as she walked up to Elijah's portrait. "I guess these things don't always work out. Give Hannah my thanks for having tried. And tell her I miss her."

CHAPTER 34

Somehow, Sophie had always known it would end this way. She and Tray were simply too different.

To stay at the cabin, as much as she'd come to love it, would only be a daily reminder of all she might have had.

After Tray left, she spent the early morning hours trying to find the strength to stay, despite everything. But the best she could do was to tell herself that someday she might return.

In the morning, she packed her things and told Maggie she was leaving. Online, she found a room in a bed-and-breakfast in Coeur d'Alene in north Idaho, and from there she planned to explore all the old towns and interesting spots along the Idaho panhandle, including areas where Lewis and Clark once crossed the state. She was going to end up with an interesting and colorful article. In it she would capture the history of this beautiful land and hoped people would realize it needed to be protected before it was too late.

"I'm sorry to see you go when you're so unhappy," Maggie said, her face filled with sadness. "Are you sure you want to leave so quickly?"

"It's for the best," Sophie hugged the older woman who she'd grown quite fond of. "As much as I've come to care about... who am I kidding? As much as I've come to love Tray, we're simply too different. Our lifestyles are crazily incompatible. I can't ask him to be happy traveling with me when he's got a son to raise and needs to make a living, and he can't ask me to spend all my time at his tree farm." She shook her head. "Anyway, I'm off."

She stepped into the foyer to see Bree hanging up the landline phone. At times, it seemed to be the most reliable thing in the house. "Were you ordering a pizza already?" Sophie asked with a smile, since that was the phone's primary use, especially for Bree.

Bree looked surprised Sophie had seen her and rubbed her hands against the skirt of the short dress she wore over navy blue leggings. "No. I mean, yes! Of course." She sounded nervous. "Can't take chances they'll run out."

Sophie shook her head. Bree was still a strange one, all right. "I hope you enjoy your stay. You've extended it again, I hear."

"Yeah. This is a neat place."

"Is the inn neat, or are you talking about a certain baker who seems to enjoy hanging out here?"

"The inn, of course!" she insisted. "But are you sure you want to leave?"

"It's best."

Sophie took her suitcase, while Bree and Maggie helped with her other bags, plus her photo booth equipment. She suspected it might come in handy if she ran out of money and found a town with a festival somewhere in the state. They somehow managed to cram everything into the Volkswagen. "Okay," Sophie said. "I just need to get my purse and camera bag, and I'm all set."

She went into the foyer where she'd left them. But when she picked up the camera bag it was far too light. She opened it. "Where's my camera?"

She turned to Maggie and Bree who were right behind her going into the foyer. "Did one of you move it?"

"I wouldn't dare touch that camera," Maggie said. "It looked like it cost a fortune."

"Same here," Bree told her.

"I'm sure I put it in the camera bag, I always do," Sophie exclaimed.

"Did you take some last-minute photos?" Bree asked.

"I don't think so. Maybe I moved it into the car with my other things and don't remember doing it." Sophie ran out to the car and looked all around the passenger compartment as well as the trunk. Her camera wasn't there.

She returned to the inn.

Maggie came down the stairs. "I went to your room to see if it was left there, but it wasn't."

"I checked the downstairs bathroom, the laundry room, and the great room," Bree said. "Even the garage. I didn't see it."

Sophie shook her head. "I just don't understand it. Oh, maybe I took it to the back porch without thinking when I went there to make sure I didn't leave anything outside."

The three of them rushed out the French doors, but it wasn't there. "This is just too bizarre," Sophie whispered.

"It's as if someone or something doesn't want you to leave," Bree whispered.

"Don't be silly," Maggie said, admonishing her as they walked back into the great room.

"There it is!" Sophie cried, and hurried to her camera which sat on the mantle in front of Elijah Donnelly's portrait.

"But we looked there," Bree whispered, her voice shaky.

"I know," Sophie said, staring at Elijah. Was he smirking at her?

"Obviously, we didn't look carefully enough," Maggie announced, her voice firm and her spine stiff.

"Well," Sophie murmured with a last glance at Elijah Donnelly's portrait, "I've got it now, so I can leave."

As they walked out to her car, Sophie gave one last look at the cabin, and then, after another hug with Maggie and even Bree, she got into the car and slowly drove along the dirt road heading toward town and the highway.

She had almost reached the Middlefork Road when she saw Tray's truck heading toward her at a fast clip, a cloud of dust kicked up behind it. He stuck his arm out the window and gestured to her to pull over, which she did.

He skidded to a stop beside her, got out of the truck, and stood beside it.

Her heart sank. It was hard enough leaving him last night, but now, after saying goodbye to Maggie and Bree, it would be even harder.

She got out of her car. "Tray, why are you doing this? We've said our goodbyes."

"I just got word you were leaving now. I had to see you."

"We discussed this last night. I'm going to take this time to finish my travel article, and you've got so much on your plate, I'm just an unnecessary distraction. I get it, Tray, I really do."

He stepped closer to her. "I came to say you have the answer for us. You said it last night."

"I did?"

He nodded. "Bi-locate."

"I don't follow," she said.

"We've looked at this as a glass half-empty, but we can also see it as a glass-half full."

She remained lost. "Which means?"

"It means, if we're in this together, we don't do things half-way. When I say I love you and want to be with you, I mean I want marriage, a wife. Maybe, God willing, more children. But the thing is, if you also want to be a travel photographer and go around the world, I realized I would have no problem with that. As I've said, it's what makes you, you. So, it's okay with me as long as I know that when you come home, it'll be to your husband, to me. Could you do that, Sophie? Could you see yourself, ever, being both a travel photographer and my wife?"

Everything he was suggesting filled her with so much relief and happiness that she wondered how she'd ever been so lucky as to find such a dear man. "You really wouldn't mind if I went off for weeks at a time to go on some kind of photo shoot?"

"That's exactly what I mean, because I know you'll be happy to do that and also, you'll have a home to come back to—our home. Hopefully, our tree farm. What do you think? Would that work for you?"

She could scarcely believe it, but she could see the possibili-ties. He'd been living alone for years, so he wasn't a needy or clingy sort who had to have his wife there every day to cook meals and take care of his clothes or whatever. And she could take only those assignments that most interested her for as long —or, or more likely as short—a time as she chose. "My God, I think you've got it."

"No, *you've* got it. It was your idea. And if anyone could handle it, it's you."

She smiled. "I'm sure, with you, it would absolutely work."

He placed his hands on her waist. "In that case, Sophie, will you marry me?"

She put her arms around his neck. "Absolutely. Especially since it sounds as if you won't mind if, someday, we'll have lots of little Christmas trees of our own."

His eyebrows rose and then he gave her that half smile she

so loved. "Well, I've never heard them called that, but believe me, I'm all in." He then took her in his arms and kissed her as if he'd never want to let her go.

"Let's go back to the cabin," he said, his voice husky. "We've got to let the ghosts know they did good."

"Yes," Sophie said, her arms still around him and heart filled with love. "They certainly did."

ABOUT THE AUTHOR

Joanne Pence was born and raised in northern California. She has been an award-winning, *USA Today* best-selling author of mysteries for many years, but she has also written historical fiction, contemporary romance, romantic suspense, a fantasy, and supernatural suspense. All of her books are now available as ebooks and in print, and most are also offered in special large print editions. Joanne hopes you'll enjoy her books, which present a variety of times, places, and reading experiences, from mysterious to thrilling, emotional to lightly humorous, as well as powerful tales of times long past.

Visit her at www.joannepence.com and be sure to sign up for Joanne's mailing list to hear about new books.